The Free Trader of Planet Vii

Free Trader Series
Book 2

By Craig Martelle

ISBN 10: 1530405270
ISBN 13: 978-1530405275
ASIN: B01CX7UPVQ

Cover Illustration © Tom Edwards
Tom EdwardsDesign.com

Editing services provided by Mia Darien – miadarien.com

Other Books by Craig Martelle

It's Not Enough to Just Exist (Jan 2016)

Free Trader Series Book 1 – The Free Trader of Warren Deep (Feb 2016)
Free Trader Series Book 2 – The Free Trader of Planet Vii (Mar 2016)
Free Trader Series Book 3 – Adventures on RV Traveler (Apr 2016)
Free Trader Series Book 4 – The Battle of the Amazon (estimate Oct 2016)

Rick Banik Thriller Series

People Raged and the Sky Was on Fire (May 2016)

For Wendy Whitehead

Table of Contents

ACKNOWLEDGMENTS

This journey started a long time ago when my brother Guy introduced me to Dungeons and Dragons™. This was early in TSR's existence, so we had to build our own dungeons, run our own campaigns. But then I attended a GenCon in 1979 where I met James Ward. I bought Metamorphosis Alpha™ and Gamma World™.

I like the civilizations that were. Post-Apocalyptic became my favorite genre and here I am, in a position to tell these stories.

Thank you Guy for introducing me and James for creating these worlds.

I also want to thank Anne McCaffrey and her wonderful Dragonriders of Pern© series. I've always believed that the world would be a better place if we could talk with our animal friends.

1 – The Companions

The companions found themselves on a hillside, enjoying a breakfast of venison, freshly reheated over a small fire of field grass. Braden and Micah had no luck recounting to the others what they'd seen in the Command Center. The Hillcat simply called it a place of terror and shut down further discussion.

The animal companions were not comfortable inside buildings, and they never would be. Only the humans would make a return trip inside.

As long as the Security Bots left the other members of the caravan alone.

Golden Warrior of the Stone Cliffs was an orange tabby Hillcat. Braden called him G-War. His back was above a man's knee, his body the length of a man's arm, and his claws were as sharp as the finest blades. With his quickness and mutant ability to see a short distance into the future, G-War was one of the deadliest creatures in Warren Deep. Despite all this, his real gift was his ability to mindlink and talk with nearly any creature. The only things he feared were the mechanical creations of the ancients known as Bots.

Skirill was a magnificent Hawkoid who had joined Braden and G-War when they found him, injured from a fight with a mutie Bear. His body was similar in size to the Hillcat, but when he unfolded his wings, they were wider than a man was tall. He could be airborne with one hop and a single beat of his massive wings. His hooked beak was a thing to fear, but his greatest weapon was his claws. He struck from above or behind, ripping and lifting. Thanks to G-War, Skirill could share what he saw as he flew. He didn't miss much as he had the eyes of a Hawkoid.

Aadi, First Master of the Tortoid Consortium, had joined the caravan as they traveled across the Great Desert. He found Braden and the others to be interesting. It was refreshing for him to speak with them, his wisdom otherwise wasted in silence. He floated and swam through the air, with a powerful beak, although his real weapon was a focused thunderclap. The Tortoid could deliver all the sound of thunder into one small space. It usually left the victims unable to move. In the case of the Old Tech Bots, it was more destructive.

Micah had been the last to join the caravan. She was from the area south of the Great Desert, called Devaney's Barren by the ancients. She was running from an arranged marriage because she had killed the groom-to-be while injuring his father, and she had taken their revered blaster on her way out. She believed that they wouldn't allow her to return to her village of Trent. Her body belied an incomparable physical strength. Now that she was free of her village, she found her place as a warrior, although she was learning the nuance of trade.

Braden was the reluctant leader of the caravan and the companions, having fallen into it when he saved a drowning Hillcat ten cycles ago. Since then, he always preferred the company of animals. His parents left the Caravan Guild, ending their careers as Free Traders, and Braden followed in their footsteps, becoming a Free Trader, plying the areas outside the influence of the Guild.

Braden also carried a weapon from the ancients, but this one needed no power beyond his own physical strength. He called it a Rico Bow, although that was an aberration of the term recurve bow. The second curve of the Old Tech material made it possible for him to shoot arrows further and more accurately than any other weapon.

Braden's greatest strength was his vision for a better future. That's why he led the caravan. The companions believed in him because he believed in what was possible. Braden's vision and planning made it possible for the caravan to cross the Great Desert, a feat no one had managed before.

The six companions of the caravan were joined by two horses that Braden had managed to trade for in Cameron, the southernmost town of the Caravan Guild's territory. Max and Pack weren't mutants, but were still equal members of the caravan, and at times, more important. During their passage through the Amazon, Aadi's negotiations with the Lizard Men had saved the horses' lives.

2 – The Power of Old Tech

Braden and Micah gnawed their smoked venison in silence. They'd argued about how to approach the oasis, neither satisfied and no decision made. Micah wanted to leave the companions at the camp while only she and Braden went in. Braden wanted the others to have free run of the oasis where they could eat and drink as they wished.

As the so-called Caretaker, Braden held some sway over the massive Security Bots. He'd found a bracelet that showed time in the ancients' way. This also identified him as the Caretaker of Oasis Zero One and gave him preferred treatment at the New Command Center. He expected that he could tell the Security Bot to log the horses into the system, so they would be free to roam the fertile area while Braden and Micah were occupied underground.

"As long as we are the only ones in the system, I think the Security Bots will protect us," Braden said, thinking out loud.

"Protect us from who?" Micah asked.

"Say that merry band from a certain village with a broken-armed old man show up looking for their blaster…"

"Then I would be happy to shoot them with this very blaster. Maybe we can shoot it before we go back?" Micah suggested, and Braden liked the idea. It was a tool and they needed to know how to use it.

They set up a patch of ground and walked twenty-five strides away. Micah held the blaster in front of her as she had seen the old man do. She pulled back on the trigger using the pointer fingers of both hands. The blaster bucked slightly in her hands. Not knowing what to expect, she had a death grip on it. After firing it, she stood, mesmerized.

The air smelled funny, as if the very sky had burned. A ragged beam of light launched forward, scorching the spot on the ground and many small areas around it. The grasses at the edge started to burn, while the center of the blast site was gone, burned to smoldering cinders.

Braden ran forward and stomped out the fires. The last thing they needed was a wildfire racing across the rolling hills. Braden, smoke swirling around his feet, looked back at Micah.

She still hadn't moved after firing the blaster, her eyes locked on the scorched earth of her target. Braden put his hands up, palms toward her.

"Relax and put the blaster down, Micah," he said soothingly. Slowly, she looked up at him. Her mouth worked, but nothing came out.

Braden let out a whoop of celebration and jumped into the air, pumping his fist as he did so. "Now that's a weapon!"

Micah put the blaster on the ground and stepped back. Braden picked it up and looked at it in awe. He aimed it at the spot, looking around to make sure nothing was coming, and then depressed the trigger as Micah had done.

It kicked in his hands, but he held it firm. It discharged its flame into the ground. Braden held the trigger down, and the blaster continued to throw flame and light forward until Micah grabbed him from behind.

"Let go! Let go!" He realized what she was saying and finally let up on the trigger. "Just pull it once and let it go. What the hell were you trying to do?"

"Sorry. I didn't know. I never saw a blaster fire before and I sure as crap never fired anything like this. I have a bow, remember?" Braden was more than a little miffed at Micah's scolding. She took the blaster from his hands and put it in the holster as she bolted toward their target.

The new fires grew quickly. She tried stamping them out, but the flames were already fierce.

Braden pulled her away and they ran to the camp to collect their stuff. Max and Pack were trying to run from the fires, but they were hobbled. Braden and Micah loosened the bonds while holding their reins, then swung into the saddles. G-War ran the opposite direction, which took him straight toward the oasis. Aadi swam as quickly as he could in the same direction. Skirill was much calmer as he took wing and flew above the mounting chaos of the wildfire.

They kicked the horses to a gallop and raced past Aadi, who was still behind the fleet Hillcat. They pulled up shortly to see the progress of the fire. It moved slowly after the initial rage. When they ripped out the prairie grasses to make their cook fires, they'd created fire breaks. There wasn't much to burn, but what there was, burned well.

Knowing they still wouldn't be able to put out the fire, they turned and continued toward the oasis.

3 – Back to the Oasis

As Braden and Micah approached the oasis, one Security Bot floated gracefully, yet quickly, toward them.

"Add the creatures we ride to your system, Master Security Bot. They are called horses."

"The horses are added," it responded instantly.

"Tell me, what is this place called?" Braden asked.

"It is the New Command Center."

"That's the place at the bottom of the little room that moves. What's the area up here called? We can't keep calling it the New Command Center." Micah looked at Braden. Of all the things to ask, this wasn't on any of her lists.

"The elevator takes you to the New Command Center. The surface area above the New Command Center is called the New Command Center."

"Elevator you called it. Okay. I tell you what, put this into your system. We're going to call this place New Sanctuary."

"I have added that name to the system."

"While we're here, will you protect us from our enemies? All of us?" Micah asked, sweeping her arm to take in Aadi, G-War, and Skirill.

"Yes. When an enemy is so defined in our system, we will protect the Caretaker and his guests. The only enemies currently listed in the system are James Warren and his followers."

"Who is James Warren?" Braden asked, although he knew that he was the founder of Warren Deep.

"James Warren is a bio-geneticist who rebelled against the proper authority of Sanctuary, ultimately waging war on the peaceful people of the south. We were programmed to protect against his forces should they try to seize the capital city. His last known location was north of Devaney's Barren."

"Warren Deep," Braden whispered. He, G-War, and Skirill were all the result of what James Warren had done in the north. That's why muties were treated as enemies in the south. Warren was their creator.

"Master Security Bot. James Warren and his followers are no longer enemies. We achieved peace hundreds of cycles, I mean years, ago. Do you agree that the last known battles were that long ago?"

"I concur. The new information is added to the system. There are no enemies currently listed in the system."

Braden and Micah looked at each other and nodded. The ability to direct the Security Bots was unexpected, but welcome.

"Without enemies, this unit has no tasks to perform," the Security Bot said as it remained motionless.

"Can you put out that fire?" Micah offered, not knowing what they could get from the Security Bot.

"Yes. Is that the Caretaker's command?"

"Yes, please. Put that fire out!" Braden said in his most commanding voice, smirking as he looked at Micah. She shook her head and smiled. Braden's smirk faded. He knew that she could take the bracelet away from him if she wanted. It was by pure chance that he had it, and luck was probably not the best method of picking a leader.

"Okay. Yes, I know. Next time we find a New Command Center, you get to be the Caretaker…"

With a couple beeps, the Security Bot bolted past the horses, scaring them. A second Security Bot appeared from behind the trees of New Sanctuary and headed toward the fires as well. The Bots bracketed the area and without the aid of water, systematically reduced the fires until only smoke remained. They hadn't gone into the flames, but stood apart as they floated back and forth.

"How'd they do that?" Braden asked rhetorically. Micah shrugged, happy the fires were out. She didn't want to be responsible for the wanton destruction of the grasslands as they struggled to grow out of the previous wasteland of Sanctuary.

That must have been one hell of a war. With creatures like the Security Bots, it was amazing that any humans survived at all.

4 – The Hologram

There was a small pond at one end of New Sanctuary, as Braden had dubbed it. There were deer, rabbits, trees, and plenty of undergrowth, including grasses. All the animal companions would be able to eat, drink, and rest.

It even had an area cultivated like Oasis Zero One, but it was orders of magnitude larger. The fields extended far beyond the oasis, over the hill to the south and west, and well into the next valley.

Fields like this meant there had to be a fabricator somewhere. Braden's mouth instantly watered at the thought. A fabricator meant brownies. He wondered if Micah would like them.

To find out, they had to find the fabricator. They had not yet gone into the third building.

They settled the horses by turning them loose, and they waded into the pond to take a deep drink. They didn't need to be hobbled because there was no reason for them to leave and nowhere for them to go. Everything they wanted to eat or drink was here.

G-War bolted after a rabbit, whose life ended shortly thereafter. Skirill also indulged while Master Aadi floated around serenely, enjoying taking in moisture through his feet.

"Master Aadi, are you going to be fine here?" Braden looked at the Tortoid, despite knowing he couldn't read his body language.

'Yes, Master Human. I have much to think about. Time is what I would like the most of. Run along, both of you. We will be here when you return.'

"Are you hungry at all? Is there anything we can get you?" Micah asked.

'No. I ate my fill at the Lizard Men's celebration and that was only a few sleeps ago. I do not need to eat for a while still. But thank you for asking. You are always so kind.'

Braden didn't know how to take that, but his ego felt bruised. He wanted to think that he looked out for all of them, then again, having five views of the same problem made him five times smarter, didn't it?

"Let's plug your blaster in while we check out the last building. I think I burned off a lot of its ancient magic. Sorry about that, by the way."

"That's okay. You'll never touch it again, so I know it won't be a problem. Boys and their toys and all that."

There were moments in life where he felt safe. This was one of them. The powerful Security Bots guarded New Sanctuary. His companions were enjoying the fruits of the oasis, while he and Micah were comfortable in each other's company. He rarely could completely be himself.

"Ass," Braden mumbled with a smile.

"I am in the exalted company of the Golden Warrior. How precious!" Micah laughed and bowed.

"The windowless building awaits. After you?" he offered.

"I don't think so. Old Tech is your thing, not mine. Lead on."

They went to the repair shop first and carefully put the blaster into the rack where they had recovered it previously. Nothing had changed in the shop, so they moved on.

The door to the third building opened as they approached it. Inside was a stairway that led down. To the side, there was an elevator. They looked at each other and together they said, "The steps."

They went down, below ground level and they kept descending. The stairs were well lit by methods only known to the ancients. Braden and Micah simply accepted the lights, not wasting time trying to figure out how they worked.

The steps ended in a hallway with doors on both sides. A hand panel was to the right of each door, like Braden had seen at Oasis Zero One. He held his hand against the panel by the first door and it flashed red.

"We have to find the hologram so it can assign us rooms, then we'll be able to enter. I suspect there's a fabricator behind each door." He left it at that, expecting Micah to ask the question.

She didn't. Instead, she turned to the door on the other side of the hallway. "What's this say?"

Before this, Braden hadn't known whether Micah could read or not. It was uncommon in the north for any child to grow up without learning to read. Braden was especially well schooled because of a trader's duty to keep the rudder up to date.

"It says Office. Yes, we should have tried there first. Good catch." He stepped forward, then hesitated. "I'm teaching you how to read."

As they stood there posturing, a scrabbling sound came from the other end of the hallway. They couldn't see what made the noise, but they sprang to action. Micah cleanly pulled her sword while Braden smoothly nocked an arrow to his bow.

A Server Bot appeared from one room and rolled purposefully to the next. As the door obediently opened, it rolled inside. The door closed behind it.

"Just a Server Bot. It cleans the rooms, if I'm not mistaken." With that, he looked for the panel next to the office door. There wasn't one. He walked toward it, where it opened by sliding into the wall. Inside, the arrangement looked exactly like what he had seen at Oasis Zero One.

"Bullseye!" he shouted and walked briskly to where the hologram should be.

Without fail, the friendly image appeared and the familiar voice greeted him.

"Welcome to New Sanctuary, Caretaker. How can I be of service?"

"It is great to see you again! You called it New Sanctuary? Why?"

"That is the most recent entry in the system for what was once called the New Command Center. Do you wish a room, Caretaker?"

"Yes, please. Two rooms, next to each other. You have fabricators, right?"

"Yes, we have fabricators. We have all the amenities of a standard residential facility."

"Tell me about this place. What is it for?" Braden asked.

"This is the New Command Center, built while war was still assumed. With the war over, as noted today, this facility will be central in rebuilding the world as envisioned by President Ansell three hundred eighty-two years ago."

"It took nearly four-hundred cycles…" Braden still had difficulty comprehending how the world clawed its way back from the destruction the ancients wreaked on it. To help him, he followed his train of thought out loud, while Micah watched. "For us to get where we are from where we were, nearly four-hundred cycles. It'll take another ten thousand before we realize President Ansell's vision, I expect, unless we turn everything over to the Bots. I don't think I want to do that, although they can make the desert grow…" Braden drifted. The Bots were built by man all those cycles ago, but now, they no longer needed man to build more Bots. The Mirror Beast, that is, the Development Unit could not be harmed. Braden also felt that the Security Bots were invincible. He could conceive of no way to defeat them.

The only way was to control them.

"Is there anyone anywhere beside the Caretaker, that is, besides me, who can give orders?"

"No. You are the only human we have been in contact with. You have the highest ranking active position."

Braden looked at Micah slyly. "What if I told you that isn't true?" He paused for effect. Micah's eyes shot wide open, but before she could say anything, he continued, "Micah is the President. Is that the highest rank? If not, then she's whatever the most important position is."

"Thank you. I will update our system. Welcome, President Micah. Your android assistant is not yet ready for service. In the meantime, will you find a Service Bot satisfactory?"

"You are such an ass! Did you ever think to ask before pulling something like this?"

Braden was crushed. He thought it was a good idea. Maybe she'd warm up to it. He would explain when they were in a more private place. "No arguing in front of the kids, please." Braden tried to lighten the mood, pointing at the hologram with a tilt of his head. "I'll explain and then you can quit if you like. Are our rooms ready?"

"Yes. President Micah, please hold up your hands so you can be entered into our system. All units will be updated with your status and let me be the first to welcome you to New Sanctuary. I hope you find your stay to be pleasing as well as refreshing." The hologram finished on sugary notes with a wide smile and grandiose gestures.

Micah held up her hands, while giving Braden a halfhearted ice-cold glare. He was relieved that she was already less angry. Someone had to be in charge, didn't they? She was mad when it was him and mad when it was her. He was convinced that he would never understand women.

5 – Sweet Suite

Braden was surprised that they weren't given rooms closest to the office, but in fact the opposite, their rooms were at the far end of the corridor. It seemed like a hassle going so far. The Service Bot waited for them as they left the office, and they dutifully followed it down a long hallway, then left, to the end of a second long hallway.

On one side was a long empty space and a single door. On the other side, the doors were spaced evenly as they were on both sides of the first corridor.

Micah put her hand against the panel as Braden had showed her. The door slid into the wall and they went inside. This wasn't a room, but a series of rooms, plush with different areas for different things. Couches, overstuffed chairs, long tables with many chairs, a kitchen area, and a large bathing area. There was even a small pond. And then there was the bedroom, the most grandiose of all.

Micah could never have imagined such a thing existed. She pushed down on the bed with two hands, feeling how soft and welcoming it was.

"Maybe it's okay to be the President," she said with a big smile.

Braden's room was like the one he had at the oasis. It was all he needed, but as he thought about it, there was plenty of space in Micah's room and he didn't like the companions separated as they were.

He suggested that they stay in the same room. The couches were far better than his usual sleeping arrangements.

Most importantly, the room had fabricators. He wanted to show Micah how they worked, so he asked her to go into the kitchen area with him.

"Oh fabricator, I would like four brownies please." The familiar hum returned along with the joyous ding, signaling the food was ready.

Micah looked curiously at him. He pushed the button to open the door and pulled out the plate. "Try these. They are like happiness and sunshine in one little cake." To show his faith in the Old Tech, he took one brownie and bit it in half. It seemed to be better than he remembered. He closed his eyes and savored the moment.

Micah's curiosity was piqued. She took one and sampled a corner of it. Then proceeded to devour it and two others while Braden watched. She was in her own personal heaven.

When she finished, Braden ordered two glasses of water. Micah came from a rough village where the drinking vessels were made of pottery, like in the north. She'd heard of glass, but hadn't seen any. Braden cautioned her not to break the glass, so she drank tentatively.

"The fabricator doesn't do meat real well, but other dishes hit the spot. Are you still hungry?"

"Not really. What do you think we should do now?"

"We have to check in with the others, make sure they're okay, let them know that we're fine. Then maybe we can go to the Command Center. Let's check with the hologram and see if she can meet us in there. We need someone to explain to us what we're seeing."

Micah agreed, although she looked longingly back at the decadence of the bedroom, the pool, the couches. Even her wildest dreams hadn't shown her such a place.

On their way out, they talked with the hologram, who assured them that there was another hologram in the New Command Center. All they had to do was ask for Holly while standing in front of the wall of screens. She didn't think it was very becoming, but that's how the original Command Center had been programmed, so the name was replicated.

6 - Peace

"How are you doing, Master Aadi?" Braden asked the floating Tortoid. Aadi slowly opened his eyes and fixed his gaze on the human.

'I was having the most magnificent dream, where I slept in peace, no one disturbing me. It was glorious, but alas, just a dream.' Sometimes it was hard to tell when Aadi was being sarcastic, but not this time.

"Well then, we'll leave you to it. Dream away, Master Tortoid." Braden bowed deeply, Micah joining him in paying homage. Master Aadi's eyes slowly closed as he sought to return to his dreams which were decidedly not about sleeping. The Tortoid's dream was about a mystical world, where everyone got along, where they explored art and nature together, respectful of each other.

That was the real dream. If only all humans were more like Braden and Micah, then maybe peace would come. But he was old. How much time did he have left? No longer dreaming, Aadi rested his eyes and contemplated what needed done to support the two humans as they reshaped the world. He knew from the moment he met Braden that this creature was different. He said that he was self-serving, but his actions showed the opposite. And then they met Micah. Braden wasn't alone in his willingness to serve the greater good.

There was much planning to accomplish if they were to change the world. Master Aadi smiled to himself at the possibilities, drifting back toward happy dreams.

Braden and Micah found G-War sleeping in a sunny spot. He was sprawled on his side, tongue hanging out of his open mouth. He looked like a snake that swallowed a boulder. His stomach was extended with whatever he had eaten. Maintenance or Server Bots must have cleaned up the kill already. They left the 'cat to himself. He was comfortable and unafraid, which was how they liked to see him.

Skirill was in a tall tree watching over the oasis of New Sanctuary. They suspected he had gone in the pond as his feathers glistened in the sunlight. He looked magnificent in the trees, sitting stately.

"Hi, Ess! Anything up?"

"I a' u' in the tree. So I guess the answer is 'e. Skirill is u'," the Hawkoid answered aloud, gently bobbing his head.

"Was that a joke? I think you've spent too much time with us, Ess." The Hawkoid ruffled his feathers in response and resumed watching. Even the Hawkoid was in a good mood. Their decision to return had been a good one. When they had to leave, they would be well rested.

They didn't have to look far to see Max and Pack grazing. They welcomed the humans because they both got their noses and necks stroked. The horses couldn't talk, but they could feel. The humans appreciated them and their role in the success of the caravan. Micah gave Pack a kiss on his nose. He snorted and shook his head, then returned to grazing.

"Well, we've avoided it long enough. Shall we?" Braden asked, although it wasn't a question. He stepped off smartly toward the elevator building.

7 – New Command Center

The Command Center was not as intimidating this time. The Old Tech was everywhere, but G-War's fear wasn't wearing on them. The room's workstations looked as if humans would be there at any heartbeat, manning their posts, doing the work of the ancients.

There was a great deal of background noise from the Old Tech, but none of it was human-made. No one was there. No one was coming.

Braden held Micah's hand as they walked together to the wall of screens. It seemed the natural thing to do. "You're up," he said.

"Holly, are you there?" Micah asked tentatively.

A young man, shimmering as holograms did, appeared in front of them. "How may I be of assistance, Master President?" Micah choked back a laugh, coughing into her hand instead.

"Yes, please, Holly. Can you explain what this all does?"

"Of course. I am here to serve. Please relax, as this will take some time. Let us start with the first workstation…" They followed the hologram as he walked to a place on a raised platform. "This is the Command Chief's workstation…"

As Braden had experienced before, the ancients' terminology was completely unknown. They stopped Holly often to define terms, explain what should have been simple concepts. The time passed both quickly and slowly as they went from station to station, from screen to screen. The capabilities of the New Command Center were beyond their understanding, but their real interest lie in the purpose behind it all.

"Thank you for all that, Holly, and your infinite patience as you helped us to understand." Braden assumed his best Trader persona. He thought there was a person somewhere behind the hologram and he believed all people deserved to be treated with respect, until they proved they shouldn't be.

"Are the people on Cygnus VI still alive?"

"I don't have that answer. Communications have not been reestablished because our system has not yet been rebuilt. It is in the construction process. It should be functional within the month. With the loss of our telecommunications, we also lost contact with Earth's Resettlement Vessel, the RV Traveler. My scopes show it still in a high orbit. It appears to be fully functional, but my data is limited. When we reestablish communications with Cygnus VI, we will also reestablish communication with the Traveler. It will be a full year before the matter transfer components are back online, assuming the systems on Traveler and Cygnus VI are functional."

"Earth? Is there another planet out there that we've gone to?"

"The people of the Cygnus system are originally from Earth, a planet located two thousand, four-hundred light years from here."

"Everyone is from there?"

"Yes. It is the home of the human species. The RV Traveler flew through space for many millennia before arriving here. The settlers were in cryo-storage for the trip, revived years before their arrival to best prepare for planetfall. Many stayed on board as the rest colonized Cygnus VII, then Cygnus VI."

"Can you show us a picture of the Traveler in the sky?" Braden asked. On the wall of screens, the separate images were replaced by a picture showing a bright spot in the sky. He had always thought that was a small moon. The space ship was yet another example of the titanic capabilities of the ancients. Capabilities that were lost to humans, but not humanity, as the Bots incrementally rebuilt the old world.

The question remained whether they could harness the power or would they end up shutting it down.

The image grew larger and larger until the Traveler filled the screens of the front wall. The ship was long, with large sections in the front and back. The middle section connected the front and back sections by use of large rods, pipes, and tubes. The back end had cylindrical shapes that were open to space with darkness filling them. From the sides of the massive ship, various lights blinked. Lights shown through rows of windows at random locations. To Braden and Micah, the RV Traveler looked very much alive.

"You said something about a transfer system. Do you have a way to travel to that ship?" Micah asked incredulously.

"Not right now, Master President. Within a year, if the matter transfer systems at both ends are functional, then we will be able to transport to the RV Traveler, and further to Cygnus VI."

8 – Two Become One

When they were back in the sunlight, they didn't speak. They enjoyed the natural light of the setting sun after the seeming confinement of the Command Center. They walked around the oasis, thinking to themselves about all they heard. It was so much.

"I can't even begin to wrap my head around all that," Braden began.

"How about a swim? I know where there's a private pool." Without waiting, Micah turned toward the entrance to the residential facility. It was cooler underground, plus they hadn't eaten since they wolfed down the brownies.

She walked with purpose. Braden expected that she was hungry. He looked forward to a pot pie and talking about what they would do next. Maybe it was as simple as waiting for a cycle and then going to the Traveler.

Micah stopped at the office so she could instruct the hologram to give Braden access to her room. After the brief stop, she walked down the corridors, slower this time. Even though they were bright, it was unnatural for the modern people of Vii to be underground like this.

Once in the room, Micah ordered two more brownies. She asked the fabricator if it knew what wine was. Of course it did and it had twenty-seven different types programmed into its database. What would she like to try? Something that went with the brownie. The fabricator recommended a fruity burgundy. She ordered two glasses.

They sat at a table by the small pool, sipping the wine and eating their first, second, and third helpings of the brownies. Micah watched Braden as he was deep in thought. She caressed his hair with one hand. He shook himself from his deep thoughts.

She stepped away from the table and removed her vest. She threw it on the floor at his feet. He looked at her, watching closely as she slowly unbuttoned her shirt and let it fall behind her. She undid her pants and let them fall to the floor, stepping gracefully out of them..

Micah was solid, her mid-section well-muscled. Her shoulders were a little wider than her chest which was just a little wider than her waist. Her hips were wide, but shapely. Her legs were strong. There was no fat on her body.

Braden tried to keep his eyes on her eyes, but failed. She was an incredible sight. She was light skinned, tanned only on her face and hands. Her skin was milky smooth.

His heart hammered in his chest.

He could see her hands shaking, ever so slightly. "Aren't you going to join me?" she said, her voice catching.

She led him to the bedroom where they laid down together.

"How did I ever deserve this? Deserve you?" he whispered into her ear.

"You're the only one I want, I'll ever want," she answered…

In the end, they giggled, covered with sweat. They held each other tightly. Micah looked up with her dark brown eyes, heavy lashes blinking away a drop of sweat.

"From here forward, I will always protect you," Micah whispered.

"And I you. I never knew I could feel like this. It's like I feel with G-War, but even better." Micah raised her eyebrows at him, as he thought about what he said. "No, I'm sorry. You're not like the 'cat at all, but the feeling, like when we first bonded, mindlinked. An incredible feeling. I don't know what I'm saying."

He looked at her and knew what he felt, but as a man, he was hesitant to say it. "Am I in love with you, Micah?"

"Yes. We are in love. And we are the same partners we were two sleeps ago. The same we'll be two sleeps from now. But, from here on, we'll only need one bed, one roof over our heads." Braden nodded. He was good with that. He felt different from the second he met her. Now he knew why.

In Micah's village, a weeding vow was sealed by the swearing of mutual protection. In her mind, they were now married.

'About time,' came a 'cat voice from seemingly far away...

9 – A New Dawn

Braden didn't know how to act. He woke up next to Micah, not knowing whether it was day or night. Had a full sleep passed? He carefully worked his way out of bed, trying not to disturb the incredible young woman sleeping comfortably cocooned in blankets and pillows.

It was too far to go outside, so he stood in the shower and let the water run while he relieved himself. The water briefly turned yellow as it swirled around his feet and disappeared down the drain. He adjusted the water a bit hotter and let it run over his head as he undid his braid to let the warmth flow through his long, blonde hair.

The door opened and Micah entered. She smiled at him as she sat on the shiny white throne. When she was done, she pushed a button on the side and the water washed everything away, refilling the bowl.

"How'd you learn to do that?"

"It's natural, I'm a human." She cocked her head playfully at him.

"Not that!" He pointed to the throne. "That."

"The hologram told me."

"When?" Braden was confused.

"While you were sleeping. You didn't feel me get up? How are you supposed to protect me if you sleep like a dead man?"

"I, well, I-I don't know," he stammered. She laughed as she joined him in the shower. They washed each other thoroughly.

Once dry, they went to the open area in search of their clothes. They found them cleaned and neatly lying on the couch. Micah stopped, instantly alert. Braden was unaffected.

"I guess the Server Bot stopped by to help." The dirty brownie plates and wine glasses were gone, too.

"Mr. Fabricator. What would you recommend for a hearty breakfast, something to put meat on your bones?"

"A nice omelet with plenty of cheese, fresh vegetables, and a healthy serving of salsa. Hash browns on the side. I suggest a glass of orange-passionfruit juice, too."

"Fresh vegetables and cheese on whatever you suggested will probably be great. We'll take two."

Braden's mouth started watering as he thought about the delightful ding that would signal breakfast was ready.

Ding. Almost drooling, Braden opened the door to the fabricator and pulled out two dishes with steaming food piled high. It looked like fried eggs with some tomato sauce, then maybe sliced up potatoes on the side? When it came to food, sometimes it was better not to look at things too closely.

"This is incredible!" Micah exclaimed, mouth stuffed with melted cheese and vegetables. She hurried through her omelet and gulped down her juice.

"What's your hurry?"

"I didn't realize how hungry I was."

"Well. We did work hard yesterday, and we didn't have a proper meal, unless you consider lady-flesh, dinner, and dessert wrapped into one."

Micah looked sideways at him. "Really? I've heard you do better when you were trying to work a trade with someone you didn't like. How about you try again."

Braden absentmindedly braided his hair as he thought. This partnership was going to be interesting. "Master President, I beg you to savor your meal. Every bite is a feast unto itself." He bowed when he finished.

"That's better, partner mine. Sooo, yesterday turned out to be a full day.

What about today?"

"I'd like to talk to Aadi, G, and Ess. They were listening when we were in the Command Center. I expect they saw something we missed, which could be a great deal. I hardly remember anything from yesterday, but then again, I remember the important stuff." He smiled and shook his head. Why was it so hard to have a conversation? Weren't they the same people they were yesterday?

No. They weren't. They had become less and more at the same time. Braden and Micah went from half of what they were to become more than they could ever be by themselves. And there came the revelation and acceptance.

"I don't think I want to take any Old Tech back north to trade. I don't think they can handle the Old Tech that we've seen. A Security Bot? In the hands of that rich guy who ripped me off in Whitehorse? I don't think so." Accepting his new role, it was no longer a finished trade when he made a decision. There were two of them now.

"What do you want to do, you know, with our lives?" he asked Micah.

"Now that's a good question. I think it's good to say what we don't want. I don't want to go back to Trent, but understand that we may have to if we're successful building trade routes. I think I want to see the north, but don't want to die crossing the Barren. Maybe we can get the Lizard Men to trade with the good people of Village McCullough. Wouldn't that be something?" Micah had thought about those things before, but didn't mention them to Braden. She didn't want to distract him, not before anyway.

"I think I want to see that ship in the sky. I can't even imagine…" Braden's mind had gone back to the New Command Center.

"Whaddya say we go rally the boys?" Braden said. Micah took his hand as they walked the corridor, side by side.

10 - Insight

Master Aadi's face remained unreadable as he blinked slowly. If the 'cat was trying to look smug, he was successful. Skirill was on a low branch, bobbing peacefully just over their heads.

Micah's face flashed red. Braden understood a heartbeat later. With their mindlink, the companions shared everything the humans did.

Everything.

There was a lot to be said for the peace of darkness.

"Ass! Can't you shut it off?" Braden scolded the 'cat.

'Why would I want to?' G-War responded calmly.

"What's a good kitty want?" Micah asked, still red from embarrassment. She started stroking the 'cat's ears, scratching behind them, under his chin. "How about the good kitty stops the mindlink every now and then?" She continued scratching him, getting under his legs and along his sides.

'No. I will never leave Braden to himself. If something happened to him when I wasn't listening, I would die. That's how our mindlink works.'

That was sobering. Micah stood up and pursed her lips. "Wow. I guess we're all partners then. I will protect all of you, to my last breath." She committed herself.

Skirill stopped bobbing. He focused his Hawkoid gaze on Micah, proud that he had joined the caravan and the companions. This was what he sought. This was the foundation of a community that he wanted to build for the Hawkoids, and they shunned him for it.

Aadi stopped blinking and stared. Braden felt the same way about his companions but he wasn't as good at saying it, so he shook his finger at the

Tortoid. "You're old enough! You should know better than to peek in the windows."

Master Aadi blinked rapidly and slowly bobbed his head. *'Yes. I know better, but it's fascinating. Tortoids don't do that. We procreate by ourselves.'*

"We weren't procreating," Braden blurted out.

'What were you doing then?' the Tortoid asked innocently.

"Umm…" Micah's face blushed a bright shade of red.

11 – The Next Move

"Our next move. I suggest we go back to Village McCullough and find their first trading partner. Any other ideas?" Braden asked the group.

G-War gave a 'cat shrug. He was indifferent to tomorrow.

"I would like to talk with the Lizard Men. I feel they're misunderstood by the humans in the border villages. Maybe they would be willing to trade," Braden said, thinking out loud. "The keys to trade, Master Aadi. What do they have and what do they want? Do we know?"

We do not. I do not. That's why I want to talk with them. I wonder if the special material they weave in McCullough would help protect the legs of the Lizard warriors as they travel through the swamps? Would they protect against a cold-water croc bite?'

"I don't know about that, but I'm sure I don't want to be the one to test your idea. Then again, maybe we do want to test that idea. If we can lure a croc with something and he bites it, we can see if it works. If it does, then they will want it. Want is the key ingredient to any successful trade. Need is better, but I doubt the Lizard Men really need anything. They've made do with what they have for as long as they've been around."

Skirill wanted to limit the time they spent in the Amazon. He was barely able to fly in the tight confines of the jungle environment, so he couldn't help the companions like in more open areas. He felt good about what he'd done for the caravan as they crossed the Great Desert. He was scorched every time he flew in the sun, but didn't share that with Braden. It was only pain. If he didn't do it, then they might not have made it. He saw the work Braden did every time he set up their camp for the day. He saw the human dig in the heat of the sun while the rest of the companions watched. He knew they all felt bad not being able to help, even the 'cat, although he would never share that.

"I think we've made good progress with the villages. If we keep visiting,

31

they'll get used to visitors, while we make sure no new strong man rises from the ashes of those who have gone before."

"I only want them to not be afraid," Braden said while staring into space. To him, simple was best. Soon the villagers would trust them and that was the foundation of trade.

12 – Leave the Soft Life Behind

Staying underground was disorienting for the humans. There were no visual cues as to the time. Their newly discovered interest in each other made time pass in an incalculable way. Braden surrendered and simply asked G-War to wake them up as sunrise approached.

Which he did, in a less than diplomatic way, by calling Braden names until he woke.

They stopped by the office on their way out so Micah could instruct the hologram to keep their room ready for their return.

"It is the Presidential Suite, after all. No one else will be allowed to use it. Are you expecting people to arrive in your absence?" the hologram asked.

"No. But just in case. We like that room. It opened many doors for us, and we have fond memories of it." She winked at Braden. He quickly turned away, smiling. "Thank you and we will return when the communications system is operational."

As they walked out, Braden said, "Spoken like one in charge. I think you like being in charge." They climbed the stairs together, each to their own thoughts, both happy. It was still dark outside, but hints of dawn shone through the trees.

The 'cat waited for them as they emerged from the building. "Blaster," was all Braden said to Micah, and she headed toward the repair shed. "Water," he said for himself as he made sure all their flasks were filled. They hadn't smoked any additional meat, but from the fabricator, they loaded up on dried fruit and other things that would keep. It didn't have to taste good, it only had to give them enough energy to make it to a place where they could hunt.

G-War and Skirill had reduced the rabbit population of New Sanctuary. The 'cat could probably make it back to McCullough before he needed to eat again. Not so for the Hawkoid. He quickly burned through whatever he ate, so eating was a constant state. They had enough in a blanket pack to keep him from starving to death at least, but maybe the Lizard Men could help find game in the rainforest to keep Skirill fit.

Max and Pack had enjoyed their stay. They seemed to have gained weight. The two horses also relished the attention from the humans. They welcomed getting saddled and the patting and stroking that came with it.

Once ready, both humans mounted their rides and urged them through the trees of the oasis toward the sparse grasses of the rolling hills as the sun peeked above the horizon.

"Next time, I'd like to get a closer look at old Sanctuary. Maybe we can take a Security Bot with us to make sure we don't have any trouble," Braden offered.

"Knowing what I know now, I think I'd like to get a closer look, too. I can't believe everything they built. And then they destroyed it all."

"It's our responsibility to not let that happen again. C'mon, G! Hop up." The 'cat didn't respond. He loped alongside the horses as they trotted through the dry grasses. The morning sun shone lightly on the patch of burned grass that dominated one of the small hills. "Sorry about that," Braden called out to the wounded land.

'Need some exercise.' The 'cat wasn't used to a soft life. On the journey from the north, he had spent more time in a cart or on a horse than he liked. He knew there was no other way, but finally decided that when he didn't have to ride, he wouldn't. He liked his body hard and ready to fight. He stretched his legs as he accelerated forward.

Max and Pack kicked themselves into a gallop, but they couldn't keep up with the fleet Hillcat. Master Aadi bounced along behind Braden, holding the rope in his beak-like mouth. He looked less than comfortable with the speed.

Skirill outdistanced all of them, circling back to let the earth-bound catch up. He loved the feeling of the breeze through his chest feathers. It was warm already, but not hot. He tucked his wings along his body, using only his wing tips to adjust his flight as he sped toward the ground. He whipped past the horses, barely over their heads, and stayed even with the ground as he shot toward G-War. He dropped dangerously close to the ground as he sped past the 'cat, then beat strongly to gain altitude.

When Braden saw that, it made him think. If G-War was able to ride on Skirill, the way they fought an enemy could drastically change. He shared that idea with them via their mindlink. Skirill was willing to give it a try, but G-War was hesitant. Since he was able to share the Hawkoid's view, he understood what it would be like to be so far above the ground.

He finally agreed to try it.

The Hawkoid was barely larger than the 'cat, so with his front legs wrapped around Skirill's neck and his back legs wrapped tightly in front of the Hawkoid's tail feathers, they tried to fly. Skirill had to run along the ground as he beat his wings. Finally, struggling mightily, they were up, horse-head high, then higher than a building, then even with the top of a tall tree.

G-War thought that was high enough. They could all hear him thinking about ways he could survive if he fell, landing on his feet, skipping off tree branches, ripping the Hawkoid's wings off and trying to use those...

Skirill had to ask the 'cat a number of times to loosen his grip around his neck. He couldn't fly if he couldn't breathe.

The 'cat liked the feeling of power he had while flying high above the ground. He felt almost invincible. Until he slipped just a little, then the thought of plunging to his death took over. He tightened his grip and let Skirill know that it was time to get back on the ground. They worked out a method where Skirill would back wing just before touching down and G-War would leap in the air. He would land running forward. If they had to fly into the attack, Skirill didn't want to land where he was most vulnerable.

It was almost perfect, but G-War slipped a little to the side as Skirill flared short of the ground. If he hadn't been a 'cat, he probably would have landed on his side. But 'cats always land on their feet. With a deft twist, he landed, running quickly to keep from planting his 'cat face into the dirt.

G-War was satisfied to be in one piece and was breathing heavily from his exertions. Skirill was also spent. Flying with the 'cat on his back was as hard as flying in a storm's wind. They would save that for dire situations only.

G-War sat and waited for the horses. When they trotted up, he leapt gracefully to Braden's lap, who helped steady him as they continued without stopping.

13 – Waiting Productively

They made camp at the edge of the rainforest, even though it was only late afternoon. Aadi wanted to go forward and meet with the Lizard Men alone. They all watched him go, not knowing if it was a good idea or not. There had to be creatures in there who thought a Tortoid would make a good meal. Once he was able to find the Lizard Men, though, they would keep him out of harm's way.

Until then, they waited. The 'cat crouched low, watching the Amazon intently. Skirill picked a high branch on a tall tree to sit on, waiting for a call to action.

Micah and Braden gathered the driest wood they could find and tried to make a fire. It wasn't cold, but they'd need the fire to cook dinner, assuming Braden was successful. "Maybe you can hunt using your blaster?" he asked. Micah looked at him oddly. "Then you can kill it and cook it at the same time!" She shook her head as he headed toward the trees, recurve bow at the ready.

With G-War's help, Braden could narrow his search to a small area. There was a wild boar in there. The rainforest itself teemed with life, but it was strange and elusive. As the barren grasslands transitioned into the rainforest, there was game and the heaviest brush. He saw why villages had established themselves along the northern side of the Amazon. The edge of the rainforest provided for all.

In short order, Braden was able to bring down a nice boar. He field dressed it and drug it back to the camp site, where they butchered and smoked it. It took well into the evening to complete their work. This also restocked their meat supply far beyond what they would need for the quick trip back to Village McCullough, assuming that Master Aadi didn't stir up the Lizard Men.

14 – A Missing Tortoid

"Have you heard anything from Master Aadi?" Braden asked G-War.

'No. But I would know if anything bad happened. Aadi is simply silent. Maybe he has not yet been successful in his search for the Lizard Men.'

"I don't think so. I expect that they saw him the heartbeat he entered the rainforest. I think we're being watched right now," Braden said, confident that he was right.

"I don't think we should enter until Master Aadi returns," Micah added.

He looked at her, then addressed the 'cat and the Hawkoid, "My thoughts exactly. Get comfortable, boys, it could be a long wait."

Night fell. They slept, but didn't get any rest. Having one of their own missing was upsetting. G-War remained alert through to sunrise. No news.

"We need to think about how we go in after Master Aadi," Braden said to Micah. She agreed, but had no ideas. Braden didn't either. The only thing he could think to do was to walk in and hope to meet a Lizard Man who recognized them.

Hope was a lousy plan.

They waited.

They spent the day taking turns hunting. Micah used string to set snares on game trails. Braden tried to bag a quail, but never got close enough. He was happy that he didn't. He wasn't sure how Skirill would react if they ate a bird.

G-War maintained his silent vigil. It seemed that the 'cat had formed a close bond with the Tortoid. Well, the rest of them had too.

As the sun was setting a second time since Master Aadi had departed, G-War spoke. *'He returns.'*

15 – The Lizard Men Trade

Master Aadi found the Lizard Men right away. They led him back to their camp where they shared a small meal of freshly caught fish. The Lizard Men wanted to share their history with the Tortoid in the only way they could. They told it to him. Once started, they could not stop. That took the rest of the night and half the next daylight.

The Lizard Men were a product of the ancients, just like every mutated animal. The Tortoid, the Hawkoid, and the Hillcats were all examples of engineered creatures. The ancients had designed each animal for a specific purpose. The Lizard Men were created to work within the rainforest where swamp and rain were constant obstacles.

The Lizard Men built the original roads through the Amazon. They maintained the roads. They held nature at bay so the ancients could travel without any problems. The ancients were masters of the air, but the heavy materials traveled overland. Once the quarries supporting Sanctuary were exhausted, they dug new quarries north of the rainforest. Those ores moved overland to the massive factories around Sanctuary.

Once the war started, all technology became targets as the ancients fought for control. The Lizard Men retreated deep into the rainforest and waited. One day, there were no more sounds from air vehicles, from the land trains, or from humanity.

When the Lizard Men left the shelter of the deep rainforest, they found that Sanctuary and the surrounding lands had been destroyed. The first ones to observe the destruction died hideous deaths as their bodies wasted away from the radiation. Only in the last hundred cycles had Lizard Men been able to venture to the southern edge of the Amazon without being affected.

The Lizard Men flourished over time. There were now thousands of them scattered throughout the rainforest. They had a number of villages and even a rudimentary government. The Lizard Man that they met on the road, Zalastar, was their senior leader. Once he guaranteed their safety, every Lizard Man was obligated to comply. The Lizard Men would protect the companions, because their leader directed them to.

The Lizard Men told a detailed story of their lineage, which they considered a key element of their history. Aadi listened attentively and remembered the ancestry of the Lizard Men leaders. The companions politely declined hearing the specifics from Master Aadi.

After Aadi shared his story, Braden only had one question. "What about trade?"

'Yes, of course. They don't make anything extra, but they could if we found something the humans needed. Do you know what that would be?' Aadi asked innocently.

"I have no idea. What do they make?" Braden parried.

'Maybe it's more like what they grow. They harvest a particular mushroom that they carry when they travel. It sustains them as if it were the best meat.'

"Do you know what it tastes like?" Micah asked.

'Master Human… I don't think you want my opinion of how something tastes. I thought it was delightful, but you should judge for yourselves.'

"Sounds interesting," Braden replied. "It would be good to have an alternative to meat, especially if it keeps without spoiling. I think that settles it. First thing tomorrow, we're going north. If you would be so kind as to arrange a meeting with the Lizard Men, Master Aadi, then we'll talk about what trade with Village McCullough could look like." Braden was pleased that the Lizard Men had thought about something to trade. It always started with one thing until the people learned more about each other, then it expanded.

They only needed to get the humans past their distrust of anything mutant. They'd made progress with Village McCullough because of his companions, but would they accept the Lizard Men?

Micah saw the excitement on Braden's face as Master Aadi talked about the mushrooms. He had sold her on his vision of a world where all creatures shared the things they produced for the things they wanted. She could see her village drying fish to bring inland for those who had no access to the sea. And from them, they could get greens, vegetables, maybe even fresh red meat. She rubbed Braden's shoulders as they both thought about the possibilities.

"Trade. So much better than war to get what you want," she said. "Why do men choose war?" It was a rhetorical question. No one knew why people chose the road to violence. She put her hand on the blaster. Maybe it was more about power. She wondered how the village of Cornwall was doing without the power of the blaster? Did they go to war with Trent?

Maybe by taking the blaster, she'd prevented war.

16 - Zalastar

Braden and Micah slept close that night. They were both relieved that Aadi was back, and they celebrated as a young couple does.

G-War and Skirill slept like the dead. They had been successful hunting, although Braden found it hard to believe that the 'cat was physically capable of eating one more bite after gorging at the oasis.

Aadi thought nothing of it all. He did what he had to do, as he had done for the past two hundred cycles.

When the sun rose, they left their camp. The only sign they'd stayed was dirt kicked over the place where their fire had been.

They set a good pace as they followed the ruins of the ancients' road north. Once in the Amazon, the air thickened with moisture and rain threatened to fall. The sun disappeared somewhere above the green canopy of tree limbs and vines. On their first trip through the rainforest, Braden and Micah had been consumed by the perpetual gloom and unknown beings that surrounded them.

Everything was different now. The rainforest was vibrant with innumerable shades of green and brown. Everything was alive. From the vines to the trees to the undergrowth to the animal life. Leaves and bushes rustled as unknown creatures fled from the caravan, forever remaining unseen.

It was almost mid-day of travel before they met a Lizard Man. Aadi was immediately excited and swam forward when they stopped the horses. They couldn't hear him when he communicated with the Lizard Men, so they had to wait, but not for long.

'Zalastar gives his warmest greetings to his friends! They have prepared a celebration in your honor.' Braden and Micah got down from their horses so they could

greet the leader of the Lizard Men.

"Master Aadi, is there any way we can talk with him directly?"

'I'm sorry, no. Even the Golden Warrior cannot talk with the Lizard Men. Odd. I'll pass on what you say. It is my pleasure to do so.'

"Thanks, Master Aadi," Braden said to the Tortoid before turning to the Lizard Man towering over him. "Zalastar. It is good to see you again, my friend. Your offer of a celebration in our honor is humbling. I suggest we make it a celebration of a long future together as friends."

It took Aadi much longer to relay that and get a response. Their communication method was frustrating.

'The celebration will be on the road ahead, so all companions may attend. Zalastar appreciates your friendship. With it, he sees a future for his people where they are no longer constrained to the swamps of the rainforest.'

"Trade it is, my good man. Trade it is." Braden reached up to slap Zalastar on the shoulder, then thought better of it. "Aadi. What is a way that I can show gratitude directly? I don't see a hug in our future, but maybe a handshake?"

After a short pause, Aadi chuckled in his thought voice. *'Very funny, Master Braden. Zalastar finds the human need for touch quite humorous. The Lizard Men never touch as their skin protects them from the harsh elements where they live. They suspect they are poisonous to pinkies, that is, you and your soft flesh.*

'A sign of respect is to simply bow your head. Others will go to one knee, but those are from the lowest order, which you most assuredly are not.' Braden and Micah both bowed their heads to Zalastar. Braden raised his hand, palm toward the Lizard Man.

"Tell him this is how we'll greet him. It shows we have no weapon in our hand and that we place trust in the one to whom we wave."

After Aadi shared that with Zalastar, he promptly dropped his spear and raised his hand. Braden and Micah waved back. Zalastar picked up his spear and waved it over his head as he turned and headed down the road.

Braden and Micah smiled at each other as they returned to their horses, hand in hand. "A leg up, partner mine?" he asked as she stepped into his cupped hands to get back into the saddle.

17 – Another Celebration

The celebration was more tame than the previous one. Without the cold-water croc episode firing the emotions, it didn't have the pizzazz. There were fewer Lizard Men around this time, as this was far from their homes, wherever those were, whatever those were.

There were plenty of fish, even deer, but as the Lizard Men did, all of it was raw. Skirill made the biggest splash by flying around the gathering, then gracefully landing in the middle of the road. One of the children, demonstrating what it meant to be fearless, ran to the Hawkoid with a fish, while his parent chased after him. Skirill gently took the fish from the lad and bowed his head in appreciation. Silent cheers filled the area; the child positively beamed.

G-War took it all in. It seemed that he was less than amused that he could not talk directly with the Lizard Men. Braden took it for granted the 'cat could talk with any creature. It was refreshing to see he had limits, although it would have been nice to converse with the Lizard Men without an intermediary.

Micah appreciated what they had accomplished. She felt that she was a part of something much bigger than herself. She was at the beginning of a movement that, if successful, could mean an era of peace and cooperation. The days of submitting to the strongest needed to be behind them.

She and her partner were creating an entirely new world.

Braden's thoughts were simpler. He liked how trade was conducted in the north. That's all he wanted. Safe roads leading to market squares filled with people looking to buy. When he left, the north was going in a direction he didn't like. When he got back there, he would have to make changes. No one could be allowed to destroy trade.

No one.

18 – 'shrooms

Micah and Braden each held one of the mushrooms, looking carefully at them. They were dark with specks that looked hideous. Despite rinsing them off with water from a flask, they still did not look very tasty. Zalastar stood patiently, watching the humans. It was good that he didn't understand human body language.

"We don't know if these are poisonous, although I suspect not. No need for both of us to try it. I'll take a bite and you watch me to see if anything changes." He hesitated as he tried to decide which side of the mushroom to try. In that moment, Micah calmly lifter the mushroom to her mouth and took a big bite. Braden's mouth fell open and he sputtered, trying to come up with the words.

"I swore to protect you," Micah started. "This is part of that. I swore first, so that means I take the risk. By the way, it tastes a lot better than it looks, maybe like a piece of overcooked quail." Braden was angry, but he shouldn't have been. One of them needed to try it. It wasn't his place to decide for them both. As it was, he made her the President, and maybe that was his last major decision. Some day he would reconcile himself with that. But not today.

"You shouldn't have tried it. It was my responsibility."

"I'm sorry, lover, too late. For what it's worth, I feel fine. Why don't you take a bite?" Not to be outdone, he bit his mushroom in half, filling his mouth completely. It had a texture like leather, and Micah was right, it tasted like overcooked quail. It wasn't bad. He ate the rest of it, chewing slowly. It was a little dry, so he had to wash it down with a healthy swig of water.

He handed the flask to Micah. She thanked him for it and chased her mushroom with the remainder of the water.

"Once you get past how it looks, it's not bad. This could be something of great value." He pulled Micah to him for a long hug. He wanted to tell her not to do that again, but knew she wouldn't listen. She took her role as his protector seriously. He wouldn't take that lightly, so he settled for, "I don't want to lose you."

Micah knew what he meant. Maybe she had acted rashly, but she trusted Master Aadi. If it hadn't been poisonous for him, she assumed that it wouldn't hurt her or Braden.

She wanted him to know that their relationship was an equal partnership. Besides bringing trade to her world, she wanted to bring equality to his. Half the people weren't less than the other half. She couldn't have it that way. Braden's actions at Village McCullough suggested he thought the same way. Everything revolved around trade. Who conducted the trade was immaterial.

She couldn't wait to get back to McCullough and see how Braden was going to work the trade between the village women and the Lizard Men. It would be interesting to say the least. She also wanted to show off their partnership. If those two little girls came sniffing around Braden, she'd slap the snot out of them.

Now where had that come from?

19 – Setting Up the Trade

The remainder of the trip to Village McCullough was uneventful. They carried with them double saddle bags filled with mushrooms. They set a date, four sleeps after they left the rainforest, to meet at the point where the road enters the Amazon in the north. They could travel that distance from the village in a single morning.

Having neutral trade sites was a less common practice in the north because every town or village had a market square. But when trust was lacking, neutral sites provided a way for trade to continue.

The women of the village rolled out to meet them. Time had treated them well. A number wore swords proudly, while others carried bows. Everyone was armed in some way. Mel-Ash greeted them kindly.

Braden looked at Micah and nodded for her to go ahead.

"What do you think about doing a little trading? We found people who have these mushrooms." She took one from the pack and rinsed it off for the Elder. "It's safe to eat. Go ahead." Mel-Ash screwed up her face before taking the tiniest bite. Satisfied it was safe, she ate the whole thing.

"Who are these people, and where are they?" she asked suspiciously. She knew there weren't any villages between McCullough and the rainforest road.

"They are the Lizard Men of the Amazon Rainforest," Braden replied. "They are our friends and provided this sample to show what they are willing to trade for your special woven material. We hope your material will protect their legs and arms from the dangers they face in the swamps of the rainforest."

"Lizard Men, you say?" Elder McCullough looked at Braden and Micah sideways. "Aren't you two the oddest. Friends with floating turtles and talking birds. And then there's him." She pointed at G-War as he bolted toward a group of children, veering away at the last second. They raced after him yelling and howling as the 'cat led them on a crazy tour of the village.

Micah took Braden's hand, holding it as they stood with the Elder.

"What's a Lizard Man anyway?" the Elder asked, smiling knowingly at the young couple while they continued to talk. Braden and Micah vouched for the Lizard Men and that was good enough for Mel-Ash. The question now was could they get some tunics and leggings done in time?

If they didn't have to hunt, that would free up people to weave. And that was the value of a good trade.

20 – Learn to Hunt

If G-War wasn't playing with the children, Skirill was. Between the two of them, they wore the children down and soon after, they were fast asleep.

Braden and Micah regaled them with their adventures in the rainforest. The attack of the killer cold-water crocs and the amazing Lizard Man celebration. The rain, the endless rain.

Before arriving at the village, they agreed not to tell them about New Sanctuary. That would have to remain secret. Even a hint of its existence could be destructive. They shared that the grasses in the rolling hills between the rainforest and the destroyed city were returning and nothing else.

Braden learned that the village hunters had only killed one deer during their absence. He committed to taking the two best hunters to show them what they needed to do to be more successful. Micah stayed behind to see how far the others progressed in their sword training. She then talked with the village leaders about ways to run the village. What did their future look like if they were to be a trading hub?

The two young vixens had seduced the remaining man in the village, so they never saw much of him. It also kept the young ladies from bothering Braden. He wanted to be far away from them. Not because he was tempted, but if he gave the wrong impression, he might get a gentle beat down from Micah. Running away was the better part of valor. Plus the village's hunters needed to learn to hunt. They couldn't live on mushrooms alone.

The next few days went by with the village hard at work weaving custom pieces for the Lizard Men. Aadi was the most helpful in adjusting the sizes. It seemed that he had an eye for girth. No one else had looked that closely. The humans could only say the Lizard Men were larger than they were, but they were wildly different guessing how much bigger.

The hunting was rejuvenated after Braden taught them the importance of wind direction, stalking, and patience. With their homemade bows, they had to be closer than Braden with his recurve bow. In the end, they were successful, bringing down a number of deer.

Micah looked at Braden and said, "No matter where we go, they are always celebrating. We must be doing something right." Braden nodded, smiling.

21 – Moving to Trade

Everyone from the village wanted to go. Braden and Micah weren't sure, but Master Aadi told them not to worry. Once they determined who would stay behind to protect the village, the rest packed up lunches and fell in behind the horses. Elder McCullough, Mel-Ash, walked for a while, but Micah encouraged her to ride in the cart. She was joined by two women with small children. Pack didn't mind. The ladies were still thin from the ordeal of their lives before the companions changed it all.

Skirill flew ahead to make sure the way was clear. G-War rode in the cart, although he could have ridden in the saddle. Braden was beginning to wonder about the 'cat. He seemed to have taken a great liking to the children and oddly enough, he allowed them to pet him until his hair was ready to come off.

He thought the kids might be happier if they could find a few dogs for the village.

'Dogs?' G-War asked sarcastically.

"Ass!" Braden said out loud. Some of the villagers looked at him oddly. He mumbled a quick apology.

"Can you hear me thinking?" he asked Micah in a quieter voice.

"Yes, but I wasn't paying attention. But I heard G-War. I can only imagine what you were thinking." She laughed to herself.

"You and G-War bonded when you were a boy. You had no worries. Your parents took care of you both. Now that you're both grown up, you don't play. The children give him that. It's nothing on you." He nodded. "When we have our own children, I expect he will be more of a parent to them than us."

That shocked Braden. He hadn't thought that far ahead. Children? "Hang on there. I'm Free Trader Braden…"

"Not so free anymore, partner mine." She leaned in close. He had been bewitched, his mind taken over! He pinched himself on the arm. Nope. Still felt that. He looked at Micah. She was watching his antics.

"I feel funny," he said to himself, smiling inwardly. "I kind of like it."

The area ahead is clear,' Skirill said over the mindlink, interrupting Braden's thoughts. *I cannot see far into the rainforest, but I don't see any movement. I do see a ground squirrel that requires my attention, however, if you can take it from here?*'

Of course,' Braden and Micah answered together.

G, are you sensing anything up ahead?' Braden asked in his thought voice.

Many creatures. It is the rainforest. I think it is safe,' the 'cat answered.

"I think we need to be ready, just in case." Braden called a halt and gathered the women together. Micah and those with swords would be on the left, close to the rainforest. Those with bows would be on the right. Braden would anchor the far right end of the line as his bow could shoot the farthest. Micah anchored the left side, closest to the rainforest. She was the most powerful warrior among them.

Mel-Ash would be behind the line in the middle, leading Max. Aadi would be next to her, to protect her.

G-War was happy to get ready for battle, although he didn't expect one. He jumped from the cart and disappeared into the edge of the rainforest.

Skirill, having finished his meal, landed on a high branch overlooking where the ancients' road entered the rainforest. He still saw no threats, but appreciated Braden's caution.

The line moved forward at a brisk walk, because the ladies from the village were anxious and excited. They were ready for a real battle!

They slowed as the rush wore off.

They moved to the designated trade location without any problems. They put the horses and the cart in the middle of the open area on the remains of the road. Braden positioned those with swords around the opening and told those with bows to put them down. The first sight of a Lizard Man could be shocking and he didn't want any accidents.

"Master Aadi, can you sense if the Lizard Men are near?"

'No. I can only talk with them when I can see them. Which is right about now.' The Tortoid swam forward as the rainforest seemed to melt. Lizard Men appeared all around them.

Even the Hawkoid's sharp eyes had not been able to see the Lizard Men, who had been there the entire time.

A couple of the women quickly raised their swords. Bows were picked up and pulled. "Hold! McCullough! Hold!" Braden shouted, jumping in front of the bowmen.

"Hold, ladies. These are our trading partners. Show them some respect!" Mel-Ash shouted in a surprisingly strong voice.

22 – Mushrooms for Tunics

"Zalastar! It is good to see you once again, my friend." Zalastar waved as he approached and Braden waved back. He then bowed deeply, as did Micah and Mel-Ash. The Lizard Man also bowed before waving forward a number of Lizard Men carrying bags made from vines and leafy fronds. They were filled with mushrooms.

Aadi introduced everyone and the humans bowed as Micah had taught them. The Lizard Men waved as Zalastar had taught them. After their initial shock at seeing the strange creatures, the villagers warmed up.

Elder McCullough signaled to the ladies in the cart. Two of them brought forward the finished tunics and leggings they had. Aadi asked if Zalastar would try them on.

He handed his spear to Braden, who took it without hesitation. Aadi told him that holding the leader's weapon was the greatest symbol of trust within the Lizard Man community. Once again, Braden had been honored.

Zalastar shrugged the tunic over his head. The neck opening was tighter than it should have been, but it still fit. It hung to his waist and could probably have been a little bit longer. The leggings tied on perfectly, covering the front half of his back legs. They had woven only two pieces for the forearms, but these also fit him well.

Braden handed the spear back to Zalastar. He moved around to get the feel of wearing the armored clothing. Lizard Men didn't wear clothes so the entire experience was new. Zalastar drew the point of his spear across his chest, then looked underneath the tunic. He went to the edge of the trees and scraped his legs and arms against the bark and the bushes.

He thrust his spear in the air and barked some short, sharp notes from his wide open mouth. He was very pleased.

23 – A Bridge to the Future

They talked about what a good trade would be for both. Neither side had any experience, so Braden bartered both ways. He asked a great deal of questions, like how long it took to pick a bag of mushrooms, how long it took to weave one tunic, and so on. He tried to match time and effort with quality. One bag of mushrooms was good for one meal for the village. Was one tunic worth one meal or three meals? Six?

In the end, they hammered out an agreement based on amount of material woven. Six leg covers equaled one tunic equaled three bags of mushrooms. Micah had warned everyone not to touch a Lizard Man as their skin was poisonous. So they kept their distance, even though the humans were naturally drawn to shake hands.

The children watched the proceedings in awe for a while. Lizard Men! As children did, they quickly overcame their fears. A very small girl walked up to one of the Lizard Men and grabbed his hand, holding it like she would with any adult.

"No!" screamed her mother, running in a panic to grab her daughter. She bodily pulled the little girl away, kicking at the Lizard Man. Instinctively, he thrust his spear at her, creasing her side. She fell, losing her grip on her child.

Braden and Micah were there in a heartbeat, standing between the Lizard Man and the woman on the ground. The humans held up their hands to stave off any further violence. Zalastar stalked forward, his spear at the ready as he approached his fellow Lizard Man. Without any warning, he thrust his spear through the Lizard Man so violently that he was lifted off the ground, before being thrown down. Zalastar stooped over him and barked at his face. This was not the sound of joy.

Micah was checking the little girl's hand and didn't find anything. She was fine. If there had been any poison, there'd be a sign. How much time had passed since they last touched a human?

"Aadi. What's going on?"

The leader is very angry at his warrior for striking a human.'

"We can see that. But what's next?"

'I don't know, Master Human. I can't talk to him right now. He is very angry.'

"The young girl is fine. I think their skin is not poisonous to humans. Tell him that. And tell him that the woman is injured, but she will recover. We apologize for this all. What can we do to honor Zalastar's warrior?" Micah offered.

Braden walked to Zalastar and without hesitation, wrapped his fingers around the Lizard Man's arm and helped him stand. Zalastar raised his spear as if to strike, then saw who it was. He dropped his spear to the ground, his rage giving way to sadness. Braden put his open hand on Zalastar's chest, now covered by the tunic, and held it there. Even through the material, he could feel the fast beating of the Lizard Man's heart. Zalastar put his hand/claw on Braden's chest.

Zalastar's eyes were difficult to read, but changed when he understood Braden's gesture and felt the beating of the human heart. Micah approached a Lizard Man by her and placed her hand on his chest. One by one, the humans and the Lizard Men paired up, hands on chests, feeling each other's heart beating. Aadi, G-War, and Skirill watched the strange proceedings, hoping they turned out well for their humans.

Aadi was relieved. He had feared the worst. The villagers were no match for the Lizard Men and they would have all died, but for the bravery and commitment of their leaders. Braden, Micah, and Zalastar had built a bridge to the future, a place where all creatures were equal.

24 – Back in Village McCullough

Back in the village, Mel-Ash berated the young mother for losing control. The young lady held her hand against the new stitches in her side. The pain caused her face to contort, but it was more than the pain of the wound. If it hadn't been that her daughter's actions helped to bridge the differences with the Lizard Men, then all would have been lost.

Mel-Ash was spent. She sat down heavily on the floor of her hut, and told the lady to get out of her sight. Braden and Micah watched silently. They absentmindedly nibbled on mushrooms while they waited.

"We need to increase the number of fibers we find and grow. If we're going to outfit the entire Lizard Man nation, we have a lot of work in front of us." With the first trade behind her, the magnitude of it all dawned on the Elder. "We need more people," she said simply.

"What would it take to share the process with the Lizard Men? Maybe they could help harvest the materials you need to produce the fibers. I don't think they'll be able to weave. Their hands don't seem to be shaped for it, although they pick the mushrooms cleanly. I don't know. You guys have a lot more to talk about with the Lizard Men," Braden finished. They agreed to meet with the Lizard Men at the same spot in seven sleeps' time.

"I think you're right, Mel-Ash. You need more people, too." Micah let that sit with them for a bit, then asked, "Where's the closest village?"

"To the east, a couple turns journey, but I don't think so. They are brutes." The Elder shook her head, unconvinced this was the way to go.

"I suspect they might say the same thing about Village McCullough," Braden said. He moved so she would look at him. "Things are different now. Maybe we can help them understand." The Elder's eyes brightened at that.

"And no. I do not intend to kill anyone else," Braden finished.

"Whether you intend to or not, I recommend you sharpen your long knife and check your arrows," the Elder said quietly.

Micah started to leave, then stopped. "Today was a good day, Elder McCullough. It could have gone all kinds of ways, but it didn't. I think we're in a better place. Braden brought us to this point. Trust him to take us further." With that, she left the hut.

Braden was again humbled at what they gave him credit for. Aadi deserved the honors. He made conversation with the Lizard Men possible. He needed to find Aadi and thank him for what he'd done to bring the humans and the Lizard Men together.

Mel-Ash waved him away, so he followed Micah outside.

"When do you want to go?" she asked abruptly.

"Probably first thing in the morning if we want to be back in time for the next meeting with the Lizard Men." Micah nodded. She was thinking the same thing.

"We better get ready then. What do you think we'll run into?"

"Misunderstandings. Bad people in power. Good people repressed. People trying to kill us. You know, the usual…" He laughed as he finished. He had confidence the companions could handle any situation. In the end, they'd win.

They always did.

25 – Three Less in Charge

They decided to ride Max and Pack as they didn't have enough to fill the cart. G-War rode with Braden while Master Aadi was pulled along behind Micah. Skirill flew ahead and watched until the horses arrived, then flew ahead again.

On the horses, the trip to Village Dwyer took only the daylight. They would have arrived at nightfall, but with Skirill's foresight, they were able to find a place to spend the night where they wouldn't be seen. It would take little time after sunrise to travel the remaining distance.

G-War watched as he did every night Braden was on the road. The 'cat reached out with his senses and knew that nothing threatened them. Because nothing knew they were there.

In the morning, after a good meal of smoked meat and mushrooms, they mounted their horses and headed toward the village.

As they got close, the uproar of a dog pack began. Braden laughed long and hard as the dogs ran up to them. Max and Pack were uneasy, the dogs incensed.

"Care to go play, G?" Braden joked. Even with the 'cat's speed, there were too many dogs. Braden couldn't let the 'cat get hurt. At the same time, Braden didn't want to hurt any of the dogs. He could feel G-War's anxiety without the 'cat having to say anything.

They decided to wait for a human rather than run the horses through the dogs.

They didn't have to wait long. Three dirty men, carrying massive clubs, approached. As they got closer, Braden saw spikes sticking out the end of the clubs. These men meant business. Mel-Ash's word for them came to mind: brutes.

With a few words and some kicking, they chased the dogs away, who only moved a short distance before renewing their barking.

"I am Free Trader Braden, seeking an audience with the leader of Village Dwyer so we may discuss the future of trade through your area." Braden ended with his usual flair, bowing at the end to the men.

"Take yur crap and git, you farging craphead!" one of the three bellowed.

'How pleasant,' Braden said to the companions with his thought voice. Then with his outside voice he added, "Are you the leader? What are you called?"

"Suck my balls, you stinking ass!" The man raised his club and waved it menacingly. Braden raised his bow and quickly sent an arrow into the club, ripping it from the man's hand.

"Git 'im, boys!" The other two men stepped forward. Braden nocked another arrow while Micah jumped down and pulled out her sword. The two men laughed at her. "A woman?" the gross man said as a question, but not.

Micah walked toward them, sword raised and back. One man rushed toward her and swung a mighty blow. He may have been trying to knock the sword from her hand, but they would never know. She easily ducked the blow, pivoted and brought the full power of a swing into the man's midsection, nearly cleaving him in half. He tumbled over backwards, or at least his upper body did. His legs remained upright until finally his still-attached spine pulled them over.

The second man looked at the entrails spread across the ground. He approached cautiously, then reared back for a wide swing. Micah stepped in quickly and thrust her sword tip into his groin. He dropped his club and bent over, howling in pain as a darkening circle of blood spread across the front of his pants. The first man cursed her and reached for his club on the ground. Micah took the delay to swing overhead toward the bent-over man. She took his head off cleanly and followed through bringing her sword up to face the gross man.

He roared, eyes wide. Braden sent an arrow into his face. He froze in his threatening pose, then dropped to the ground. The wound bled little.

"I had him!" Micah growled.

"I know you did, lover. Look. We have more company," Braden said calmly.

The entire village had turned out in the brief time it took to dispatch the rather rude greeting party. She wondered what the villagers were in a hurry to see. Odd to think of that while three dead men littered the ground.

"Please, please don't hurt us!" an elderly man pleaded. Braden and Micah looked quickly around. The three men on the ground seemed like the only ones ready to fight. Everyone else looked like farmers, gentle folk.

'G, do you sense anything?'

'Only those stinking dogs. The smell is disgusting. I think I'm going to be sick.' The 'cat started gagging.

"I am Free Trader Braden, come to talk with the free people of Village Dwyer about the possibility of trade." He bowed only slightly, so he could keep his eyes on everyone. No one moved. No one spoke.

"Who's in charge?" Braden asked loudly. A younger person pointed at the men on the ground, where Micah was wiping off her sword on one of them.

"Not anymore, they aren't. Why isn't anyone willing to talk?" Braden was angry and started to yell. Leaving the heaving 'cat on the saddle, he jumped to the ground. He screamed at the dead bodies, "Why did you make us kill you? Why?" He forced himself to relax. "We only wanted to talk. Now, is there someone here willing to talk with us about trading with Village McCullough?" He looked from face to face.

"If that's all you wanted, why didn't you say so?" the old man said under his breath, but everyone heard.

"We did!" Braden lunged forward, but Micah grabbed his arm. More calmly, he added, "We did, but these idiots threatened us. We didn't take that too well."

"Neither did they, it seems," the old man mumbled in response. Braden was beginning to like him.

"What's your name, Elder?" Braden asked. Micah stood next to him, sword still in her hand.

"I am Old Tom. That's it, Crazy Old Tom."

"Well, Tom, I'm pleased to meet you. This is my partner Micah. The Hillcat's name is Golden Warrior. The Tortoid is Aadi, First Master of the Tortoise Consortium. And up there is Skirill, a Hawkoid." The crowd of people started to grumble. The word "muties" came through.

"They are our friends. They are a crapload nicer than these idiots." Braden pointed with his bow at the three corpses. "Assuming these things don't rise from the dead, who is next in charge?"

"Probably Gravenin, but he's hunting right now. Not sure when he and his party will get back."

"That's great," Micah chimed in. "Am I going to have kill them, too?" The people shied away from her. They had seen the last of the battle, especially the part where she cut off the man's head, well, both of his heads if you looked at it a certain way.

"Maybe. Maybe not. I expect he won't like that you killed his brothers," the old man answered.

"I hope for his sake that he's the smart one." Micah knew that they couldn't kill their way to a trade deal, but they couldn't have a blood feud between the villages.

"When will this Gravenin return and from where?" Braden saw people turn and look in a certain direction.

'Skirill, if you would be so kind. See if you can find who they're talking about. It would be nice to know where they are, how many, and what they look like. Will we need to run?' Braden asked over the mindlink.

Skirill leapt into the air and beat skyward, soon disappearing into the distance in the direction the villagers had looked. He made a lazy S in the sky, widening his search the further he got from the village. He saw a thin tendril of smoke rising. Staying high in the sky, he made a beeline for it.

Three men stood around while the haunch of a boar hung over a fire pit. They would not return today.

"I think they'll be back mid-daylight tomorrow," Braden said matter-of-factly. "Between now and then, we'd like you to get to know us. We can be great friends to Village Dwyer. You see what can happen if you are our enemy." Braden said the last part sadly. He didn't want to threaten them or for them to feel threatened, but this was two villages in a row. When Braden arrived, the men in charge died.

Micah finally put her sword away. They each led a horse as they walked into the crowd of people. There must have been some forty or fifty there. No warriors in this group. No mutants of any sort, either.

Once in the middle of the village, Braden and Micah realized it was more extensive than they thought. Maybe the husband trade could be lucrative as Village McCullough was short on men. They were short many men, owing to Braden and Micah.

"Why are the men such asses in this part of Vii?" Braden asked Micah in a low voice.

"Are they that different up north?"

"No. Not really," he said, exasperated. "You know that if you kill too many men, I'll have to expand my man duties in each of these villages?" He smiled evilly at Micah.

"I get your point." She leaned heavily on the pommel of her sword. "And if you want to get my point, you'll say something like that again." She nodded toward the man without a head and a large pool of blood around his groin.

He couldn't help but smile at her. They locked eyes. His heart skipped a beat. They heard someone clear his throat. They looked toward the sound.

Old Tom stood in front of the rest of the villagers.

"Tom. So glad you could join us." Braden clapped the man on the back. "Do you bury your dead?"

It turned out they did, so Braden offered to help dig the graves. They made quick work of it, and dropped the men unceremoniously in. Braden waited to see if they would say something, but they didn't. They simply threw dirt on top of the bodies, then tamped it down firmly and walked away without emotion.

'G, I need you. I can't figure these people out.'

26 – Clean It Up

The Hillcat couldn't deal with so many dogs clamoring for a piece of him, so Skirill helped out by flying above the dogs' heads and getting them to follow him. He flew low and slow. Incensed, they ran and nipped at his tail feathers. He kept going as long as they followed.

This lightened G-War's burden. And Braden's too since he had been carrying the 'cat to keep him out of the dogs' reach. Once on the ground, G-War shook himself and sneezed a couple times. He looked up at Braden and Micah with a dismal expression on his 'cat face. The ground must reek of dog.

It was hard for them not to laugh, but they restrained themselves.

They discovered that Old Tom wasn't crazy at all. He was sharp, using sarcastic wit to keep himself sane. At one time, Tom thought he had a future in the village, a future where he could invent tools and things to make their lives better. But then the brute brothers grew up and took over. They wouldn't allow anything they didn't understand, so that's how they ended up armed with clubs.

Tom hated them for dumbing down the village, for taking out their ignorance on him.

Micah was disgusted at the displays of brute force throughout her land. Some humans were the worst example of humanity, and she was embarrassed for her people. She had seen things might not be right, but she hadn't considered how wrong they could be.

And she was proud to be at Braden's side, trying to reclaim humanity's place. The companions showed her what was possible when creatures of different types banded together for a single cause. At times, they each showed their vulnerabilities, but when one was weak, another was strong.

They carried each other until they could stand on their own again.

That showed what was possible for them all. That showed what Micah wanted for the south. Braden called it trade. Micah called it civilization.

Braden looked at the newly liberated village. No one wanted to take charge, for they were still afraid as long as one of the brothers lived. They looked to Braden to lead them.

He knew he had to, until he and Micah could talk with the remaining brother and his two hunting partners. Those three would have to see reason.

"When killing becomes easy, we will go to the oasis and live out the rest of our lives. Deal?" he asked Micah.

"I enjoyed killing those men, I'm not sorry to say. At the time, anyway." She hesitated and hung her head. "It doesn't make sense. We have to be ready and willing to kill, but opposed to it at the same time. All in the name of free trade." The warrior in her stood proudly, but the human in her deplored the killing. She was torn, but in the end agreed.

"Deal. Killing is never the first choice."

"Everyone in the square! I want to see everyone out there. Right now!" Braden yelled, not in anger, but like a trader setting up for an auction.

There was nothing to stand on to rise above the crowd, so he climbed into the saddle. Max stood peacefully. G-War was nowhere to be seen. Aadi and Micah stayed close to Pack. Skirill watched from a high branch, having only recently returned from leading the dogs deep into the wilderness.

"Good people of Village Dwyer! I want you to take pride in your village and yourselves. Here is what we're going to do…" Braden laid out a plan for everyone to clean the village, then clean themselves. They would restock their water supplies, dig a hole for an outhouse, tear down the shacks that looked ready to fall, and then put things in order. Where Max stood now would be the market square. They would bring logs to build the vendor stalls. He was going to drag them kicking and screaming into a world where people traded freely. Where people trusted first.

The villagers got to work under the watchful eyes of their liberators. These people weren't afraid of hard work. There was hope for them.

27 - Hope

While Micah stayed behind with Aadi to ensure work got done, Braden took two youngsters, G-War, and Skirill hunting. From the size of the village, they needed at least one deer for a single meal. Braden knew the power of a good celebration, and he wanted to reward the village for embracing a new way to treat visitors.

G-War gave them the direction to go. Then, Skirill scouted ahead, easily finding both deer and wild boar.

Braden decided to go with the boar as it was big enough. Plus he'd grown accustomed to pork, preferring it over venison.

With G-War's help to scare the boar into the open, Braden took a long shot, wounding the animal. It led to an unfortunately lengthy chase until he was successful in bringing it down with a second, better placed arrow.

They cleaned it and then hurried to drag it back to the village. As they approached, G-War grew anxious. He could feel that the dog pack had returned. Skirill flew ahead to try his trick again, but the dogs were tired and wouldn't chase him.

G-War refused to go any further. He ran off perpendicular to the return route, to head upwind to avoid the unpleasantness of dog smell. He'd find a tree and wait for Braden and Micah to leave, even if it took a few turns for them to finish with the villagers.

Braden let him go without question. G-War would show up if things got bad. He had his intuition of imminent danger. Although with all the dogs, Braden couldn't be sure that the 'cat could do anything.

The sun was setting when they arrived at the village. The change was dramatic. The village looked warm and like a place one would enjoy being. The people were clean and cheering as he and the two lads pulled the boar into the market square.

"Let's get this pig on a spit with a roaring fire. For you, Village Dwyer! A celebration of life," Braden bellowed in his best trader voice. Micah welcomed him back with a hug and fierce kiss. He liked coming home to that.

During the day, she'd discovered that the villagers were rather good at growing. Their fields produced a variety of crops, as they rotated the crops so there was always something ripe to pick.

Old Tom, it seemed, had the potential to be a master blacksmith. Metal was lacking in this village, but Tom had already bricked out a furnace that he would use as a rudimentary smelter. He had more work to do to build a bellows and other things he needed to start his smithy. It would take a long time before he could produce anything, but after that, there was a limitless number of metal items that would vault this village forward technologically. He would help them closer to the technology level in the north.

Micah let Tom work on his smithy, even asking a few hearty souls to join him. It appeared that few people thought of him as crazy now that the brothers' influence was gone.

More people wanted to be like Tom, and Micah encouraged them to come forward with their ideas to help the village grow into a better place.

Two middle-aged women took over the boar roasting duties, chasing Braden away, probably with some urging from Micah. They let the fire burn the skin, before they skillfully carved it away with old, small knives. Braden couldn't wait until Tom's smithy was operational. There was so much he could do to help these poor souls.

As the meat on the outside cooked, they trimmed it away, letting the fire get to the inside before peeling another layer away. They piled it into a mound on wood trays. The people lined up as the women offered the first helping to Braden and Micah.

Braden stood up, holding his hands high for silence. "From here forward, the young and the weakest of you shall eat first, then the others. We--" He indicated Micah and himself. "--will eat last." Some villagers cheered, while others looked confused. Braden asked the women to put the trays next to the fresh vegetables and greens put out for the celebration.

Braden and Micah picked up the serving utensils themselves. "Children first! Come on, bring your bowls!" And they started serving. A hearty cheer resounded through the market square. It took so little for people to start believing again. Maybe Braden would post the minimum standards for anyone who would lead a village. First, he'd have to teach them to read.

So many hurdles stood between where they were and the place they wanted to be.

As with all journeys, it started with a single step.

Now that they were walking, he hoped the surviving brother would be reasonable.

28 – The Last Brother

In the morning, people woke to bright sunshine. Braden and Micah helped clean up the remnants from the celebration, while wishing people well as they went to their work in the fields or at the river. Everyone's job was important to the village.

The villagers' attitudes had changed significantly from the turn before. Even if the last brother tried to reassert a brutish form of control over these people, they wouldn't have it. Braden decided to let them take the lead.

He and Micah stood in the background as the last brother and his fellow hunters walked into the village.

Their reception instantly alerted them. The whole village had turned out. The three men stopped as soon as they saw the people in the new market square. They saw the two horses, a creature unknown in the south. They saw the Hawkoid in the tree, but thought it was a rare eagle. They saw Braden and Micah in the back.

"Where are my brothers?" one man shouted. He looked around and saw only hostile faces looking back. The crowd slowly pressed inward toward him. He lifted his spear.

"Who dies first?" His threat stopped the throng.

Braden and Micah elbowed their way into the crowd, and the villagers allowed them to pass to the front.

Micah drew her sword while Braden nocked an arrow. The three men looked at the weapons.

"There's no reason to resort to threats, don't you think?" Braden stated in a low voice.

"Who the crap are you?" the man continued shouting. Maybe that was his speaking voice, Braden wondered.

"I'm Free Trader Braden. This is my partner Micah. We're here to talk about trade with Village McCullough and any other village willing to trade."

"You're not from Village McCullough," he said, finally lowering his voice to a reasonable level. "Where are you from?" The two hunters who arrived with the brother starting moving to the sides. *Here we go,* Micah thought.

"Micah, if you would be so kind, that man needs his spear cut in half." Micah angled to Braden's right, the villagers giving way. The man hefted his spear and tightened his grip. She continued to move toward him, rushing the last few feet. He jabbed quickly, but was off balance. Micah swung and lopped off the spear tip. She continued spinning in a complete circle, bringing more power into her follow-through. She hacked through the spear, just above the man's hand.

His eyes went wide as she continued with a side kick to his groin. He went down like a sack of potatoes.

The man to their left raised his spear as if to throw it. Braden let fly his arrow at the man's arm, breaking the bone in half as the arrow drove through it. The spear fell from nerveless fingers.

"Would you be willing to talk to us, or do we have to kill you, like we had to kill your brothers?"

"They're dead? All of them?" The man looked at his two companions, so easily felled by the strangers.

"All your filthy brothers!" Old Tom yelled from the crowd.

"Well now, that changes things, doesn't it? I had to act this way otherwise my brothers would beat me senseless." The man threw his spear down and wiped the sweat from his forehead. "Why do you people think I was the one to go hunting? I always left in search of one thing or another. I couldn't stand those three. They gave the family a bad name." He leaned his head back and gave a full belly laugh. He held up his hands, palms forward to the villagers.

"I'm not your enemy," he continued. "They were." He looked around. "I like what you've done to the village. How can I help?"

Old Tom rushed forward, stopping in front of the last brother. He pointed his finger, almost touching the man's face. "Don't believe him! Don't believe him! Kill him now!" he shouted hysterically.

"Let it go, Tom," Micah said as she moved next to him.

"Yeah, Tom. Let it go," the man said sarcastically. Braden didn't like the way he changed from big and loud to just another hard-working member of the village in the space of a few heartbeats. The brother angled closed to Micah. In a quick movement, he had his arm around her neck, the other on the hilt of her sword.

But she was lower to the ground and ready for the move. She pulled her head under his arm and pushed him forward, pulling back on his arm at the same time. He flipped onto his back, landing hard. Micah pulled his arm and twisted it viciously, ripping the muscles and tendons in his shoulder. He howled in pain.

"Micah!" Braden yelled when she raised her foot to stomp on his throat. She looked angry, but calmed at the pleading look in Braden's eyes. She put her foot on his throat and held it there to control him, not kill him.

"You!" Braden yelled to a villager near the man who had been kicked in the groin. "Bring him here." Three of the villagers responded by grabbing the man's arms and dragging him across the ground. They threw him in a heap at Braden's feet. The man surged forward.

Right into Braden's knee as he drove it forward, breaking the man's nose. "So this is how you want it, huh?" Braden asked in a normal voice, but he was seething mad. "Is this what you want?" he screamed as he kicked the man in the side of the head.

Braden got down so he could get close to the brother's face. He wrapped an arm around Micah's leg, for his support, and hers.

"Say the word and we'll kill all three of you, right now. Can't you see you've lost? Your way of leading this village is done. You're done, unless you agree to our way." He paused for effect. "I told these people I didn't want to kill you. That was true then, but not now. If I don't kill you, I'll have to watch my back, won't I?" Braden pinched the brother's mouth and nose closed. "Won't I?" The man started to panic, his eyes shooting wide as he tried to shake Braden off so he could breathe.

Braden let go. The man gasped for breath. Braden reared back and punched the brother in the middle of his forehead, smacking his head into the ground. His eyes crossed as he tried to stay conscious.

Braden waved at Micah to let him go. His arm dropped to the ground, causing fresh anguished cries. The three men were down, incapacitated in one way or another. The question was, what to do with them?

'G, Master Aadi, any ideas?' Micah nodded at him. G could look into the men's minds. Their lives depended on what the 'cat saw.

'Master Human. I fear they have sealed their own fate.' Master Aadi was the first to respond.

'Yes. Even now, as they are, they plot the demise of our humans,' G-War provided.

'Our humans? So unlike you, G. You must still be swimming through a cloud of dog breath.'

"Old Tom. These men are plotting their revenge, even as they lie here in their own blood. Fools. How do you deliver justice in Village Dwyer?"

"We kill them!" Old Tom screamed. Maybe he wasn't the best one to ask, Braden thought. He looked for someone else.

"You, what's your name?" he asked an older lady. He always trusted older ladies as they reminded him of his mother, not afraid to speak their mind and wisdom, brought by a life of listening and watching men do stupid things.

"I'm Betty Dwyer," she said softly. The crowd moved away from her.

"What's your relation to that?" Braden said a little more caustically than he meant as he pointed to the last brother.

"He's my son. My last son." The breeze could be heard rustling the leaves. Skirill ruffled his wings to balance on the branch. A dog barked in the distance. Someone shuffled their feet. A child sniffled.

"What do you recommend we do with him and these other two?" Braden asked as he moved closer to her.

"They aren't bad boys. They've only lost their way. They only need a firm hand, but they can be good members of the village again if we give them a chance."

"How do we do that without them turning on us? We can't watch them every heartbeat. I know a way we can be sure they don't hurt anyone ever again." The crowd started to grumble, calling for the men's heads. But Betty stood firm.

"I'll be responsible! I'll keep them under control!" she cried above the calls for their heads.

"Should you fail, your life is forfeit along with theirs." Braden said, pointing at the men.

'G-War! What are they thinking now?' Braden asked over the mindlink.

They are in a great deal of pain. They seem to be receptive to anything that spares their lives,' the 'cat answered.

Braden moved close to the last brother, leaning close so he could speak only to him. "If you ruin this deal, I will let her cut you up into little pieces. The last thing you'll remember is your head falling off your body. If you betray your mother, great pain will come to you all. Now nod to let me know you understand." The man nodded obediently.

"Everyone listen to me!" Braden stood tall to address the crowd. "Betty Dwyer is responsible for these men. She will personally ensure you are safe from them. Then she will put them to work, beside you in the fields, in the woods, on the river. The trade is made!" Braden smacked his fist into his open hand. That was the sign of a completed deal.

"I need three people to lead Village Dwyer, to help set us up for trade, to help us grow…" He continued his speech on leadership, on turning excess into items for trade, on defending themselves while still welcoming strangers, on everything it took to be a civilized society.

Braden and Micah walked hand in hand to a hut with the three people selected to lead the village. They had many details to discuss. There was much work to do. Betty Dwyer gathered her three charges and ushered them to her hut. She believed that the odd strangers would kill them all, but that these very strangers wanted Village Dwyer to be a better place. They didn't want the power for themselves.

She started to see the wisdom. She'd had no control over the boys as they grew. Once they were old enough, they killed their father. Only now did she have the authority over them she had needed all along. She gripped her son's injured shoulder until he winced in pain. "You'll do as your told or I'll kill you myself," she growled. He recoiled, and for the first time in his life, he was afraid of his mother.

29 – Masters of the World

Two turns of the sun later found Micah and Braden on the horses with Master Aadi, G-War, and Skirill in their usual places. They were pleased with the progress they made. Once the villagers learned they could take pride in their home and themselves, they embraced what Braden and Micah tried to teach them.

For trade, they would start with vegetables, but they had no way to move large quantities over long distances. They wanted Pack's help, but Braden would never give up the horses. They needed to find a work animal, like the water buffalo he'd used in the north.

"How do you think that all went, Master Aadi?" Micah asked.

'You two are getting better at finding ways to not kill people. I feel the pain it causes you both.'

"How did we get to this point, Master Aadi? Humans once relied on the power of their minds; they now rely on physical strength. Where have we gone wrong?" She had been born into this world, but refused to accept that the way things always were was the way things had to be.

'You saw Sanctuary. They used the power of their minds to overwhelm their enemies. The goal remains unchanged, to have the most power. Only the methods have changed. Until the power of the mind returns, physical strength will matter. You will fight this everywhere you go, Master Humans.' Master Aadi spoke with passion.

'I have to add that you two are different. You were the first humans I met. I see now that you are not the norm. You use your strength to help others. Your hearts are pure. Please do not call me master anymore. I don't deserve it, compared to all you've done in such a short time. You are the masters of a new world.'

"Master Aadi, you're kind, but..." Braden began, but was interrupted.

'No! I am just Aadi, Master Braden, Master Micah. Please. You have shown me a new world where I want to live.' Aadi's thought voice had a begging tone to it.

"As you wish, Aadi. How about A-Dog? Everyone gets a nickname here," Braden joked.

'I'm not sure I like that,' the Tortoid responded. G-War snickered in the back of their minds. Skirill screeched in delight from a distant tree.

"We'll work on it. What about pack animals and carts? Anyone have any ideas? Trade is not going to go well if people have to travel two turns one way with only what they can carry on their backs."

"I heard stories of large creatures, south of Cornwall, but I never saw one for myself. Maybe we can take a look," Micah offered reservedly. Braden knew it was difficult for Micah to suggest going near her home village.

"Maybe we can find something closer to here. Skirill, how big were the biggest boars you saw?"

'Big. Their backs were higher than the horse's belly.'

"Hmmm. And they are close, too. I think boars of burden could be the future of Village Dwyer trades. We only have to find a few people who believe and then turn them loose." Braden looked around. Max and Pack were guiding themselves and they seemed to be going in the right direction. "Next time we go back, we can float the idea. They have good woodworkers there. We'll take the cart and show it to them. I expect they'll be churning out carts and trained boars before too long.

"Until then, we'll help them. Mushrooms for vegetables. It looked like more men than women at Dwyer. We'll see if that goes anywhere." He looked at Micah. She was smiling at him.

"How did we get so busy?" he asked.

"If we weren't busy, then we wouldn't be making a difference. It's an incredible feeling having a purpose that's bigger than just us." She reined Pack in close to him. Her competence in handling the horse had vastly improved. "We don't have to make it back today, do we?" She looked at him, a sparkle in her eye.

No. They didn't need to get back today. A little time to themselves would do them both good. They stopped by a stream where soon, their clothes were abandoned on the bank, while the rest of the companions watched over them, patiently waiting.

30 – Building Trust

"We have been able to double the amount of material we can weave!" Mel-Ash said proudly. "Since we have to hunt less, we're able to put more manpower, ha ha, womanpower into our trade items." She was pleased and her joy was infectious. Everyone around her smiled broadly.

Braden pulled the Elder into a bear hug. He could not have been more pleased. They already grasped the significance of trade and how it helped them get better at what they did. They were accelerating toward their place in the bigger trading world.

On the next turn, they would take their wares to the meeting spot with the Lizard Men and trade. The ladies of Village McCullough looked forward to it. No children could come. The woman injured on the last trip would not be coming either. They weren't sure when Mel-Ash would stop being angry with her, although Braden and Micah said that her actions, although unintentional, vaulted the groups together.

After sunrise, they loaded the tunics, leggings, and forearm covers into the cart and they headed out. The trip seemed to get shorter each time they made it. They rolled into the clearing without hesitation. Braden and Micah dismounted and they waited for the Lizard Men to appear.

Which they did, not by materializing from the trees, but by approaching as a group from within the rainforest. They traveled in the open, without using their chameleon powers to hide. Zalastar's village-woven coverings were unique, and he stood out as he approached. Maybe they were trading stealth for the safety that the tunic material provided. The Lizard Men couldn't have both.

Before Zalastar and his people entered the open area, they stacked their spears against a tree. They then walked independently toward the humans. As each met a human, they put out their hands. Everyone paired off, hands on chests.

This gesture put them at ease and each side showed what they had. The Lizard Men had great sacks of mushrooms, in addition to braided vines that looked like a thin rope. They hoped the humans would accept it in trade.

Braden checked out the vines. They were strong and lighter than what he carried. Through Aadi, he asked what they wanted for them. For one deer, they would give him that and as much more as he could carry.

Always the trader, Braden asked if they would be willing to wait, while he, G-War, and Skirill went hunting. When they agreed, he jumped on Max's back and bolted for the edge of the rainforest. With the 'cat's guidance and the Hawkoid's incredible vision, they tracked down their prey in short order. He downed it with one shot. Knowing what the Lizard Men liked, he didn't clean it but hurriedly threw it on Max's back, turning the horse back to where the Lizard Men waited.

Braden had a hard time telling the mood of the Lizard Men. Aadi assured him that they were pleased with the speed of the kill. They took the deer and handed over a great quantity of rope.

Braden would have gotten a deer for the Lizard Men even if they had nothing to trade. He was always happy to hunt with his friends. They made hunting almost too easy. Maybe he'd come up with some kind of contest to keep them all sharp, including Micah. Aadi seemed disinterested in the hunt, but always happy to enjoy the fruits of their success. Then again, no one else in the caravan could knock down six people in one heartbeat like Aadi could.

Braden asked Aadi if the Lizard Men could tell them about any other human villages they knew of or any animals that could work, like the horses. In this, the Lizard Men turned out to be a wealth of knowledge. Braden felt like giving their rope back, but he promised himself that he would bring them a fresh-killed deer next time to thank them for the information.

A number of small villages followed the edge of the rainforest to the west. In the far west, there were strange creatures, bigger than the horses. Braden looked at Micah and she nodded. She preferred going west into the unknown rather than anywhere near Trent. Braden also preferred the Lizard Men's facts to fishermen stories.

Without further conversation, they parted with the Lizard Men, as friends, having traded to the benefit of both parties. Braden was pleased with the trust that the villagers and the Lizard Men shared. It was simple, but too many people found it difficult. Say what you are going to do, then do it. That's what trust was all about.

31 – Going West, No, East

The group returned to Village McCullough, where Braden and Micah prepared to go west. They needed those animals to pull carts, wagons even. They needed more villages on the trade circuit.

Traders driving big animals pulling magnificent wagons overflowing with both exotic and routine trade goods. People filling the square, traders shouting. Braden found it intoxicating.

Braden still had his saffrimander. He still had platinum, gold, and silver. He wondered what kind of value saffrimander had here. He suspected none, as no one knew what it was. Plus, he had yet to run into anyone he would consider wealthy. As he thought about it, he and Micah could be the wealthiest couple in the entire south.

That wasn't what he had expected when he set out from the north. He figured he'd find some Old Tech trinkets and take them back for a big profit, then retire comfortably.

Instead, he was here, with a partner, teaching the people about the basics of trade. In other words, he was saving the world.

He stopped unloading the rope from the cart. "I think we need to make a quick run back to Dwyer and check up on them. We can take some mushrooms and rope. I'm pretty sure they aren't ready to stand on their own feet yet."

Micah was anxious to go west, but she understood the burden that Braden carried. She recommended that they take Mel-Ash with them and maybe one of the younger women. If Village McCullough wanted to grow, they needed more men, or at least the opportunity to decide whether they wanted to invite men into their village. The opportunity, she thought, and smiled to herself.

32 – Loading Up

Braden loaded the cart quickly, hurrying Mel-Ash and Ipso-Ter, the younger woman, to their positions inside with the trade goods. Micah was concerned that he was angry at something.

"Slow down," she said, trying to calm him. He looked at her, his face showing near panic. She pulled him into a hug and whispered in his ear, "It's going to be okay. Wherever we go, that's where we were meant to be."

He relaxed in her arms. He pulled back a little so he could look into her big brown eyes. Yes. Everything was okay.

He smiled. "What would I do without you?"

"I don't know. Make bad decisions? Do stupid things? Be bored out of your mind?"

He slapped her firm butt cheek, lingering and thinking how good she felt. Shaking those thoughts from his mind, he knew that getting to the west would wait. He had other trades to complete.

It was time to get back to work.

"You ready?" he asked, pointing at the two women in the cart. They waved back, smiling. They sat among bags of mushrooms, a great deal of the Lizard Man rope, and a small sampling of McCullough's special material.

As Braden resigned himself with the trip to Village Dwyer, he became curious about many things. He looked forward to seeing Tom's progress on the smithy, Betty Dwyer's progress with the three miscreants, and if there were any trade stalls completed. That would show the villagers on both sides what trade was all about. They'd set up the rope in one stall and the mushrooms in another. And then start hawking their wares.

Micah saw the change in Braden's demeanor. He was happy and looking forward to a trip that moments before he was dreading. *What changed with Braden, Golden Warrior?'* Micah asked with her thought voice.

'My human is excited about the prospect of normal trade. Arriving in a town, as we used to. Setting up in a trade stall, like we used to. Calling all near or far to trade, as he loved to do. This is less about saving the world and more about normalcy.'

'Am I good for him, G?' she asked.

'Yes,' the 'cat replied simply, then added, *'Hungry.'*

"Yes, G, I know you're hungry. Go on ahead, we'll be on our way shortly. You know the route we'll take." Braden watched as the 'cat jumped from the cart and bolted away. "Good hunting, my friend."

Micah wondered if Braden heard the rest of her conversation with G-War. No matter. Between them, there were no secrets. The companions guaranteed that.

33 – Market Square: Open for Business

As they pulled in to Village Dwyer, Braden and Micah both let out sighs of relief. A number of trade stalls had been completed. The village and the people looked clean.

A cheer went up from those who saw the caravan arrive. Others rushed to the square. The three village leaders--Mick, Destiny, and Fen--pushed to the front of the group to welcome the visitors from Village McCullough.

This trip was good for them all. It reinforced what Braden was trying to teach them. This is what good trade was all about. Trust, not fear.

Braden asked for a little time to get set up in the stalls and asked people to bring the items they were willing to trade. In the meantime, he introduced Mel-Ash and Ipso-Ter to the leaders of Village Dwyer. They talked as they unloaded and prepared to trade.

People looked curiously at the rope, but the mushrooms drew furled brows. Micah strolled up next to Mel-Ash. "We may have to give out samples. Once they try them, they'll be hooked," she said confidently.

Micah stood back and watched her partner as he turned into Free Trader Braden. He moved with a purpose, set up, always watching for customers. G-War's observations were perfect. This is what he loved.

When they were set up, Braden climbed into the back of the cart to stand taller than the growing crowd. "Come one, come all! See these magnificent products, fresh from the Lizard Men of the Amazon Rainforest! Free Trader Braden's Caravan knows no limits to the trade! We bring you treasures from across Vii! Come! Look! Rope, stronger and lighter than you've ever seen before! Look! Mushrooms that take the place of meat. They last longer, an easy meal to keep up your strength while you work away from the village. You've never seen anything like them! What do you have to trade? Come one, come all!" Braden projected his voice and waved his arms, entertaining more than driving trades.

The villagers had limited items, although Ipso-Ter eyed a number of the men. She picked out potential 'volunteers' to move to McCullough.

Braden hawked and cajoled, but most importantly, he taught them that nothing is free. Trade had a price, even if it was only time. In some cases, he traded things now for promises of items in the future. That wasn't the best trade, but it was the right thing to do by Village Dwyer.

Old Tom stopped by, delighted with the prospect of the ropes. He needed something strong to help him build his bellows. Braden traded him a few spans of the rope for an axe head, nails, and a hammer that Tom would produce at some time in the future. These were necessary if Braden ever wanted to build a home. It also showed the villagers that Braden placed a high level of importance on building.

Tom had plans to produce weapons, swords and spear tips, but those would take time. Braden wanted him to work on more important items like the metal parts necessary to build carts and wagons. Many in Village Dwyer saw how such vehicles would help them, even something as simple as making their lives easier moving vegetables from the fields to the village. Braden assured them that he had a good lead on getting beasts of burden. When they left, they'd begin that quest.

Braden had earned their trust. They believed he would deliver for them, so they could help him expand the trade, build routes that the Free Traders would use.

Some children stood around, mimicking what Braden was doing. "We want to be Free Traders!" they cried as they bargained among themselves, for rocks and sticks. Micah ruffled their hair and traded a mushroom each for a good rock, which all the children were able to produce.

The other children spent their time playing with G-War. The villagers took mercy on the cat and made sure that the dogs were under control. They were either closed in the huts, or away from the village with the workers.

Aadi and Skirill watched from afar. They weren't fully accepted by the village, but they weren't shunned. They wanted to give Braden his moment.

After the trades were complete, they loaded the cart with vegetables, various wood items, and promissory notes that Braden drew up. He read them back to the villagers, one by one. They giggled at their words as they were memorialized in charcoal on stripped bark.

With one last wave, the caravan rode from Village Dwyer.

34 - Karma

They welcomed the vegetables, the wood plates, and the utensils. But the best thing that came back were the stories that Mel-Ash and Ipso-Ter told about Village Dwyer's friendliness. They felt welcome and had already made friends. They looked forward to returning. They knew they could make it on foot, without Braden, they assured him. They could trade with the Lizard Men without Aadi as well.

Micah knew what they were doing. They were helping Braden be free. To do what he felt he needed to do, find more villages and bring back creatures that could pull the wagons and carts that Dwyer committed to building.

They weren't sure what the terrain was like for the trip west, so they decided to leave the cart behind. By traveling light, they could go further faster.

They decided to leave when the sun rose. As the villagers were getting accustomed to, whenever the caravan returned from a successful trade, they celebrated. This turn was no different. They celebrated together and then Micah and Braden celebrated in private, with the minds of their companions keeping them company.

'Don't you feel bad listening in?' Micah asked over the mindlink after they were finished. She had thrown off their blanket as she was covered in sweat. Braden was already drifting off to sleep.

'We've already had this conversation,' the 'cat answered.

'Sorry, just thinking.'

'That is how you are afterwards. Your mind is excited and difficult to follow.' G-War had grown friendlier after their interactions with Village Dwyer. He was almost personable.

She still felt like he looked down on her as he talked, like a parent talking to a child. *'Are you and I bonded, G?'*

'Yes. When you partnered with my human, you became my human too.'

'But we didn't partner for a long time after we met, and you talked with me right away,' she said, a bit surprised.

'In your minds, you did, the moment you met. It was very Hillcat-like. I was impressed.'

'I didn't know. How could you feel what I couldn't?' she asked, confused.

'Because humans are stupid,' the 'cat said without hesitation.

"I guess we are, compared to the all-knowing ass, I mean 'cat. At least I didn't get sick at the smell of dog," she countered out loud.

'Despite the size of human noses, they are poor at what they do. I can't imagine the meaningless existence of humans who don't have a 'cat to tell them what's important.' Micah felt Aadi in the background of her mind, laughing the slow, full laugh of a Tortoid. Skirill's quick chirps of laughter were there, too.

When Skirill saw her fishing all those moons ago, karma took over and brought her to this point in her life.

And she wouldn't have wanted it any other way.

35 – Mutie Birds

They left as the sun rose. Braden felt lighter than he had in many turns. He galloped ahead, Micah raced to catch up while G-War crouched low, hanging on during the wild ride. Aadi bounced along happily behind Micah. Skirill soared overhead.

Things were as they were meant to be.

They passed the rainforest road quickly and kept going, keeping the edge of the Amazon in their view to the left. They took a break at mid-daylight so each could hunt. Even Aadi was successful in his hunt, when he found grubs infesting a sodden tree trunk. The daylight was perfect. Not too hot, not too cold. The sun shone brightly.

They should have known that perfect wasn't meant for them.

'They come,' was the first warning they received from G-War. *'From the north, coming fast.'* They looked, but couldn't see anything.

'The sky,' Skirill added, panic in his thought voice. They looked up and saw a cloud that wasn't a cloud. Black birds packed a spot in the sky so densely, light couldn't get through. The dark spot in the sky bobbed and weaved as it approached.

"Skirill, I think you should get down here." The Hawkoid agreed and made a turn to come back, flying as hard as he could.

Suddenly, the cloud of birds stopped their dance in the sky and headed directly for them, cutting Skirill off.

"Find cover!" Braden yelled as he and Micah jumped on the horses and raced for the tree line. Aadi was already there and G-War was under a tree, safe from any attack from above.

The cloud of birds arrived as Braden and Micah reached the edge of the rainforest. Sharp claws hit, but their tunics protected their backs. Their exposed arms and heads were raked, as were the horses' flanks. Max and Pack plunged into the woods, crazed from the pain. The humans jumped off. Micah pulled her sword and started waving it in a circle around her. Braden had his recurve bow out, swinging it like a club, knocking down some of the grisly creatures.

A thunderclap sounded in the opening before them, knocking a great number of birds from the air. The rest flew out of the rainforest, but circled for another attack. The humans stomped the birds on the ground to kill them. These weren't normal birds.

Mutants.

Their wings had some feathers, but were mostly fibrous skin. Their claws were oversized and sharp. They had faces with mouths, not beaks. They looked like bats, but with the bodies of ravens. Braden thought this in an instant before the mutants were back. He pulled his long knife and swung it, trying to cut their wings. Micah was jabbing fiercely and rapidly with her sword. The 'cat prowled the ground, dispatching wounded mutants. The scratches on his back and bite out of his ear suggested he was less than successful in avoiding their attacks.

Skirill screeched as he attacked the cloud from behind. He was far bigger than the mutie birds, but he was vastly outnumbered. Skirill used his speed and size to crash against them, knocking many out of the sky, before trying to fly away for another attack. The smaller mutie birds were on him in a heartbeat. He rolled, attempting to shake them off, but failed. They went down in a heap.

Braden's long knife was a blur as he sliced his way through the biting and scratching cloud. Micah stopped their attack as her sword danced in a tight circle around her, too fast for the eye to follow.

Another thunderclap and a large hole was punched into the cloud. The attack let up as the mutie birds quickly flew from the woods to regroup.

Braden ran toward Skirill, using his long knife to peel two of the mutants off the Hawkoid. Skirill raised his head and a dead mutie bird dropped from his beak. A mutant struggled in each claw as he shook one to death and bit the head off the other. He staggered a few steps and flopped over.

Braden stood over him, ready to face a new attack.

The remaining mutie birds had no stomach for more. They left their injured fellows behind as they flew away to the north.

The companions made quick work of the survivors. Aadi was the only one not bleeding. He swam after the horses so Braden and Micah could tend to the 'cat and Hawkoid, as well as to their own wounds. They needed Aadi to come back quickly with the horses because their numbweed was in the saddle packs. They had some in their belt pouches, but not enough. Even with that on the horses, there wouldn't be enough to treat all the wounds.

G-War was in pain, but his wounds weren't bad. The bite out of his ear wouldn't grow back. He was scarred for life. It added personality, made him look mean.

Skirill had the worst of it. His feathers were pulled out and he bled from numerous bite marks. It would be a while before he would fly again. They rubbed numbweed on the bites at his wingroots. These were the most important to heal properly. They used almost all the numbweed on those wounds, which left the ones on his neck and chest. They needed their flasks to wash the injuries. Where was Aadi?

Micah tried to rub the last of her numbweed on a deep scratch on Braden's neck. He winced and pulled her hand away. If anyone was going to get the last of it, he wanted it to be Micah. She adamantly refused, so they settled on using the last of what they had on a deep cut in G-War's side.

36 – Treating Wounds

Micah stood guard over the Hawkoid and 'cat as Braden jogged into the woods in search of Aadi and the horses.

The Lizard Men found him first, surprising him as they materialized out of a tree. The Lizard Men looked alike to him, so he wasn't sure if he had met this one before. It wore no leggings, so maybe he hadn't. They stood there looking at each other. Braden realized that he still had his long knife in his hand. He put it into the sheath on his belt, then reached forward to touch the Lizard Man's chest. The Lizard Man raised his spear in a flash and knocked Braden's arm away, then thrust toward him. Braden twisted just enough so the spear hit him at an angle and slid off the firm fibers of his tunic.

Braden grabbed the spear with one hand and the wrestling match began as they each tried to throw the other off. Braden would have liked to take his long knife back out, but feared he couldn't hold the spear with one hand. They pushed and pulled, trying to knock the other from his feet. Braden was starting to weaken, the Lizard Man gaining the upper hand.

Micah's sword chopped through both of the Lizard Man's forearms in one mighty downswing. He looked at her, confused, before running off into the rainforest, dark red blood spurting from the stumps of his arms.

"What the crap was that about?" Micah blurted out. "Aadi!"

Aadi finally showed back up with the horses in tow. They told him what had happened with the Lizard Man. Aadi was not surprised. Not all of the Lizard Men believed in Zalastar. There were some renegades, but they were very few, Aadi assured them.

"You couldn't have told us this before?" Braden asked incredulously.

'How would you have acted if I did?' The Tortoid answered the question with

a question.

"We would have been more careful!" Braden exclaimed.

'Exactly. You would not have trusted all of the Lizard Men because of the beliefs of very few,' the Tortoid responded. He was right, they thought. The Lizard Men as a whole did not hold the actions of the young mother against her when she kicked at one of them. The humans should show the same level of trust.

"You continue to be wise, Master Aadi, I mean Aadi. Thank you for that, but next time, please be wise before I get a spear through my heart, not after." He patted the Tortoid's shell, before stroking his neck a few times.

They used the remainder of the numbweed on Pack and Max, who had significant rips across their flanks. Braden and Micah would do without. They used all their water washing out their wounds. They put Skirill into one saddle, using some of the light Lizard Man rope to hold him in place, and put G-War on the other. Braden and Micah walked to keep the load light on the injured animals.

"Creatures like that exist? They're horrible," Micah offered. It was still the same daylight from when they left Village McCullough earlier. Braden absentmindedly turned back the way they'd come.

"The world conspires against us. I guess we're not allowed to be too happy." Braden rested his hand on her shoulder. She winced as claw gashes criss-crossed what had been milky smooth skin. Her wounds would leave scars. The scars on his back from G-War were far worse than the scratches from the mutie birds. *What's one more scar*, he thought.

"Should we go back?" he asked, holding her face in his hands.

"To do what?" she asked. She was leading to something. Braden didn't answer her, only waved his hand, motioning her to keep talking. "I say we go on. We could slink back to the village where they might see us as weak. Or we go on, injured, damaged, sore, but we go on. We show them what real strength is.

"Our goal hasn't changed, Braden. We continue to the first village and show them how being a trading partner will benefit them. Then the next village and the next until we find these land creatures, bigger than a horse. And we do what we can to bring a couple back. By then, we'll be healed and ready to rip the heads off sharks."

"Sharks?" Braden asked. He didn't know the word.

"Sharks! They are the predators of the ocean. They are shaped like this." She drew the shape in the dirt on the ground. "Their mouths are filled with sharp teeth. I saw a dead one on the beach once; it was twice the size of Max. They would swim by our boats when we were cleaning fish. They're drawn to blood."

"That's pretty scary. I think that confirms I'll never go out on the ocean."

"What? My big tough man afraid of a little fish?"

"Yes, I am," he said, proudly defiant. "And I'd smack you, but I'm too sore. I think I finally scabbed over. I don't want to start leaking again." He smiled. "Well, then. I think we're going the wrong way," he said as he turned back west, moving deliberately and slowly.

Aadi floated barely above the ground behind Pack. Skirill squeaked in the way that Hawkoid's express pain. G-War's pain was funneled directly into their brains via the mindlink. Their own injuries probably projected back to the companions as well. Even Max and Pack were skittish.

The caravan stopped when they came to a stream. Ice cold water ran rapidly through the shallows. Braden and Micah helped Skirill into the water and washed out his wounds. No numbweed remained to redress the Hawkoid's injuries, so the cold of the stream was all the help he'd get to take away any of the pain. The cool stream was so soothing that Skirill fell asleep as the water ran over him.

G-War avoided the water, preferring to lick his wounds. He kept his tongue away from the ones with numbweed on them, for now anyway. He was already healing. His wounds looked bad because of his cat hair, but they weren't deep below the skin. He'd be back to hunting by the next daylight.

Braden and Micah led the horses into the stream. The cold water numbed their cuts and helped calm them. The horses were tough animals, but later they needed to trade with Village McCullough for horse blankets made from their woven armor. It hurt the humans to see the injuries to the horses. Max and Pack had been with Braden longer than anyone except for the 'cat. They were the foundation of the caravan. Without them, it would be the companions walking across the world.

That would take all the fun out of it, Braden thought.

Aadi only needed rest. After a good sleep, he'd be able to protect them again. With his second thunderclap, he had broken the back of the attackers. After that, they couldn't regroup. He saved Skirill's life, maybe even all of their lives.

They camped at the stream, everyone licking their wounds in their own way.

"We need more numbweed," Braden said, breaking the silence.

"I don't know what it looks like wild." Braden drew an outline of the leaves in the dirt. He stood up, holding his hand mid-thigh--they were about that tall. About this big around--he held his hands wide apart. He drew a picture of the branch, with bunches of leaves on it. She shook her head.

They would look in earnest starting in the morning. They stayed closer to the rainforest. It seemed like everything grew within a hundred strides of the big trees. Braden didn't say that if the mutie birds came back, they'd be closer to shelter. If a cloud that size attacked again… Braden shuddered. Maybe they should have gone back to McCullough. They were vulnerable like this.

And he didn't like being vulnerable.

"Micah. Next time, don't hesitate to use your blaster, for all our sakes." She had completely forgotten about the weapon. It would not have been effective in close as she would have risked hitting one of the companions, but as the mutie birds approached, she might have been able to kill them all with a single blast.

She hung her head in shame. "I don't think of it as a weapon. I've carried it all this time, but never used it against an enemy. I'm sorry, Braden. I could have gotten us all killed."

"Stop it, partner mine. I didn't think of it until just now. Ha! Does that make me the smart one?" He threw his head back and laughed, ending with a choking cough. "Oh, that hurt." He winced as he stretched against his injuries.

"Serves you right, smart one." Carefully, she snuggled close to him, checking in with G-War. He was with them and watching. They were safe. For now, anyway.

With daylight came fresh pain as each of them worked sore muscles and healing skin. They all had wounds that oozed. A fresh dip in the stream was both refreshing and cleansing. Everyone got a thorough washing before they walked, the morning sun at their backs. Their destiny lay to the west.

37 – Continuing the Journey

They stayed close to the rainforest as they spent the day leading the horses. G-War was almost himself as he rode on a blanket across the saddle. Skirill had to be tied down to keep him on Pack. He was still in bad shape, but he'd started to heal. If they could find numbweed, then they could greatly accelerate the Hawkoid's return to health.

Braden was angry at himself for not looking for numbweed earlier. Maybe he had started to think they were invincible. They would all suffer their wounds that much longer because of his arrogance.

Micah noticed Braden digging a hole for himself. She didn't know what it was about and it didn't matter. He carried the responsibility for their security and health on his shoulders.

Always.

"Stop it," she said, trying break him from his reverie. "I'm adding this to the list. You're up to three gut punches and one head punch as soon as I'm well enough to give them to you."

"Like crap you are," he shot back. He stopped and looked at her. She stood calmly, looking at him with her big brown eyes. There was no reason to be angry with her. She was right. Maybe not about the gut punches, though. If she tried, that would lead to an exciting wrestling match where he would win, even if she said he lost.

"G-War, my friend, is there any game around? Maybe a rabbit or squirrel, something for Ess to eat?" In response, the 'cat jumped off the horse, landing softly. He stretched right, then left, then dashed into the undergrowth.

Soon there was a brief skirmish, and G-War returned with a small squirrel. *That felt good. This little guy was quick.*' The 'cat was proud of himself.

Braden took the squirrel and held it up for the Hawkoid. He couldn't move his neck all that well, so they cut the squirrel in smaller pieces for him. His metabolism demanded that he eat often, so they needed to keep him fed so he could heal.

Aadi was back to himself, floating gracefully along. Since they were walking, he kept up by swimming along next to the humans. Each of them took responsibility to look out for the others. Aadi felt as if he were the most powerful among the companions as he was the only one uninjured. He wanted to put himself in a position to react if needed. He was obvious in his movements, even though he was trying not to be.

"Aadi, are you trying to protect us?" Micah asked. "That's so nice of you. But if they get past you, I have my blaster handy and we won't let anything bad happen." She patted the butt of the ancients' weapon for emphasis.

G-War bolted into the brush again, this time returning with a rather plump rabbit.

"Let me guess. This one wasn't so quick." The 'cat held up his furry paw to Braden. "I learned to be an ass from you, G. I learned from the best."

G-War disemboweled the rabbit, a little messier than usual in order to make a statement. The 'cat wanted Braden to know that he could kill him any time he wanted, so every day he let Braden live was a free day. Braden was immune to the 'cat's jibes, because this had gone on for nearly eleven cycles.

They kept walking, knowing that G-War would eat quickly and catch up. They weren't traveling very fast, as no one was in shape for it. Without Skirill flying overhead, they couldn't see ahead. They'd gotten used to having few surprises, things that were normal for the rest of humanity.

So they pressed ahead slowly, taking care not to rush headlong into trouble.

But nothing threatened them that turn or the next. By the third turn after the mutie bird attack, they arrived at a small village.

38 – Village Greentree

They stopped on a small rise outside the village, watching, waiting for someone to see them. That would tell them what they wanted to know. Would they raise the alarm and get their weapons or would they be curious, maybe prepare to defend themselves.

The companions waited a long time. The sun approached mid-daylight before someone made an appearance. A person came from the rainforest. First one, then another, then a few more and finally, what looked like the whole village streamed back to their thatch-roofed huts. They looked exhausted. Tired people were less alarmed.

Braden and Micah mounted the horses, taking care not to scrape the scabs on the horses' backs and flanks. Micah had G-War in front of her and Braden held Skirill in his lap.

They slowly walked into the village, stopping where all the huts were still in front of them. Micah loosened her sword in its scabbard, just in case. Braden put a hand on her leg. He had high hopes that they wouldn't have to kill anyone.

"Hello! I'm Free Trader Braden and I'd like to talk to your Village Elder!" Braden projected confidently in his trading voice. An older couple stumbled out of their hut, then others young and old came into the open.

"What do you want?" the old man asked simply.

"We wish to trade with this village. I am Braden. This is my partner Micah. The Tortoid is Master Aadi. The Hillcat is Golden Warrior. The Hawkoid is Skirill. What is the name of your village?"

"We are the Village of Greentree. I fear we have nothing to trade, though." The old man looked sincere.

'He tells the truth as he believes it to be,' G-War offered. *'They are in anguish.'*

'Ask them, Master Human,' Aadi chimed in.

"I see a great darkness hanging over you. What troubles the people of Greentree?"

"You are very wise to see how distraught we are. One of our children has disappeared in the rainforest. We fear she was taken by the shadow people. Our search has been fruitless," the old man answered.

Braden looked at Micah. She nodded almost imperceptibly. They would join the search.

"My friends and I have some experience in tracking within the rainforest. We've run across these shadow people before." The Lizard Men, no doubt.

"Who are you?" the old man asked with renewed interest.

"Travelers. Traders. Trying to make tomorrow just a little bit better than today for the people of this world. I want to thank you for not attacking us when we rode in. You are kind and for that, you've earned our gratitude and our help."

"I'll stay with Skirill and the horses, maybe even look around a bit. They may have plenty to trade and don't know it. Do what you do best. Find the child; save the village." Micah leaned sideways, almost falling out of the saddle in order to give her partner a good luck kiss. Braden obliged her, holding her head with one head, letting the kiss linger.

"Time to go, G, Aadi. We have a child to find." G-War was first to jump off, then Braden got out of the saddle. Aadi swam forward to join them. The villagers parted to let them through. Braden stopped before the old man.

"A little girl, ten cycles old," was all he said, hope welling up in his tired eyes. They grasped hands, briefly, then Braden was off. He jogged into the trees. Aadi struggled to keep up as G-War raced ahead, found a perch in a tree, and sat there, watching.

39 - Bronwyn

'Any ideas, G?' Braden tried to read the signs, but it looked like the entire village had been through there.

'Joy. I sense her joy. She is not afraid.'

"Joy? How odd. She's alive, though. We just need to find her. Do you feel anything, Aadi?" Braden asked.

'Nothing, Master Human. I must be able to see the Lizard Men to talk with them and I don't see any at present.'

Braden stepped carefully through the underbrush as he moved deeper into the rainforest. It became darker, hotter, and more humid with each step. G-War indicated a rough direction and they set out. Braden fought his way through the puddles and the undergrowth, while Aadi floated majestically above it all. The 'cat acted more like a squirrel, using the dense lower tree branches as his road.

An untold number of villagers attempted to follow. Braden didn't care if they followed, but expected he would do better without them. He didn't know the forest-sense of the villagers, if they would slow him down or not. He ignored them and forged ahead. They soon fell far behind.

The 'cat came to a stop, crouched on a branch, and listened. *'Not far now,'* he said. Braden waited as he wasn't sure what direction they needed to go. The Tortoid swam forward, gently bumping Braden aside. He floated upward and faced a tree.

Braden looked closely. A Lizard Man leaned against the tree, perfectly blending into it. Braden had been a mere arm-span away and never saw him.

'She is with the Lizard Men,' Aadi said.

"That's good. Thanks, Aadi. I'm here to take her home." Braden said aloud to the Lizard Man. Braden was careful not to expose his chest to the spear. One act and he lost his ability to trust them freely. He fought with himself, but could move no closer to sharing his heartbeat.

'She is with the Lizard Men because she can talk with them. She sees them when no one else can.'

"I'd like to talk with her if I can. She sounds like a gifted little girl." Aadi took a long time before answering.

'Yes. Follow Akhmiyar. He will guide us.' The Lizard Man stepped away from the tree, leaning his spear against it before turning back to the human. Braden breathed a sigh of relief, as they reached out at the same time to put their hands on the other's chest.

Akhmiyar grabbed his spear and set off, jogging lightly through the swamp. Braden rushed to keep up. G-War bounded from limb to limb, seemingly enjoying the footrace. Aadi struggled to keep up, his thick legs swimming furiously.

Fortunately they didn't have far to go. Running into a clearing, Braden saw the child, sitting peacefully among a number of Lizard Men. Akhmiyar waved them away after briefly communicating with the girl. She stood up. The 'cat vaulted from a branch above, landing soundlessly next to the human. Aadi swam up, blinking rapidly as he joined the group.

"Oooh, how cute!" she said and leaned down to pet the Hillcat. G-War looked back up at Braden. If a 'cat could have a smug expression, that was it.

"Who are you, pretty thing?" she asked the Tortoid.

"Aadi. What an intelligent name. Mine is Bronwyn. What does your name mean?" she asked. Braden was shocked. She was able to talk with all the companions, but he couldn't hear her.

"The One. You are the one, the only one like you I've ever seen, but I'm only ten. I haven't seen that much."

"I'm Braden," he said as he kneeled so that he was on her level. She seemed disinterested. "G-War, can you tell her we need to take her back to her village, please?"

"Oh, I don't want to go back," she answered G-War instantly. "I'm perfectly fine here. The Amazonians will take care of me."

The Lizard Men? Has she seen how they eat, Braden thought to himself.

"G. Please. I need to talk with her. Can you get her to acknowledge that I exist? Aadi, a little help please…" Braden pleaded with his friends.

Aadi floated upward where he could face Akhmiyar and talk with him. The 'cat continued to enjoy the child's attention. Braden shook his head. *'Skirill, can you hear me?'*

'Yes, Braden,' answered a tired voice over the mindlink.

'Tell Micah we found the child. She is with the Lizard Men and she can talk with them, as well as the companions. The only one she's not interested in talking with is me. Let the village know that Bronwyn is safe and we'll return as soon as we can. By the way, the Lizard Men are friendly here.' Braden figured Micah could hear him as well, although he always felt weird talking with her over the mindlink.

'I don't know why,' she answered, having clearly heard everything he said and thought.

'The child is safe, but she wants to stay here. Don't tell the villagers that. I'll see what I can do, but maybe it's time for the Amazonians, as she called the Lizard Men, to introduce themselves. We're working on it, lover. I'll let you know when we're on our way back,' Braden said in his thought voice.

'These are good people, Braden. They will be partners on the trading circuit. Be safe coming home to me, partner mine,' Micah answered.

40 – Ear of the Amazonians

Aadi convinced Akhmiyar to introduce himself to Village Greentree. With Bronwyn to interpret, they would quickly have close relations. The Lizard Man said that he would bring a small party and that they could round up a pouch of mushrooms to share.

Bronwyn had picked up the 'cat and was holding him awkwardly while still petting him.

'G? There's no way you're comfortable, and there's no way you're enjoying this. Is there?' Braden asked.

'Yes. She is delightful. But it grows old. Time to go back to the village where it is dry and warm. Did I mention that I looked forward to being dry?'

Braden laughed softly. The one constant in the universe was the 'cat's ability to hold his own comfort above all things.

"If we must, Golden Warrior, we'll go back to the village. I feel my home is here, though. Yes, I know they miss me, but I'm not really like them. I'm more like you. Oh, thank you!" She squealed, smiling from ear to ear. Braden had no idea what the 'cat told her, but if it enticed her to leave the rainforest, then it was the right thing to say.

Akhmiyar took the lead, while four Lizard Men fell in behind. Braden stayed beside Bronwyn, although he wasn't sure that she knew he was there. She was holding Aadi's shell with one hand, while G-War was draped around her neck like a scarf, his long legs dangling well below her waist. Braden didn't care as long as they were headed in the right direction.

It took to the end of the daylight before they reached the border between the Amazon and the Plains of Propiscius where the Village of Greentree sat. Micah let the villagers know when Braden and the others would arrive, so they were waiting. She also talked to them about the Lizard

Men, the Amazonians.

Micah told them that the Amazonians had saved Bronwyn when she got lost. She hoped this would make their appearance less startling.

It didn't matter. When Akhmiyar stepped out of the rainforest, he had to cover his eyes. The Lizard Men weren't accustomed to direct sunlight. His skin looked a sickly green, where in the rainforest it had been a vibrant shade of nature.

A couple, who Braden assumed were Bronwyn's parents, ran forward to her. She took their hands and introduced them to the Hillcat, who had gotten down to walk into the village. He looked stiff from his ordeal, and Braden told him that it served him right. The child then introduced Aadi, and finally Akhmiyar.

The villagers were relieved at the child's return. They slapped each other on the back happily and gave approving nods to Braden.

Bronwyn knew her parents couldn't hear the other creatures, so she told them what they were saying. Braden urged everyone into the shade, which he knew Akhmiyar had to appreciate. There were too many people crowding around for Braden to be sure.

Braden shouldered his way to the front, dragging Aadi along with him. When he reached Akhmiyar, he turned around and held his hands up, trying to get the crowd's attention. Once the villagers settled down, he assumed his best trader voice and projected as he had been taught.

"Meet Akhmiyar, Amazonian leader. He's brought a sample of their wares: mushrooms that can take the place of a meal. They aren't much to look at, but they taste fine and they keep you healthy. He is willing to trade. What do you have that he could use? Any fresh meat?" Braden watched the people carefully. They looked away.

'Micah, what do you think they have to trade?' he asked using the mindlink.

'Ask about their songs.'

'Songs? Did I hear that right?' The villagers looked at him as he made faces trying to figure out what Micah said.

'Songs. Music. We know the Lizard Men make their own music. Maybe something new and fresh would be of interest.'

"Micah! You're a genius," Braden shouted above the growing din. "Villagers of Greentree! Would you have music that you could share with Akhmiyar?"

The old man who talked to them when they first entered the village stepped forward. "They would trade food for music?"

"I believe they would. They are a very cultured people. Aadi? Bronwyn? What does Akhmiyar think of the offer?"

"Yes!" shouted the little girl. "We would love to hear the village play!"

"Get your instruments!" directed the old man. People raced away, returning quickly with odd instruments of all kinds, made from wood, hide, strings, and even stone.

One young man beat a large hide-bound bowl using a rock tied to the end of a stick. The sound was deep and bold. Other instruments joined in, weaving a sound around the regular beat. More joined until the sound was full. Voices were added, singing notes and dancing within the tune. The players played, the villagers swayed, and if Braden and Micah could put an emotion to the music, they would call it happiness.

Aadi bobbed his head, slowly, letting Braden and Micah know that the music was well received. The trade had been made and it was a good trade, because everyone was happy with what they received.

G-War found Bronwyn in the crowd and stood next to her as she stroked his fur, with her eyes closed, completely giving herself over to the music.

When the playing finally stopped, everyone clapped, even the players themselves. After watching the humans, Akhmiyar tried to mimic their movements, but his clawed hands were not made for clapping. The sound he made was a click, click as his heavy claws rapped against each other.

Bronwyn let go of G-War and ran to the Lizard Man, wrapping her arms around his waist and giving him a hug. The villagers stopped and watched. The little girl finally released Akhmiyar and waved good-bye as he and his four fellows made to go back into the rainforest. He handed her a bag made of leaves and vines, then turned.

'Aadi, can you ask Akhmiyar if he's seen numbweed anywhere?' Braden formed an image of the plant in his mind, hoping that Aadi could share it.

'Yes, yes, it grows everywhere. Look for where the sun shines through the overhead in the rainforest. You'll find the plants there,' Aadi said. With that, the Lizard Men faded into the dark interior of the Amazon.

Bronwyn handed a leafy bag of mushrooms to her parents, who handed the bag to the old man. He looked at Braden and Micah. Micah took one of the mushrooms, rinsed it off, then broke it into pieces. She ate one to show the villagers that they were safe. Soon, all the villagers were eating them.

"Congratulations. You've made your first trade," Micah said to the old man.

41 – Lots to Trade

His name was Ditarod. He was the Village Elder, although they didn't seem to have anyone in charge. People did as they always did. No one needed to be told. That made Greentree unique.

This community was the closest knit that Braden had run across in all his travels. Everyone was equal here. He liked that, but understood that it wouldn't work in all places. He was happy that he didn't have to install new leadership, and happiest that he didn't have to watch Micah kill anyone. She was good at it, and that was disconcerting.

As Braden looked around, many villagers wore well-tanned hides. Good tanning was not easily come by. He thought they could trade tanned hides, or even the knowledge of the tanning process. They could trade musical instruments. As villages became more civilized, music could become important. The Amazonians were willing to trade for it and maybe others would too, but how did one move twenty villagers and their musical instruments?

Animals. Big animals pulling wagons. Traveling musicians? What a concept. They could travel the rainforest road, bringing music to thousands of Lizard Men along the way. Braden was concerned that traveling musicians might stumble across New Sanctuary, but that concern was far away. They needed to find animals first.

One step at a time, he cautioned himself. Relax and enjoy the moment.

And the company. He looked down at his hand, fingers intertwined with Micah's.

Enjoy the moment.

As soon as I check on Skirill, he thought.

42 – The Good Companions

The Hawkoid was still in pain, and with the darkness of evening, Braden couldn't search for numbweed. First thing after sunrise, he'd go into the rainforest and find where the light penetrated to discover the numbweed plant. He'd make the mixture that would return the injured Hawkoid to health.

Braden's rescue of the little girl turned into two different tales. Bronwyn told the story of the Golden Warrior, Master Aadi, and Akhmiyar. Braden was nowhere in her version of the tale. She was different and had always been treated differently. She said that she could talk to animals, but no one listened, just like they were barely listening to her now.

Braden and Micah knew she was exceptional. He once thought G-War could talk with any creature, but not so. Bronwyn could. He wondered if they would allow her to be his Trade Apprentice? But then again, she would have to acknowledge his existence.

Micah introduced herself to Bronwyn. The little girl waved with one hand while the other continued to stroke G-War's fur. "Would you like to meet Skirill? He's a Hawkoid. He's injured and it would be nice if you could talk with him." The little girl brightened as she took Micah's hand and skipped as they walked to where Skirill was standing on a log, covered with a blanket.

"Hi! My name's Bronwyn. Can I see where you hurt?" she asked merrily.

Micah lifted off the blanket. The little girl leaned close, angling away so the firelight could shine through. She put her hands on his wings, very gently. "It's going to be alright. My! Aren't you a big bird?" She stroked the feathers along his back, then under his chin and down his chest. The Hawkoid closed his eyes and craned his neck in pleasure. Micah watched, fascinated at the transformation.

"The 'ain is gone!" Skirill exclaimed aloud. He stretched his wings. The wounds were there, not leaking, but they still looked painful. Skirill expanded his chest as he took deep breaths.

"Hang on, Ess," Micah cautioned. "Don't go flying anywhere just yet. The pain may be gone, but the wounds remain. You don't want to tear anything. We'll find numbweed tomorrow and start you on the path to a real recovery."

"I 'eel good!" Skirill stated.

"Thank you, Bronwyn. What did you do for him?" Micah asked.

"I just pushed the pain away. He is such a noble creature. Do you think I can ride him like Golden Warrior did?" Micah was taken aback. She must have abilities like those of the 'cat to look into a being's mind.

"No, sweetie, I think you might be too big. And when Golden Warrior rode on his back, he was afraid and didn't like it."

"I know, but it sounded like fun." The little girl hung her head for a heartbeat, then skipped away toward the horses. Micah ran after her. She didn't want the horses to accidentally step on Bronwyn. But, Micah should have guessed.

Bronwyn could talk to the horses.

"Hi, Max!" the little girl said in greeting as she approached. "Hi, Speckles!"

Braden joined Micah as they watched Bronwyn in her element, with the creatures of Vii. "Speckles?" he whispered to Micah.

The little girl interrupted Micah's shrug. "You call him Pack, but he prefers Speckles. See the dots all over his body?" Braden took it in stride.

"Is there anything else we should know about our friends, Max and Speckles? We can't understand them when they talk to us."

"They like you very much. Aadi, Golden Warrior, Skirill. They all like you so I've decided it's okay to like you." For the first time, she faced

Braden directly and looked into his eyes.

"Thank you, Bronwyn. We will accept your help any time. Do you know anything about flying mutants, birds of all black, with skin like a bat, a face with fangs, not a beak?" Micah looked harshly at Braden for asking a little girl such a question.

She shivered. "Yes," she said in a low voice. "My bird friends told me about them. They come from the north, in a cloud, once or twice every moon. Everyone must hide. Is that what happened to these two glorious creatures?" She stomped over to Braden, making a fist, preparing to swing at him.

"You don't let them get hurt like that again!" she cried. "You hide like you're supposed to!"

Braden and Micah both raised their hands. "To the best of our abilities, we will protect our companions," Micah said for both of them. Bronwyn calmed immediately.

"Bronwyn, can you help us? We are looking for big, strong creatures who are able and willing to pull a cart or a wagon. That's a way for us to move large quantities of trade items between the villages. Max and Pack, I mean Speckles, have helped us so far on our journey. They are the heroes of our caravan, but they need help."

"Yes. I've heard of large creatures, but they won't come with you, not unless I'm with you and can talk with them."

"Ooh. I'm not sure about that. It's dangerous where we travel, sweetie." Micah offered. The little girl stamped her foot and pouted.

"What if she's right? If she can talk with the creatures, then this could go much easier." Braden resigned himself to it. They'd have to talk with her parents and see if Bronwyn could come along. Braden looked at Micah and shrugged. So much for any private time with his partner while plying the trade routes.

Bronwyn's parents were fine with her traveling with her saviors, Braden and Micah. The little girl explained it to them as necessary to help the village. She was right, but only in a small way. She would be helping the entire south. All of the villages would grow to depend on these new beasts of burden, and that included the Amazonians.

43 – A Growing Caravan

In the morning, Bronwyn was ready to go early, but Braden had to find numbweed first. They all had wounds to heal.

Braden wanted to go into the rainforest at first light, but Micah convinced him to wait until the sun rose higher in the sky. She wanted his search to be as short as possible. Bronwyn said she would go, too. G-War and Aadi would keep her company. Braden noted that she didn't consider him to be company.

"Well, maybe they'll keep me company, too," Braden suggested. She shrugged her little shoulders. Even though she decided to like him, she preferred creatures other than humans. Braden felt sorry for her. Such a gifted child, but humans had not treated her well. She was loved, as shown by the way the villagers felt when they thought they lost her to the rainforest.

"G. Aadi. You guys up for a trip to find some numbweed?" Braden asked.

"Of course they are, silly!" Bronwyn marched off smartly, Aadi at her side, the Hillcat running ahead. Braden looked back at Micah, holding his hands up in surrender, and jogged after the little girl.

The first numbweed bush was less than a hundred strides into the rainforest. Braden was embarrassed at how easy it was to find. Bronwyn walked right to it and pointed.

"Let's take this back to the village. I'll start preparing it and then you and Micah can come back and find more. The sooner I get started on it, the sooner we'll have Skirill back in the air. Is that okay?" She waved him off.

'G. Convince her to come back to the village and then you can come back in to find more. I've got work to do for Ess and the horses. Do you need any?'

'I'm fine. Yes. We are going back to the village.' On cue, the little girl turned and skipped through the underbrush, avoiding puddles as she headed back.

'On our way back with the first batch,' Braden sent to Micah.

'Already?' she answered.

'Yeah. It's a real short story...' he said. The villagers hadn't noticed they'd left, so they didn't get a second glance when they returned. Micah took Bronwyn's hand as they turned around and immediately went back into the rainforest. Braden and Micah exchanged looks as they passed each other.

Braden put the small pot over a fire, added a small amount of water, and crushed the numbweed leaves into it, creating a pungent mixture. As the water reduced without boiling, he added water, small amounts at a time. Couldn't let the leaves get too wet and couldn't let the water boil. He filled the pot with the first batch. When it was ready, he put it into an oiled pouch that had remained empty of numbweed for far too long.

He had started working on the second batch when Micah and the companions returned. Aadi didn't have facial expressions, but his head hung low and if he could look sad, that would be it. Numbweed bushes were piled onto his shell and tied in place. He didn't seem to relish his role as the group's cart. Micah and Bronwyn skipped along beside him, hand in hand, singing merrily. G-War was nowhere to be seen, but Braden could feel that he wasn't far.

"It's okay, my shelled friend; we'll have this off you in a heartbeat." Braden undid the Lizard Man rope that he grew more fond of with each use. It would be hugely popular in the north, where ropes tended to be dry and stiff, bulky and weak.

The bushes fell to the ground. Braden decided they'd leave at sunrise. In the interim, he had a great deal of numbweed to process. Maybe he'd show someone in the village how to do it, too. Everyone could use numbweed. This could be one of their trade items, especially since the bushes grew so close. They had a ready resource.

The power of numbweed was unknown in the south.

It was time that changed. With enemies like the mutie birds, everyone needed to know about numbweed.

Micah took the completed first batch to Skirill and applied it liberally to his wounds. To get at the scratches and scabs on the horses, they had to be washed. With Bronwyn's help, they walked to a nearby stream. The little girl didn't need to lead them by a rope, Max and Speckles simply followed her and did as she told them.

When they were washed and while they stood in the stream, Micah applied numbweed to each of the many wounds on their backs and flanks. Micah took the time to wash herself and asked for Bronwyn's help to put the numbweed on her scratches. The little girl was impressed by the scars.

"Is this how a real warrior looks?" she asked innocently. Micah flexed her muscles, showing off.

"Yes. I guess it is. You should see Braden's scars if you want to know the burden that a warrior carries."

"I don't know," the little girl answered.

"He is my mate and I ask that you treat him with respect. He would give his life to protect you or any of the others. He saved the Golden Warrior's life, many times."

"Okay," she finally said. "He can be my mate, too." Micah laughed until she choked. The innocence of youth. Yes, they would all be friends, but Braden only had one mate.

44 – Village Coldstream

Bronwyn was a handful and a huge relief at the same time. She wanted to ride with Micah, holding G-War on her lap and pulling Aadi close by. If she could have figured a way to wedge Skirill next to her body, she would have.

Braden kept Skirill with him. The Hawkoid was healing well. The injuries lessened with each turn, with the most progress since they discovered the new source of numbweed. Skirill had no pain since Bronwyn first touched him. She didn't heal his wounds, but she made him forget they were there. That could be dangerous if Skirill attempted to fly before he was ready.

It wouldn't be long now. Braden figured that within a couple turns, Skirill would be able to take some test flights, maybe they would find a breeze he could fly into to lessen the strain.

When they approached a new village, Bronwyn reached out and talked with the animals. As they entered, she was greeted by her new furry and feathered friends. That seemed to remove any tension that the villagers had toward the strangers. Nothing like a happy little girl to keep everyone calm. This village, like the last, was a community. No one in charge, everyone going about their business. Nothing unique to trade.

The same story as Greentree. Village Coldstream was unique in its own way. It was smaller than Greentree, but they favored bright-colored clothing. The colors were so vibrant that Braden felt like squinting when he looked at them.

The companions were welcomed because Bronwyn would have it no other way. She introduced each of them, with a story. Even Max and Speckles were included. Braden and Micah ended up introducing themselves.

The Elder couldn't move like he used to, so his son took care of the business of greeting strangers. Other people did not travel to the village very often. They thought it had been three or four cycles since the last, but no one was sure. People kept to themselves in the south. *But they have plenty to offer each other*, Braden thought.

"The colors? Oh, that's just a little something we do. We never really thought anything about it," Dantan said. He remained non-committal, but Braden saw the light of potential in his eyes. If they spent more time making and dying fabrics, then they would have to spend less time in the fields or with the animals.

The pens contained a good number of pigs. Pork was their staple. They treated it with syrup from a nearby stand of unique trees. Braden thought he was in heaven eating the meat. Bronwyn promptly disowned him, informing all present that she did not eat the friendly animals. Someone made a quip that they were only eating the unfriendly ones. Everyone laughed but Bronwyn, who stormed off to talk with the pigs.

It wasn't long before she returned and apologized to Braden by giving him a hug. When he looked at her curiously, she answered that the pigs told her that their purpose was to get big and die gloriously to help the humans live. With that, she thanked the pig and bit deeply into the syrup-cured meat. Her eyes lit up.

"Yup," Braden said to Micah. "This stuff will change anyone's life." Micah couldn't respond as her mouth was stuffed, sweet juices running down her chin. She nodded instead. *Who cares about pretty clothes*, Braden thought.

Braden traded half their rope supply and some mushrooms to get a couple big handfuls of the sweetened, smoked pork. He didn't care. He even contemplated trading the saffrimander, but they probably wouldn't appreciate the spice.

They left Coldstream in high spirits, another village added to the trade route.

Two more turns and another village. Another addition to the trade route. More fields and vegetables. Village Bliss didn't quite live up to its namesake, but at least the villagers weren't hostile.

Another couple turns and Skirill was flying again. He flew tentatively at first, but Braden kept him on the ground so long that his injuries were fully healed. It was his muscles that needed work. The Hawkoid was at home soaring high above the ground. He raced far ahead, then circled back. Braden cautioned him from getting too far away, in case the mutie birds returned.

Skirill kept his Hawkoid eyes pointed northward. He wouldn't let those flying terrors sneak up on them again. He didn't know what their minds would do to Bronwyn, but he knew uncomfortably well what their claws and fangs could do to flesh.

45 – Never a Dull Turn

With the Hawkoid watching far in front of them, they were able to pick up the pace. Max and Pack trotted along happily, guided by Bronwyn.

Braden still couldn't call him Speckles.

Had it only been a cycle since he and G-War drove the water buffalo and their wagon on the trade routes west of Cameron? Not even a cycle.

And now, he was a family man with responsibilities. Although he could look at it as being the best trader in the entire south. He laughed to himself. Change was constant. Change was good. Bronwyn sat in his lap, stroking Max's mane, humming to herself. With the animals of the world as her companions, she was always in a good mood.

Micah looked at him as he watched Bronwyn. She caught him smiling. He mouthed the question, *'What?'*

"You. Tough man." Her tone was kind. Yes, change was constant.

"Next stop, big scary animals that can pull a whole village!" he exclaimed, trying to change the subject.

"They aren't scary. You just have to love them. You are so mean!" Bronwyn said in her little voice. The 'cat had been running alongside to get some exercise. He vaulted into a tiny space between the little girl and the horse's mane. She threw both arms around him, pulling him in tightly.

He started purring, the sound deep within his chest, shaking him and Bronwyn. Braden wasn't the only one who changed. The 'cat was getting soft in his old age.

'I'm still young, in 'cat years. I just decided to enjoy the finer things in life,' G-War said.

"Bronwyn. Do you know Golden Warrior's true name?"

"Oh yes," she answered brightly. "But he told me not to tell you."

"Of course he did." Braden put his hands over the little girl's ears. "Ass!"

"Stop that, it tickles." Bronwyn fought back as much as she could, but her arms were filled with 'cat and she was wedged in front of Braden. Micah laughed out loud as she rode alone. Skirill was ahead, perched on a high branch of a tall tree, carefully watching the sky.

Aadi watched them all, pleased with his decision to join the human called Braden. There was never a dull turn for the Tortoid as he contemplated all the things he'd seen and what else he might see. Maybe it was time for him to expand his family. There was much that Tortoids could bring to the good people of the south, as well as the Amazonians. *Ambassador Aadi of the Tortoid Nation*, he thought. That had a nice ring to it.

46 - The Aurochs

As Skirill scouted ahead, he spotted a herd of large creatures grazing the western grasslands of the Plains of Propiscius. He swooped in for a closer look, passing the image via the mindlink.

"Wow," Braden said. "Those look much bigger than the water buffaloes I used to have."

"Let's hurry. They look wonderful!" Bronwyn exclaimed and immediately Max and Pack broke into a run.

"Farging crap!" Braden yelled as he almost fell off. Micah glared at him in harsh rebuke, pointing with one hand at the little girl as she held on tightly with the other. They all leaned lower in the saddle as Bronwyn urged the horses on.

There is a village, not far. I see many people,' Skirill shared.

Bronwyn slowed the horses as they approached the grasslands. The creatures towered over them. Bronwyn struggled to get down, but Braden held her back, not knowing why.

"Let me go!" She continued to struggle until Braden lost his grip, G-War going one way and Bronwyn going the other. She tumbled to the ground, brushed herself off, and ran toward the creatures. Braden's instinct was to race after her, but G-War stopped him. Aadi stopped him. Micah stopped him.

Although she was only ten cycles old, this was Bronwyn's strength. She had nothing to fear from the beasts.

She reached the closest one, a massive brute with shoulders nearly as wide as Max was long. They looked like water buffaloes, but far larger and their horns were immense, on top of their heads, above their ears, wide at the base, curving gracefully forward to end in sharp points. Braden wondered if the horses would be safe.

The beast bent down to the little girl who lovingly stroked his head. She patted his forehead, her hand a tiny spot on his thick brownish hair. Other beasts ambled over. They varied in size and color, large to small, thick dark brown hair to light, one color to splotches of dark brown, light brown, and white. They continued to join the large bull until Bronwyn was completely encircled. Braden and Micah could no longer see her.

"G, a little help please," Braden asked.

'She is safer there than anywhere else she could be. They call themselves Aurochs,' the 'cat said.

"Aurochs." Braden looked at Micah and shrugged uncomfortably. "I guess we wait." He got down from Max, gave him a couple pats on the neck, and turned him loose to graze. Micah followed his lead. Bronwyn must have told the horses that the Aurochs were friends, because no one seemed concerned besides Braden.

Micah took his hand as they stood watching the Aurochs. "It's not knowing that bothers you," she started. "You've taken responsibility for all of us and that means you can't let go." She squeezed his hand tightly and leaned into him. "Sometimes you have to. What would you have done if she wasn't here?" Micah nodded toward the circle of Aurochs. They still couldn't see the girl.

"Probably screwed things up," Braden answered. "I think I would have gone to the village first, hoping that they had domesticated these creatures and would be willing to trade for some." He shook his head. "We still need to go to the village. They might think they own these beasts."

"I agree." Micah put her head on Braden's shoulder. He wasn't sure what exactly she agreed with. It didn't matter. He felt better.

"Bronwyn!" Braden said in his loud trader voice. "Can you introduce us?" He hoped that she heard him. He was impatient. He expected that if he didn't help them focus, Bronwyn would spend the day playing with her new friends. But she had heard him and, surprisingly, acknowledged him.

A couple smaller females, cows, moved aside so Bronwyn could exit the circle. She skipped as she joined Micah and Braden, wedging between them so they each took one of her hands. The Aurochs she first talked with followed her. The others fell in behind.

"This is Brandt Earthshaker. He's King of the Aurochs." Braden and Micah didn't know what to say. How did one greet a king?

"I am Free Trader Braden and this is my partner, Micah," Braden started and both of them bowed deeply. "We are searching for someone who can help us establish trade routes. We need your strength." Braden didn't know if Brandt could understand him directly or if Bronwyn was translating what he said, so he waited.

"Greetings Brandt Earthshaker, King of the Aurochs," Micah said in her own greeting. They bowed a second time.

Finally, the king bowed back, dipping to one knee, then standing up straight. His horns were bigger than the humans and when he dipped, they were treated to an alarmingly close look. It took all Braden and Micah had not to step away from the King.

These are intelligent creatures,' G-War offered, before opening the mindlink with Brandt. The King's thought voice rivaled his size and boomed within their heads.

Welcome to our herd, humans.' Although his voice was loud, it was friendly and filled Braden and Micah with warmth. Their fears melted away.

"You are magnificent!" Braden blurted out.

"Do you mind?" Micah said, already beside the creature's great head, stroking his ears and his neck. His hair was thick and coarse, but not long. She could feel the muscles rippling beneath his skin. His strength had to be incredible just to hold his head up. Micah knew she would be unable to lift even one of his horns.

Not at all, my lady. I've never talked with a human before. I find it exhilarating,' the King answered.

Bronwyn stretched as far around Brandt's nose as she could reach to give him a hug. He raised his head, lifting her into the air. She scrambled over his head, turned, and straddled his thick neck. She sat there, radiating joy.

"Have you dealt with humans before?" Braden asked.

'Yes. Dealt with, but never talked to. From the edge of our grassland, the villagers think they can control us with fire. We stay away from them. If the grasslands burn, we will all die.'

"We won't let that happen, will we, Braden!" cried the little voice from high above the ground.

"No. We won't, little sweetheart. Have you talked with Brandt about what we'd like?" Bronwyn shook her head as she leaned down to rub the huge neck with both her hands.

"King Brandt, we are creating a world of trade here in the south. We've gotten a number of villages to believe what is possible. If we had wagons, a great deal of products can be moved between all the villages, helping them become civilized. Good trade can stop conflict, help people be better, be happier..." Braden's thoughts drifted back to Sanctuary. *Good trade can make people envious, destroying the world,* he thought. *But this time was different. He could influence things the right way.*

'We can pull your wagons, but there will be conditions.' Braden waited, but the King of the Aurochs didn't explain.

Never agree to a trade without knowing all the conditions. "What are your conditions, King Brandt?"

'We are never to be tied up. We are equal partners with the traders. We determine how far we go in a day and we determine how much time we need to feed.'

"Shrewd! Understand that you'll have to wear some kind of harness to pull the wagons. Outside of that, you will never be tied up. Anyone who tried would be foolish. Those are easy conditions. Now, how do you define equal partner?" Braden asked, now in full trader negotiating mode, despite the fact that he was speaking with an Aurochs.

'If we find something we like, a grass, a vegetable, we will want our fair share as part of the trade.' The great beast shook his head to chase away a few flies. Braden fell backward trying to get away from the horns. *'Sorry,'* Brandt said in his booming thought voice. *'Not used to humans.'*

"Not yet, my friend. I hope you'll grow to like us. Yes, getting vegetables as part of the trade is certainly possible and a good thing. Try this." Braden pulled a mushroom from his belt pouch and held it before the King's great head. The Aurochs looked at it briefly before carefully taking it from Braden's hand and eating it.

'We usually avoid these kinds of things as they are too often poisonous. But this is good. I've not seen its like before. Where did you find it?'

"This is something that the Lizard Men trade, the Amazonians that is, the people who live in the rainforest."

'We have seen these creatures, but we don't go into the rainforest. We don't fit!' He started shaking his head. The other Aurochs standing close by were shaking their great heads as well. Were they laughing?

"As to your other points, I can't say how far you go and when you eat. If we trade, it is nice to keep to a schedule, but that schedule can be whatever we make it. We'll need to travel a certain amount each turn. I expect that, as big as you are, you cover a great deal of ground in a very short time. I don't think it will be a problem, so yes. You determine how far and when you feed. How much do you eat?" Braden asked without thinking.

'That is an ongoing battle, I'm afraid.' The Aurochs all started shaking their heads.

'That's it, then, shall we go?' the King of the Aurochs asked.

"Now?" Braden was surprised. "How many would come with us?"

'Well, all of us, of course,' Brandt answered without hesitation.

"But we probably only need a couple of you..." Braden stammered. Micah stepped up.

"We have one village where we stay. We travel from there and then return. A couple of you could come with us. The trade route can end here. I'm afraid that if all of you come on all the trades, then there won't be enough vegetables or mushrooms to go around."

'*Show me,*' Brandt asked cryptically.

Skirill stepped into the conversation, showing images of the villages and surrounding areas to the Aurochs. The Hawkoid showed broader swaths of land between the villages.

'*There. That will be our new home.*' Brandt selected an area with fields and grasslands with streams flowing throughout.

It was Greentree, Bronwyn's home village. Braden suspected she influenced Brandt's decision, but it could not have been better, in his opinion. There would always be someone who could talk with the Aurochs and make sure that they were happy. He didn't want to think of the damage any of these great creatures could do if they were upset.

"Yes! I will take care of you all. Mushrooms and cabbages!" the little girl shouted gleefully.

"I'd like to talk with the villagers near here, if I may, and then we can get going."

47 – Too Many People

The Village of Westerly had few houses and huts, but a lot of people. Braden and Micah wondered where they all slept.

Although they didn't raise the alarm and come at Braden and Micah with weapons, the reception was cool. They did not get down from their horses as they waited for someone in charge. An older man finally strolled up, making it clear that he was important.

"Someone said you wanted to talk with me?" he asked in an imperial voice.

"I am Free Trader Braden and this is my partner Micah. The Hillcat is G-War. The Tortoid is Master Aadi. The Hawkoid--" He pointed to a tree. "--is Skirill. We are looking to open a trade route, from east to west on the north side of the rainforest. We already have a number of villages with trades ongoing." Braden left it there, assuming that the man would want to know more information.

"We already got one of those. No need for more." He looked skeptically at the companions. He mouthed the word 'muties' as he turned away.

"Wait! You already have a trade route established? What do you trade? Maybe we have a better deal," Braden offered, not knowing what the old man's intent was.

"Trade. Everyone shares a bit of what they grow or make with me and I share my wisdom and leadership with them. That's our trade." The old man hesitated. Those standing around seemed interested, others joined them.

"If there is enough to share, there might be enough to trade. What do you grow that you could expand, grow more of? What do you want that you don't have?" Braden decided against getting down. He didn't like this self-proclaimed leader. If he was face to face with him, Braden would probably end up hurting him. He put a restraining hand on Micah's knee. She was ready to change the village's leadership.

He looked at her out of the side of his eye and shook his head, just enough so she would understand. She took a deep breath, trying to force herself to relax.

"Maybe I can talk with someone who grows the food, who might want to trade?" Braden suggested, knowing that it might make the old man angry. Braden's anger was rising. He wanted the old man to do something so they would be justified in killing him.

Braden struggled with his thoughts. He had to talk his way out of this.

Maybe the old man saw the danger he was in. "Talk to whoever you want. I'll have no part of it." He turned and walked away, much more quickly than when he arrived.

"You, my good man!" Braden called to one individual who seemed ready to burst with excitement. "Are you interested?"

"Yes! Take me with you!" Choruses of "and me" followed until the whole group pressed in on the two horses.

"Whoa! Wait a minute. What's this all about?" Braden tried to regain control.

A number of people started talking, then talked louder trying to speak over the others.

"You!" Braden pointed to the first man who spoke up. "Why are you begging to leave?"

"Look how we live! There has to be something better than this. We sleep in shifts, some during the day, some at night," the man said.

"Why don't you just build more places to live?" Micah asked.

"He won't let us," they answered as one.

"Why does he have that much power over you?" Braden asked, looking from face to face. People looked down, shrugging. No one answered. "He only has as much power as you give him."

"Yes!" the young man shouted, trying to reassert himself. "We can build them ourselves and still provide for him."

"We're not going to take anyone with us," Braden stated firmly. He held out his hands to calm them down. "But we will be back. I want to see new homes and I want you to be able to tell me what you can trade. I don't know when we'll be back, but we will. By the way, the Aurochs are coming with us." They looked at him. Without being able to talk with the Aurochs, these people didn't know what they were called.

"The great beasts roaming the grassland. They have agreed to come with us."

"Agreed? How did they do that? They are just beasts. We use their droppings for fertilizer."

"We can talk with them," Micah said.

A startled cry of 'Mutants!' came from someone in the crowd. The people backed away.

"We're not mutants," Micah said coldly. "But they are." She waved her hand in the direction of the 'cat and the Tortoid. "And they are good creatures, better than you. The great beasts? They're mutants, too, and their waste fertilizes your crops. Think about that." She pulled on Pack/Speckle's rein, turning his head away from the village. He danced in a half circle, scattering some of the people.

"We'll be back and we expect to see changes if you want to join the trade route." Braden gave Max a light kick and he was off. They urged the horses into a gallop to put as much distance as possible between them and the village.

48 – An Injury and a Bond

The herd of Aurochs made great traveling companions. Bronwyn refused to ride with Braden and Micah, preferring to sit astride Brandt Earthshaker's broad neck. Besides Brandt, there were three young bulls and twenty-five cows. As Braden suspected, they didn't walk fast, but their strides were so long that they moved a great distance in a short amount of time. They stopped often to graze, but not for too long.

The Aurochs had trouble with obstacles. They spent their lives grazing grasslands, not climbing over rocks or fording streams. The horses, though smaller, negotiated these obstacles without issue, compared to their larger companions.

One of the younger cows slipped while climbing a rocky slope, and tumbled down the hill, crashing against a tree near the bottom. It left a huge gash in her side.

Brandt was beside himself. He was responsible to protect the herd and with this, he was helpless.

"Braden and Micah will help her and I will take away her pain," Bronwyn said softly to the King of the Aurochs. Braden gave the pouch of numbweed to Micah while he got his needle and the precious bit of remaining thread out of his saddle bag.

Bronwyn stroked the large cow's head, singing happily. Even the cows had horns, but these weren't as big as Brandt's. Micah cautioned the little girl to be careful that she didn't get hurt if the cow moved suddenly.

The numbweed helped stop the bleeding, while Bronwyn took away the cow Aurochs' pain. Braden asked the cow to remain still while he sewed up the wound. The little girl kept the great beast calm as Braden worked the needle and thread. He ran out of thread, but by putting the stitches further apart, he was able to close the majority of the gash. They cleaned it with water from their flasks, then applied more numbweed. Braden suggested they remain here until the next daylight when he knew the cow would be able to continue.

Brandt's gratitude was as big as the Aurochs himself. He showed his affection through nuzzling, which ended up knocking the humans to the ground. Bronwyn, the smallest of them all, was first up and first to nuzzle back, wrapping her small arms as far around the Aurochs' face as she could reach. He lifted her in the air repeatedly. She squealed in delight each time.

The herd closed in around the humans, each taking a turn touching them. G-War adeptly danced around the hooves, but once he'd had enough of that, he vaulted onto Brandt's face and ran up his head and down his neck to the King's back, where he crouched low, before lying down. Aadi hovered higher to stay above the fray. Skirill perched in the tree that the cow fell into.

This was a good spot to camp, so they stayed. With the Earthshaker Herd watching over them, there was nothing to fear. Bronwyn slept between Brandt's front legs, as comfortably as if she were in the finest bed. G-War slept on the King's neck. Warm and soft, it was a perfect 'cat bed.

Sunrise brought rain. Braden thought the horses smelled bad when they got wet, but that didn't compare to the smell of a wet Aurochs. Bronwyn seemed oblivious to it. They applied more numbweed to the injured cow. The rain would wash it off shortly, but then they'd apply more. Their supply was virtually unlimited.

Brandt continued to be effusive in his praise of the humans and their ability to heal such a fearsome wound. Braden explained that it was because humans were so frail that they had developed the techniques for better healing.

Bronwyn turned out to be the one who got the herd moving, including the horses.

Braden leaned close to Micah. "Did you ever think that we're simply watching events as they unfold?"

"Watching? I'm not sure you were watching when the three of you went into the rainforest after Bronwyn. Remember the part where she wanted to stay with the Lizard Men, the Amazonians?" Micah reminded him.

"Okay, maybe we pushed this raft into the river and we're hanging on for the ride. Is that better?"

Micah nodded. "Yes. We are hanging on, watching a beautiful world go by. We stop here and there to clean up the shore, make sure things are right, then we push back into the rapids."

"Maybe we can stop at Coldstream for some of their sweetened smoked pork? I think I like that better than the brownies, although I have some incredible memories that go with the brownies."

Micah blushed. Those were a few of many great memories.

"We don't have anything left. Maybe the Aurochs can knock down a few trees for them?"

"That's a reach! If the Aurochs work for them, wouldn't that be their trade?" Micah suggested.

"You got me there. But Brandt feels like he owes us for working on the cow's wound."

"Listen here, my lover. As long as I'm your partner, you will never trade doing the right thing. The villagers didn't owe you for going after Bronwyn, and Brandt doesn't owe you for sewing up a cut." She lifted her eyebrows to solidify her point.

Braden raised his hands in surrender. "And since you'll be my partner until you die, I guess it's settled," she said ominously.

"Since you'll be my partner until YOU die," Braden started, but he didn't have anything else, so he ended with a shrug of his shoulders. *Let her wonder about that,* he thought.

'*There's nothing to wonder about,*' she replied in her thought voice.

"Crap! Would you stop doing that?"

"Can't you hear me when I think?" she asked. He scowled in response.

She held his face in her hands, looking deep into his blue eyes. *What about now?'*

"Yes. I heard that," he answered.

'Not with your outside voice,' she responded. *'This is without G-War's help. I think some of his ability to mindlink rubbed off on us.'*

'Or maybe he shared it with us because the number of companions has grown rather large. And he is a selfish ass, you know.' They laughed. The 'cat's indomitable spirit loomed large. The Golden Warrior was a stalwart companion, always there in time of need, and by sharing his ability to speak with others, he helped them get where they were.

Micah stopped thinking about G-War. She looked back over at Braden. *'I love you,'* she said simply. A thought voice couldn't lie. It was one's thoughts after all. He could feel the emotion behind it, too.

'Until we die,' he responded, realizing that her earlier statement was not a threat. They were bonded to each other. Simple as that.

49 – Needing a Wagon

As they rode to the outskirts of Village Greentree, someone raised a cry of welcome. The villagers ran from all directions to meet Braden and Micah. Bronwyn's parents looked for the little girl, alarmed when they didn't see her.

"She's coming, and she has something to show you." Micah smiled.

As the Earthshaker Herd came into sight, everyone's eyes went wide, until they saw Bronwyn waving from the great neck of Brandt, King of the Aurochs. She stopped the herd before they got too close and carefully climbed down.

Brandt stamped his mighty front hooves and shook his head as he looked over his herd and their new grazing lands. *'On behalf of the Earthshaker Herd, I accept these grasslands as our own,'* Brandt said to his people. The herd spread out to graze.

Bronwyn's parents ran to her, sweeping her up in their arms. She wanted down, taking a hand of each and running with them back toward the herd.

Braden and Micah explained to the villagers that the herd had chosen this area as their new home. They would help pull the wagons on the trade routes. They would be partners in the trade, not beasts of burden, as they were mutants, and like the Amazonians, they were friends. Plus, their droppings made good fertilizer, or so they heard.

The villagers nodded knowingly. Bronwyn could talk with the Aurochs. At ten cycles, she was going to be in charge of the herd, or more likely, she was the liaison between the herd and the village, between the Amazonians and the village.

"We would like to set up our trading base here, in Greentree. We can go both east and west. The Aurochs are here. We can swap who pulls the wagons as we pass through," Braden said.

"What wagons?" someone asked.

"At Village Dwyer, they are working on some right now. Maybe they'll be ready when we get back there. We'll also need harnesses. The ones we have for Pack, I mean Speckles, won't fit any of the Aurochs. Do any of your people work with leather?" *Maybe the new ropes from the Amazonians would help. Hmmm. All kinds of work to do,* Braden thought to himself.

"Welcome home, Micah. We need to build a house." Braden gave his partner a hug, then walked toward the grasslands where the villagers were strolling to get a close look at their massive new neighbors.

Someone clapped him on the back. "They are something, aren't they," the villager said with a big smile on his face.

Yes, they are, Braden thought.

I couldn't agree more, he heard Micah think.

It didn't take long before the village suggested a celebration of the caravan's successful return. Music and food.

Bronwyn suggested they move to the edge of the grasslands so the Aurochs could attend and listen. The village brought all the vegetables and all the mushrooms they had. There wasn't very much, not enough to feed a single Aurochs, let alone twenty nine of them. But the King of the Aurochs was gracious, refusing to accept anything, until there was enough for all. The villagers still managed to put together a sampler tray, with one small treat for each of the new arrivals.

Brandt had the Aurochs come up, one at a time, so Bronwyn could introduce them and give them a treat. "This is Ackla," the little girl said, carefully holding a piece of cabbage in her small hand. The Aurochs cow's mouth was as big as Bronwyn's head, but she managed to gingerly relieve the human of her prize. The cow bowed as she left.

"This is Wen…" Each in their turn greeted the villagers.

No one saw Aadi leave, but everyone saw him return. As dusk arrived, the Tortoid escorted Akhmiyar and four Amazonians to the celebration. Braden and Akhmiyar greeted in their new way, hands on each other's chest. Then Bronwyn introduced them to the King of the Aurochs.

The Lizard Men bowed deeply, which Brandt returned. Then they stood facing each other. Brandt shook his head. Akhmiyar made some signs with his hands/claws.

"Bronwyn, do you know what they are talking about?" Braden asked.

"The ancients, old times, survival, I really don't know what any of it means," she said before skipping away to scoop up G-War and carry him around.

"Unfortunately, we do," Braden said to Micah. "More creatures created by the ancients, and then left behind after the war to fend for themselves. Well, we see who the survivors are. Without the ancients, we wouldn't have the pleasure of their company. G-War, Aadi, Skirill. I wonder how Bronwyn got her ability to talk with all Vii's creatures?"

Micah shook her head. Some questions were better left unasked.

When the Amazonians finished talking with Brandt, Bronwyn ran up to them. Taking Akhmiyar's hand in hers, she took him to various villagers, where they conversed briefly. Akhmiyar had an agenda and it probably involved trade.

Braden was pleased. He wanted to drive trades because that was in his nature, but he was happy making sure that trade happened. Maybe he could start a Guild and be the Guildmaster.

"Well done, Master Aadi," Micah said as the Tortoid swam up to them.

Just Aadi, Master Human. And it was my pleasure. I saw them standing on the edge of the rainforest. They deserve to be a part of this celebration, too.'

50 – Trade!

The King of the Aurochs said he would accompany Braden, Micah, and the companions as they traveled east to McCullough and Dwyer. Brandt brought one cow and one bull along. They would learn the route and when the wagon was ready, they would take turns pulling it.

Braden wanted to stop at the meeting site with the Amazonians, hoping to work a deal to get more of their rope to help him build a harness for the Aurochs. The Amazon rope was the best until they could have a proper leather harness made.

It took work to convince Bronwyn to stay behind, but going with three Aurochs while twenty-six remained behind wouldn't work. No one could talk with them if she left. Reluctantly she agreed.

She was ten cycles old and they had to get her permission. One never knew who could make or break a trade.

Also, without Bronwyn, Braden felt less guilty taking down a couple deer to trade with the Amazonians. They left, feeling good about their progress.

Brandt expressed some reluctance to go into the rainforest. He was comfortable in wide open spaces, not the confines of a narrow road wedged between foreboding trees.

Once in the Amazon, Brandt realized the road was wide enough for him to turn around. He was much relieved.

The Amazonians appeared at once. After bowing and showing proper deference. they conversed with both the King and Aadi. Brandt conducted the negotiations for the rope, but since the Amazonians were pleased with his presence, they included a great volume of mushrooms. The Amazonians had no trade goods with them, so the companions waited while they disappeared into the rainforest to get them. Braden told them to take the two deer so they wouldn't spoil.

It wasn't long before Zalastar himself showed up. He greeted Brandt, and they bowed to each other as leaders of their people. Akhmiyar had passed to Zalastar that the Aurochs had joined Braden and Micah. Zalastar was also pleasantly surprised that the Amazonians had been invited to participate in the human celebration at Greentree.

"We're all in this together, trying to make tomorrow just a little bit better than today." The trade route would go from Dwyer to Westerly. He didn't expect many items would be traded initially, but their exchange of information, sharing of knowledge, and partnership would build a strong foundation on which future trade would flourish.

The Amazonians wanted to travel on the trade route, but Braden wasn't sure how they could survive in the dry of the open air. Zalastar said he'd ask his best people to come up with a way.

Mutants and humans working together. Although in Braden's mind, they were all mutants. None of the ancients were left. Everyone and everything had changed since the war destroyed the tech.

Which reminded Braden that it had been a while since he last waxed his bowstring. He always took care of his recurve bow, because it took care of him.

Skirill grew restless so he flew out of the rainforest and waited in the open.

Amazonian villages were initially established along the road and edges of the rainforest. Once the war started, the Amazonians moved deep into the Amazon, as far away from humanity as possible. Over the last hundred cycles, as their numbers grew, they spread back toward the edges.

Zalastar wanted to improve the road through the rainforest. He was currently working with his people to start moving the villages closer to both the road and the northern border. As they moved, they could reestablish regular interaction with humans.

This time as equals.

As Brandt and the Aurochs were doing with the humans.

Braden showed them it was possible for humans and mutants to share equally, although they didn't consider themselves mutants. They were a different race, that was all. Braden committed to remembering that. They were different races, working the same trade.

As the conversation wound down, Brandt called to get everyone's attention. He wanted to discuss the matter of New Sanctuary with the leaders of the peoples of Vii. Micah was the President, with Braden her mate and the Free Trader. Golden Warrior was a prince among his people. Master Aadi was the First Master of the Tortoid Consortium. Skirill was the Hawkoid with a vision for building a community. He had been cast away from his people for that, but he was still the best to represent them.

How could he refuse? He flew back to the Amazonian's Market Square, rejoining the others. With Brandt's permission, he landed gently on one of the King's great horns, gripping it tightly with his claws.

Braden tried not to laugh, stifling it with a cough as the 'cat sat on the Aurochs' head, Skirill perched near the point of one horn, Aadi floated close by, while Zalastar stood like a statue.

Once Braden returned to the topic at hand, he sobered quickly. *They know about New Sanctuary*, he thought. *How do we prevent a second human war? The easiest answer was to deny access to the Old Tech.*

Micah assured the others that they set up security when they left. No other humans would be granted access. This gave them some relief, but what was a long-term solution?

Braden felt like he was over his head. He didn't think that far ahead. Micah hadn't either, not to the degree that Brandt and Zalastar had. How could they memorialize their commitment to long-term peace, ensuring that others followed suit? Braden and Micah both were in awe in the presence of real leaders like Brandt and Zalastar.

The companions wanted future generations to think as Braden and

Micah, that the good of all was more important than personal power.

Braden shared his caravan's adventures with Zalastar, noting the growing problems with power-hungry individuals in the north. Braden and Micah had greatly reduced the number of strong-men in the south, but the problem would rise again if not carefully watched. The others seemed fascinated by Warren Deep's civilization. Braden thought it was better than the south, more mature as a civilization, but not fully civilized. When he saw the mob in Binghamton hanging the trader, he didn't equate that to a good society, but rather the breakdown of civilization.

Maybe the north was preparing to fight themselves again, but he escaped it when he came south. They needed people of vision to prevent another civil war.

Well, Micah is the President, Braden thought. *Where is that rope?* They would have to think about this and talk more. Braden was most comfortable trading. With powerful allies like the Aurochs and Amazonians, he felt that they could maintain a balance of power. No one could be allowed too much.

He'd seen what power did to people.

He was Free Trader Braden and always would be. His mate was Micah, a Warrior. He kept repeating this to himself and it helped ground him. When he opened his eyes, not realizing he had closed them, everyone was looking at him.

"I could really use some of that sweet smoked pork right about now," he said. He needed time to think.

51 – Muties Attack

With plenty of rope and the Aurochs well fed with mushrooms, the companions continued their journey.

Micah wasn't surprised to see a number of men, formerly of Dwyer, working in and around Village McCullough. Everyone waved happily until they saw the Aurochs, but with Braden and Micah's assurances, the groups met without reservation and greeted each other.

Braden asked if they would consider weaving a saddle blanket from their special material that would cover the horses' back and flanks. When Mel-Ash saw the scars from the mutie bird attack, she committed to helping out, saying that she'd cut Braden a deal.

After a short stay, they continued to Village Dwyer to check on the status of the wagon. They had both woodworkers and a blacksmith working on it. If they couldn't build the wagon, then no one could. Braden put the thought out of his head. He needed that wagon, but worrying about it wouldn't help.

The changes in the village were monumental. The villagers greeted the caravan as if they were long lost sons. That was the reception. As usual, the villagers were impressed by the Aurochs.

What wasn't impressive was the progress they made on the wagon. As in, they had cut a few planks, but nothing else. There were too many distractions. Braden expressed his dismay, probably a little too vocally, until Micah calmed him down. With renewed determination, he brought together those building the wagon and laid out the details, sketching everything thoroughly on the inside walls of Old Tom's smithy. They measured the Aurochs a number of times. The wagon could be far bigger than what Braden had previously envisioned. The wagon he designed was better than anything they had in the north.

He couldn't wait for it to be completed, but he'd have to.

In the interim, he drew up a drag cart, a very simple design of ropes and poles, that an Aurochs could drag. They could put a great deal of material in one of these. They wore out quickly, but they'd serve the purpose until the wagon was ready.

In less than a turn, they had their first drag cart ready for testing. They loaded it with vegetables and headed to Village McCullough. The Aurochs wanted to prove themselves, so they powered through. Often, Max and Pack had to trot to keep up.

They made the trip in record time. Village McCullough took the vegetables and loaded up half their stock of Amazonian mushrooms for a return trip, along with another sample of their protective material.

With sunrise, the second Aurochs took the cart, trying to outdo the first. It was a little much for the drag cart, which broke halfway there. Micah and Braden were able to fix it, but it took Brandt lifting the cart into the air on the ends of his horns to do so.

Even with the fix, they made it to Dwyer in the daylight. Old Tom needed more ore. There was very little close to the village, but he knew a spot not far away on the Plains of Propiscius.

The villagers built a second drag cart and both Aurochs pulled them into the grasslands, with the King and the companions following. Once at the spot, Tom and his workers started digging. The Aurochs spent the day grazing while the companions hunted. Skirill was readily successful, but G-War had to work much harder to corner a ground squirrel and make the kill.

They come! Skirill screeched in his thought voice. Time seemed to slow as Braden and Micah looked northward, seeing the familiar cloud of mutant birds heading toward them.

There was nowhere to hide.

The Aurochs stood back to back to back, with the villagers in the middle. Aadi and Micah lined up on either side of Braden. Skirill returned, his wings pounding the air to get more speed. G-War left his kill behind, his paws barely touching the ground as he raced to join his humans.

Micah unholstered the blaster, held it with both hands, and aimed. Aadi prepared himself. Braden pulled out his long knife, but hoped he wouldn't need it. The horses were near panic. Brandt attempted to calm them with his powerful thought voice.

"Now?" Braden asked. Micah nodded and pulled the trigger. A flame of light shot skyward, tearing into the bird cloud. Black shadows fell. The cloud broke apart, then swirled back together, continuing its approach. Micah fired again. The cloud broke apart again, more bodies fell from the sky. They regrouped into smaller clouds.

'You will leave us!' boomed Brandt's thought voice.

'You will all die,' came the response in unison from hundreds of small voices.

Micah renewed her efforts, firing short bursts at the smaller clouds of birds. They started to fly erratically, making her miss often. But when a strike was successful, many mutant birds died.

They were getting close, approaching from three directions at once. Braden stepped away to give himself room to swing his long knife. Micah fired relentlessly, at times depressing the trigger and waving the blaster to spread the light of flame across more of the sky.

But the blaster ran out of power. She threw it to the ground as she pulled her sword.

A cloud headed for the Aurochs. Aadi delivered a thunderclap into the middle of it and most of the mutant birds fell, flopping on the ground after they hit. The rest swerved away.

Micah twirled her sword around her as she stepped into a cloud of birds skimming along the ground. She knocked a few down, but the rest flew past her toward the 'cat, who was flying over the ground to get under the Aurochs.

Brandt swept his great head from side to side, but the mutant birds were too fast. He wasn't hurting them, while they dove in, leaving razor thin creases across his back.

The mutant birds had learned. They were avoiding the humans with the sharp blades and attacking the creatures that couldn't defend themselves.

Skirill launched himself and flew hard. None of the mutant birds could stand up to him one on one, so he danced in the sky, staying away from groups, isolating and killing them one by one.

Golden Warrior climbed to Brandt's back and kept the birds away. Any that approached were quickly slashed. Once on the ground, Tom and his fellows dispatched them with their shovels.

The birds stopped their attacks and flew away, where they regrouped into a single cloud.

"Get back here, Skirill! You! Get on their backs and get ready to fight!" Braden yelled. The men climbed up the Aurochs, backs sticky as they bled from numerous scratches. Their hide was thicker than a horse's, but they weren't invulnerable. The horses also bled from a number of new cuts, but Brandt was keeping them close. Braden feared if they bolted, the mutant birds would swarm them and bring them down.

As the mutant birds headed back toward them, Aadi let loose with his final thunderclap.

It broke their attack.

'We will hunt you down and kill you all!' Brandt swore as the remaining mutant birds flew away to the west. There weren't many, but the villagers from McCullough could suffer if they were caught unaware. Braden couldn't do anything about that except hope the villagers could get inside.

'And that's how wars start, my friend,' Braden said as he dug into their stock of numbweed.

'No. This war was already underway, so that's how wars end,' Brandt replied.

I'm sure that's what the ancients told themselves, Braden thought. Micah put a hand on his shoulder and hung her head. She retrieved her blaster and put it back on her belt. Then the humans took turns applying numbweed to the numerous wounds on the Aurochs and the horses.

"Farging crap!" Braden shouted, hands red with Aurochs blood. He sighed and hung his head low. Micah looked at him questioningly. "Bronwyn is going to be so mad at me."

Micah laughed, while Brandt bobbed his mighty head.

52 – Through the Rainforest

Once the mutant birds were gone, there was no reason they couldn't continue digging out the ore. They needed ore to make the metal to forge more swords so they could protect themselves while digging ore to make more metal.

It made sense once Braden stopped thinking about it.

They worked out a system where the Aurochs could communicate with people who didn't have the mindlink. Head motions would mean one of a number of things; unhook me, hook the cart up, need to eat, leaving, I'll stomp you to death if you do that again…

Things like that.

The King and the companions returned to Village Dwyer, where they set out planning their return to New Sanctuary. If they were at war with the mutant birds, they wanted to win, without destroying the world.

If the New Command Center didn't want to help, then they would take that as a good sign. If they could convince the hologram that nobody won the last war, the ancients destroyed themselves, then maybe it could build in a counterbalance to prevent a recurrence. Braden had the utmost confidence in the intelligence of the hologram and the New Command Center.

They decided to return to New Sanctuary immediately. They needed help.

As usual, the companions left at sunrise. Max and Pack carried the humans. Skirill flew ahead. Aadi was towed along behind Pack. G-War took to riding on Brandt, which the Aurochs approved of. He couldn't protect his back from the fast flying mutant birds. The 'cat was there and could fight the things off while the King sought shelter. Once in the rainforest, the birds would no longer pose a threat, but Braden expected G-War would remain on the King's head, perched high above everyone else.

Who else got to ride on a King?

Besides Bronwyn, that is, but she didn't do it for her ego.

Braden and Micah rode in front, side by side, and even held hands when they could. No one needed to talk. This was a journey where they only had a few questions. Once those were answered, there'd probably be more.

Then the rain started. The smell of wet Aurochs. The Hillcat looked miserable. Skirill tried to perch on one of the King's horns, but he slipped too often, using his wings for balance, which blocked Brandt's view of where he was going. He was polite about it, but he made the Hawkoid get off.

The humans explained that rain was the nature of the rainforest. That's why the Amazonians developed as they did. The Aurochs was not relieved to hear that the rain would last only a few turns, as long as they were in the Amazon.

G-War traded his spot on Brandt's head to wedging between Braden and Max, where some of the rain didn't fall directly on him. Skirill rode with Micah while Aadi bobbed along merrily behind. Braden wondered if the Tortoid could smell the wet Aurochs.

The caravan kept going. They were surprised when they reached the southern edge, having not met any Amazonians. They stopped as soon as they stepped into the daylight, exhausted from traveling without a break once the rain started.

The humans took off their clothes, laying them in the sun to dry. Those with fur spread out, letting the sun work its celestial magic on them. If anything smelled worse than a wet Aurochs, it was a wet Aurochs as it dried.

Everyone moved upwind of Brandt. He didn't take offense. Although he was oversized in many areas, smell wasn't one of them. He couldn't tell the difference between a dry or a wet Aurochs.

Braden and Micah had nowhere to lay as the dry grass was stiff and uncomfortable, so they went to the edge of the rainforest, where they could hold each other while standing, leaning against a tree. They talked quietly, simply enjoying each other's warmth, but not going further than that. They looked forward to a night in the Presidential Suite, and selfishly, having their clothes cleaned for them while they sampled more of the fabricator's menu.

They weren't far from the oasis if they traveled quickly.

They'd spend the night here, leaving at sunrise, and go quickly over the hills and grasslands. They'd reach the oasis before nightfall next, and they'd sleep in that comfortable bed while enjoying brownies and wine.

Maybe they could leave before sunrise...

53 – New Sanctuary

Braden and Micah didn't have to rouse the others as everyone was ready to go early. They went slowly at first as it was still dark.

When the false dawn came, it showed the rolling landscape before them. Brandt got excited at the broad expanse and started running, his strides eating away the distance. Braden and Micah spurred the horses to a gallop to keep up.

The 'cat ran alongside, but it wasn't long before he leapt into the saddle and clung to Braden. Skirill flew low to keep the others in sight as the darkness gave way to daylight. Then he flew high overhead, correcting their direction as they had veered too far south. They pulled the horses to the right and slowed.

They would reach the oasis a little after mid-daylight. Brandt was worn down from not getting a good meal for a number of turns now. Grazing in the rainforest did not suit him. He needed to eat. They'd already given him the rest of their mushrooms for his breakfast. That explained his earlier burst of energy.

Watching him try to eat the dry grasses was frustrating for the companions, but most of all for Brandt. He ate and ate, but it wasn't nourishing. It took a lot of work to get a little to eat. If he could get to the oasis, then he would be able to eat his fill. He could graze the extensive growing fields, once they alerted the Security Bots.

He finally gave up and committed to moving on. He struggled with each step, making progress but painfully slowly. G-War and Skirill stayed with him while the humans rode ahead quickly to get some fodder from the oasis and bring it back.

As they rode up, one Security Bot greeted them and confirmed who they were. President Micah informed them of the new arrival, the Aurochs. The Security Bot knew of the Aurochs from the before time.

"Can you take fodder to the Aurochs for us? He is dying of hunger," Braden asked. The Security Bot would not, but he dispatched a Development Unit, a Mirror Beast, to carry as much fresh pickings as possible.

They let the horses drink and graze briefly, then they raced back into the rolling grasslands. The Development Unit effortlessly kept up with them as the horses ran. On its top and trailing behind it was a mass of freshly picked vegetables and sweet grass. It reminded Braden of how hungry he was.

When they reached Brandt, he apologized for not having gone farther. He was almost at a standstill. The others worried, until they saw the Bot loaded down with choice foods.

Brandt ate slowly at first, but as he built strength, he dug great swaths out of the vegetable pile, until nothing remained. He laid down and was soon fast asleep.

"It's not important if we get there today. What matters is that we get there together," Braden said, more for himself than the others. At least they were dry.

Brandt was not out long. When he shook himself awake, he stood and bugled into the waning sunshine. He took a few steps, then jogged, then broke into a run, taunting everyone left behind. Braden and Micah vaulted onto the horses' backs and were off. Aadi barely got the rope in his beak, while G-War ran to catch up. He tried to catch the King, but he had too big of a head start. The 'cat finally settled for riding with Micah.

They ran into the welcome green of the oasis before the sun set. Brandt looked around. Many paths weren't wide enough for him, so he chose his path carefully. He enjoyed the grasses and even some of the bushes that grew throughout. He looked at the fields greedily, but Micah stopped him. She had yet to clear that with the Security Bots.

The others drank from the lake, G-War even managed to get himself a fish, which Skirill flew by and took from him, thanking him profusely as he carried it away. G-War continued fishing, but wasn't lucky a second time as the fish shied away from his furry orange body.

"We'll be down below. Call if you need anything," Micah told the companions.

54 – Preparing to Fight a War

The evening was for recovering. Once in the room, Braden and Micah put the thought of everything else out of their minds. They enjoyed the fabricator, their time together, and the divine comfort of that bed.

In the morning, they explored more of the menu options from the fabricator. Most they liked, some they didn't. The sun was well up when they made their way back outside.

Micah gave her blaster to the Security Bot to recharge/repair. Then they went to the New Command Center to talk with the hologram.

"Holly, are you there?" Micah asked. She led as the hologram recognized her as the President.

"Master President, I'm so glad you returned. How may I be of assistance?" Holly said in his pleasant voice.

"Do you know about the mutant birds? All black, like a cross between a bat and a bird," Micah asked him.

"Yes. It sounds like one of Professor Warren's failed experiments. He had many, unfortunately, which is why the war started. The ideas between the north and south were far too different."

"But I didn't see destruction like this in the north, not like what happened to Sanctuary."

"That's because the destruction in the north was far more complete," Holly answered. "The destruction here was due to last acts of desperation. According to our calculations, the south won the war by a considerable margin."

Micah stepped in. "And that's what we're here to tell you. No one won.

Everyone lost in that war. Now, these mutant birds threaten us. We need to defeat them, keep the peace in the south. Then we need to make sure that war never happens again. Can you help us with all that?" Micah sounded sincere, but sarcastic as well. Holly took it all in stride.

"Defeating the mutant birds will not be difficult. I can prepare a nerve agent that you can deliver to their nesting grounds."

"What's a nerve agent?" they asked together.

"A toxin that attacks the living being's nerve center, where they lose the ability to control their muscles and organs. Eventually they beat themselves to death."

"What happens to the person who delivers it?" Braden asked, already thinking he would be that person.

"Unfortunately, they won't make it, unless they wear full chemical protective equipment, including a supplied air mask. I do not have any missile delivery systems available, so it will have to be delivered in person."

"That won't work for us, Holly. What other options are there?" Micah asked, refusing to accept a suicide attack.

"We have a number of hand blasters available as well as the capture nets, but I recommend expanding the Tortoid ranks. Tortoids are effective in knocking the birds from the sky, where they can be dealt with by any ground-based creature." The hologram stood, waiting patiently.

'What do you all think?' Micah asked over the mindlink.

'Although I'm honored to be considered an answer to the mutant birds, I don't think creating more of one thing effectively solves problems. Whenever we upset the balance of nature, something else will have to change, too,' Aadi suggested.

'Blasters for humans we trust to clean out the nest. Then we destroy those blasters. They have too much power. Even the Aurochs would be helpless against them,' Brandt said.

"Holly, if we take the blasters, how can we destroy them when we are done?" Micah, looking hopeful, asked the hologram.

"We can store them here, securely. We have a fully functioning armory guarded by an integrated sensor-response system as well as access to multiple Security Bots. Or we can recycle the blasters, whatever the President wishes."

"An armory?" Braden was intrigued. Micah put a hand on his arm and shook her head.

"Holly, please ensure the following security measures are in place. The armory is to open only when Braden and I are together. No one is to enter the armory alone."

"Does that include you, Master President? You can change the protocols at your convenience. If you don't want Braden to enter alone, that will be logged and enforced. If you want to make sure that you also don't enter alone, that will require a second executive endorsement."

"How do I do that, Holly?"

"Braden, as the only other human available, is assumed to fill all other roles the President requires. As such, Braden's concurrence will lock in the desired two-person security protocol."

"I agree," Braden said simply.

'If anything happens to one of us, what do we want to do? Say I die when we go after the mutie birds and then we discover we need more blasters...' It was a sobering question that Micah posed.

"Holly, what if something happens to one of us. How would you know?"

"We can access your neural implant at any time, then this system would know instantly. Authority would revert to the surviving member. You don't have the neural implants. Would you like them installed?"

"What is that and what do you mean by installation?" Micah asked, not feeling comfortable with the hologram's suggestion.

"It is a device that resides in your brain. It is smaller than a grain of rice, powered by your biological energy. We can access the implants from anywhere due to our satellite monitoring system. Installation is a process completed in the New Command Center's medical laboratory. A fiber probe is inserted past the eyeball, along the optic nerve, and into the visual cortex. This gives the human the impression that they see the information directly."

"You want to shove something into my eyeball?" Braden asked sarcastically.

"Past the eyeball. There is no incision and no damage to a person's body. This process is well refined. There will be no complications."

"I'll do it," Micah said quickly.

"What the crap are you doing?" Braden grabbed her by both arms to face her.

"Let go of me," she said coldly. He released his grip, his fingers white and shaking, his head hung low. "It'll be okay, Braden. If they can create all of this, they can do a simple procedure. We need to be able to fight these things. And we have to win. We have to win for the world you're trying to create." She hesitated. "I want you to get it, too. If the hologram can share information with us over a mindlink, then there's nothing we won't be able to accomplish," she finished, confident and strong.

"Listen to yourself. The power draws you in. I don't want it. I don't want a blaster. I don't want to see you like this." Braden started to get frustrated and angry.

'Braden,' the King of the Aurochs said in his booming thought voice. 'That is why you are the right person to get it. You get this. You get the information. You carry the blaster, because you don't want it. Be afraid of a person who wants this, for they will want it for the wrong reasons.'

'A trade then, my friend. If I start to embrace the power, you will spear me with one of your great horns. You will save me from myself?' Braden had no choice but to get the implant. The balance had to be maintained. As long as no one had the power alone, then there was hope for an uncorrupted future.

'Agreed. We all agree,' Brandt spoke for the companions. Balance had returned.

"I'll get the implant as well. Then we'll need blasters, Holly. So where is this laboratory and the armory?"

55 – Building a Better Human

"I don't feel any different," Braden said to Micah as they looked at each other, trying to see any sign of their implants.

"What is it supposed to do? Holly, are you there?" Braden and Micah sat in an Old Tech laboratory. Bright white Bots of all shapes and sizes stood about. Many had arms or snake-like tendrils, and all had screens on them to show processes. There were two tables in the middle of the area where Braden and Micah had been directed to lay.

The next thing they knew, they were awake and looking at each other.

"The procedure is complete. Please wait while I bring your systems online. Lie down, please, as there may be an initial disorientation."

They both felt the sensation. Their right eyes fogged, then the laboratory came back into focus. In one part of their vision, a window opened. Braden reached in front of him, trying to feel if something was physically there. He saw his hand behind the window.

It was only in their minds. Information started scrolling past. Numbers and letters. Braden could read it. Micah could not. She started scratching at her closed eye. "Please don't touch your eye, Master President," Holly said calmly, but firmly.

A medical Bot moved close and grasped her hand. She kicked it violently. Straps slipped out of the table, wrapped themselves around her flailing limbs, and pulled her down. She heaved against them, arching her back, her muscles straining with the effort.

"Micah!" Braden shouted. "Micah, what is it? What's happening?"

"I can't understand what it's showing me. I can't! It's frying my brain!" she screamed hysterically.

"It's not. It's not. You see that little window, right? Those are numbers and letters. I will teach you to read. Then you'll know what it's trying to tell you." He switched his attention to the hologram. Micah strained against her bonds, but more weakly.

"Holly, what's it showing me?"

"Those are your medical vitals, Braden. Let me highlight each of them for you." The numbers stopped scrolling. The first pair of numbers loomed large, taking up the entire window. "This is your blood pressure, systolic and diastolic."

"That doesn't mean anything to me. Just tell me what blood pressure is and what the numbers should be," Braden directed.

"Your current blood pressure is 128 over 70. Normal range is 120 over 80, but in your currently excited state, it is well below a norm. Master President's numbers are 152 over 103."

"Micah. Can you see them? I taught you the numbers. Do you see them?" She stopped straining and relaxed back onto the table.

"Yes. The number now shows one four zero over nine two. It continues to get lower." She watched, carefully reading off the numbers as they changed.

"Good, Master President, Braden. Next is your pulse, that is, how many times a minute your heart beats. Normal is fifty to seventy for you, Braden, and sixty to eighty for the President."

"Why is hers higher?" Braden asked suspiciously.

"Women have higher blood pressure and pulse rates by a small margin. Please understand that these are averages. It appears that you both are well better than the average." Holly finished and waited.

"Yes, I see mine is fifty-nine," Braden said.

"Mine is also fifty-nine," Micah added.

"Please release Micah's restraints, Holly." The straps quickly receded into the table. Micah tentatively sat up.

"Will the window always be there?" she asked.

"The neural implant will respond to your commands. It will disappear on the command 'Sleep,' or shrink to a dot on the command "Minimize.' It will reappear on the command 'Wake.' It will fill your entire field of view on the command, 'Expand'." Holly continued through the ways to control their implants. He told them about requesting information, but they had no reference to work with, not knowing what a database was.

"Holly, at Oasis Zero One, the hologram there told me she could download maps of Vii directly to my implant. Can you do that for me, please?" The maps that Braden had diligently copied from the computer screens appeared before his eye. He scrolled through them as Holly directed. Micah followed along, not knowing exactly what she was looking at but realizing the full potential of having so much information.

"Can I add things that I know to these maps?" Braden asked the hologram.

"Yes, Braden…"

When they finally tried to stand, they couldn't. Their heads were swimming, nothing seemed steady. "Sleep!" Braden commanded. His normal vision returned and he started to orient himself. Micah followed his lead.

Braden shook his head. Where once he sought out the Old Tech, he was now uncomfortable. The ancients were permanently in his head. And Micah's, too. He knew she regretted her decision, but wouldn't admit it. They'd use this tech to rid themselves of the mutie birds, then they'd return the blasters.

Then maybe the ancients in their minds would sleep. *It's about the trade, to help people live better lives, be something more,* Braden thought to himself. He looked at Micah as she rubbed her temples. *I already have my reward. Once the trade routes are established, we'll move away from all this, live by ourselves. Raise our children.*

'That is the best thing I've heard all day,' Micah thought.

"To the armory, Master Holly!" Braden commanded loudly. Micah punched his arm and they both gasped with the sudden pain in their heads. If it was going to be like this, they would let the ancient beast sleep.

"Once in the elevators, tell it to go to the Armory Level."

"Besides the New Command Center, how many levels are there?" Braden thought the elevator only went to one place, but learned that it went there when it was not told one of the other destinations. There was the medical level, the armory, storage and distribution, the factory level, and finally raw materials processing. The bottom two levels were the most extensive with the factory level appearing to be endless, massive machines and systems to move materials. The factory level built everything that was used throughout New Sanctuary, including the Bots that did the building.

The armory was big. When Braden and Micah walked in, they were instantly afraid. Weapons of all types were in racks and on shelves. There were even wagons, which Holly called armored vehicles. When everyone has power like this, everyone loses. No wonder the destruction from the ancients' war was so complete.

"Just the blasters, Holly. Two for each of us. When one runs out, we'll have a backup. If we had four of these, we would have been able to kill all the mutie birds at one time." Braden was certain of it. Micah had done a great deal of damage with only one blaster.

"May I recommend you take a field charging unit as well." Holly pointed them to the wall where the hand blasters were neatly arranged. Next to them was a small unit with an attached pack. It had a place where a blaster could be plugged in.

"How does this work?" he asked.

"Open the pack and spread the solar collector to face the sun. Plug in your blaster and it will be recharged. The solar collector will also recharge its own battery so you can charge your blasters when the sun is not available." The hologram waited while they took two blasters each and belts that were nearby. They were specifically made for carrying two blasters, with additional pouches for other equipment.

Holly talked them through their new equipment until they were comfortable with how everything worked. The blasters had a wide setting that would be most effective at close range against the birds. Each blaster could also be programmed to only work in the hand of the owner. Once they learned of this feature, Braden and Micah insisted on activating it. Braden tested it by trying to fire one of Micah's blasters. Nothing.

Perfect. Power to the good guys only.

Holly recommended a form fitting body armor, along with special boots that could increase a person's jumping height. They took the boots, but declined on the armor as they wanted to fit in when they visited the villages.

If they took the armored vehicle, then they'd be completely protected, but everyone would run away. They needed people to accept them, to trust them. The people wouldn't do that if they were armored in Old Tech. They could hide the belts under their tunics, covering the blasters as well. The boots would soon be dirty and muddy. No one would notice them.

As they were preparing to leave, Braden had a thought. "Can you do anything for our friends? You know, give them a little extra kick or something."

"No. Engineered creatures take generations to change. If we took a sample of each of their DNA, we'd be able to build clones within a couple cycles. This facility has not been set up for cloning, but could be configured if the President requested it."

"I don't know what any of that means, but I don't think I like it." Micah crossed her arms, waiting for the expected unacceptable answer.

"Cloning is a way to make an exact copy of a living creature."

"I knew I wouldn't like it. The answer is no. We won't sample our friends. We don't need any copies; we're satisfied with the originals."

They stepped into the elevator and Braden said, "New Command Center, please."

When they entered the Command Center level, Holly instantly appeared, waiting for direction. "Have you reestablished communication with Cygnus VI? And the ship in the sky?"

"Your timing is impeccable. The system is going through its final function checks now. We should be able to attempt communication later this evening." Holly seemed to brighten with the good news.

"Can you let us know when you're ready to try? We'd like to be here." Braden was infinitely curious. Once he heard of humans living on another planet, he wanted to know. He wanted to see how they lived, how they traded. He wanted good news about the ancients.

"Yes, I will notify you via your neural implants."

With that, they needed to get back into the sunlight.

"Let's go for a swim," Braden suggested.

"I don't want to go back inside, lover, not yet anyway," Micah said sadly, not wanting to disappoint her mate.

"No, I meant in the pond. We'll have to share it with the fish, but at least there aren't any cold-water crocs!" He ran through the open air, stripping off clothing and dropping it as he went. He kept the belt and the blasters with him, finally dropping them on the beach as he waded, naked, into the pond. Micah followed his lead, leaving everything on the beach. She sauntered toward the water, her bare skin a creamy white, except for her shoulders and arms which now showed the scars from the mutant bird attack. Braden stopped swimming, watching as she slowly and gracefully entered the water.

She dipped low and dove beneath the surface. He watched as she swam along the bottom toward him, pushed off and grabbed his legs. She pulled his head under, then pushed him away. As he surfaced, sputtering, she splashed his face, then with her feet, pushed off his chest and swam quickly away. He pummeled the water with his hands as he swam after her.

56 – Contact

Braden and Micah didn't know how late it was when summoned to the New Command Center. It was dark outside and they'd been asleep, but not for very long.

When they arrived, Holly escorted them to the wall of screens, where all the images faded out and blended into one massive picture of some kind of drawing. Braden read the words that wrapped around the outside for Micah. "Cygnus VI – A Refuge For Humanity, A Gateway To The Stars."

"The signal has reached Cygnus VI and the auto-response sequence has been activated. This is a very good sign!" Holly exclaimed. They watched as the screen changed, showing a room, much smaller than the New Command Center, but of similar configuration with the desks, screens, and raised platform.

A single human was there, sitting in the chair on the platform, engrossed in the screens that surrounded him.

"Hello! I'm Free Trader Braden of Plant Vii, I mean, Cygnus Seven." They waited, but the man didn't acknowledge they had spoken. "Holly?"

"There is a delay of nearly four minutes, twenty-three seconds before they will hear you."

"I guess we'll wait." During the delay, they watched the individual as he never took his eyes from what he was working on.

"And it will take another four minutes twenty-three seconds before you hear and see his response."

"Well, now. That takes all the fun out of it. How did the ancients carry on a conversation like that?" Micah asked.

"They prepared their information and sent it over the computer. They delivered messages but they didn't have conversations."

"No, I wouldn't think they did. What about the RV Traveler?" Braden hoped that they would find humans alive on the ship as well. If he had heard correctly, in one more cycle, they could travel to the ship. He wanted to make that trip, with Micah and their companions, too.

"The delay with the Traveler is only three seconds. I've been able to establish only a base communication link. It recognizes the signal, responding with its own code, but it won't open a telecommunications channel. I'm attempting to query its systems for diagnostic information now."

They continued to wait until the young man's head popped up, looking around. "Hello? Who's there?"

His eyes found them. He looked directly at something, Braden and Micah felt like it was them. His mouth was open, working, but no sound came out.

He did something with the arm of his chair and a red light started flashing. A horn sounded intermittently in the background.

"That's the emergency klaxon," Holly answered before they could ask. Holly continued to interpret what he saw for Braden and Micah, who were still mildly in shock from watching what was happening on another planet.

An older couple rushed in, disheveled and half-dressed. The younger man pointed at Braden and Micah.

"Hello!" the older man said before turning to the young man. "Shut that damn thing off!" he barked.

"I'm Doctor Johns of the Cygnus VI Research Station. Are you the relief convoy from Earth?" He waited, watching, then asked the young man to replay the original message. The three of them looked at a different place on the screen, watching closely.

Braden and Micah had not yet responded, not knowing what to say.

"You're from Cygnus VII? But Cygnus VII was destroyed some four hundred years ago. Are you the relief convoy? Did you land on Cygnus VII first? We could use your help here. Our population is in rapid decline and I'm afraid there aren't many of us left. I'm a clone, as is my son. My wife is the last surviving natural human. There are only twenty-three total of us. I'm afraid we can't clone anymore. We don't have the materials for it. When we die, we'll be the last. We've learned so much since we lost contact with you. We don't want to lose that. We will transmit all of our information, but that could take months. There is a lot of information."

"Only twenty-three left," Micah said softly. "I'm Micah, President, for what it's worth. What happened to the others?" She waited impatiently, forgetting about the delay.

"It'll be four minutes," Braden said, parroting the hologram.

"What is a minute?" she asked. Braden shrugged and shook his head.

"Holly, can you give them the history of the war and the intervening years after we tell them about the north and the south as we know it?" Braden and Micah started telling their tale, as if they were around a campfire. Holly assured them that he could hold the others' message until they were ready to hear it. After they finished, Holly started with what he knew, ending with the rebuilding of the Command Center by a single surviving Bot using materials recovered from the destroyed city.

When they finished, Holly allowed the Cygnus VI message through, where they talked about meteors and environmental leaks, and research into improved propulsion systems resulting in failures that killed a great many of their good people, but in the end, they believed they had vast improvements for in-system transit. They only needed rare elements that were now depleted on Cygnus VI. None of that mattered to the companions. Maybe the Bots who built the New Command Center would someday build a space ship, but that wasn't going to happen in their lifetime.

Braden and Micah waved good-bye, wished them well, and told them Holly would be in touch. The matter transfer system would be under construction for almost an entire cycle. Once that was ready, then maybe the people could travel to Cygnus VII and return to humanity.

57 – The Return Trip

The companions heard everything that was said, but they didn't see the information from the neural implants. If there was anything that the companions needed to know, Braden and Micah would have to consciously share it.

As was their new routine, they loaded up on foods from the fabricator for their trip. Brandt, Aadi, G-War, and Skirill ate their fill of grasses, bugs, and javelina as the time of their departure neared.

Brandt remained uneasy throughout their stay. Any civilization that could build itself up like this, then destroy it, was not to be trusted. He committed to watch over Braden and Micah, to keep them from enforcing their will on others through Old Tech. The Old Tech weighed heavily on them. They needed his broad shoulders to carry some of their burden, even though physically their greatest weight was no bigger than a grain of rice.

Mentally, it was the size of all Vii.

And there were people on Cygnus VI.

Barely. They couldn't do anything about them, but they could do something about the mutie birds.

And they needed to do that soon.

So they left New Sanctuary, with instructions that no humans besides Braden and Micah were allowed into the buildings. No mutants besides the ones already categorized--Golden Warrior, Aadi, Skirill, and finally Brandt-- were allowed. Any of the companions could ask questions of the hologram by way of the Security Bots.

Everything was agreed to. Braden and Micah had clean clothes and plenty to eat. The companions had eaten their fill, although the hologram had asked President Micah to limit Brandt's forays into the fields as he had eaten nearly all of their monthly production in less than a day. They laughed at the enormity of the King's appetite.

Sounded about right. Micah informed the hologram that New Sanctuary needed to expand the fields as the Aurochs would return and maybe next time, they'd have more of the behemoths with them. New Sanctuary needed to be able to provide for them. The hologram sounded contrite as he said that all efforts to expand the fields would begin immediately with the production of three additional Development Units.

"I think it was pretty simple. Either they grow more or the King of the Aurochs eats less. I am not going to tell him he needs to lose weight!" Micah said to Braden. "Sometimes, it's good to be the President."

They headed out, better than they arrived as they were all healthy. A Development Unit was dispatched to follow them all the way to the rainforest with fodder for Brandt and the horses. Once they entered the Amazon, the Development Unit would return and begin work on the fields.

Since they knew they could eat, the Aurochs and the horses ran. It wasn't much of a race. Skirill always won. G-War could outrun any of those stuck on the ground, but only for a short distance. After that, he was comfortable riding, like now, where we crouched on the King's head. Skirill circled lazily not far ahead of them.

Braden brought up his neural implant window, showing healthy vitals, as the hologram called them. He queried Holly, to see if he could hear. He could. Holly informed him that they could talk anywhere Braden was. Braden asked if the factory could make metal hubs so the wagons would roll better. Holly asked a few questions, which Braden answered. Holly said that eight of them would be ready when Braden returned. He asked for a spare for each wagon, but Holly said that a spare wasn't needed. These would hold up under any circumstances.

Braden told the window in his eye to sleep. *Wasn't that convenient,* he thought.

He looked around him to see his growing caravan. He started with two water buffalo and a 'cat. With the Aurochs running ahead and a Mirror

Beast skimming along behind, his group looked nothing like a traditional caravan.

In this case, he saw the group as a war party with the singular purpose of finding the nest of the mutie birds and wiping them out. For that goal, they were well suited.

They reached the southern edge of the rainforest just after mid-daylight. The Development Unit unceremoniously dumped the fodder and departed toward the oasis at a high rate of speed.

Good, Braden thought. *You have a lot of work to do if you want to be ready for our return. Brandt is going to be hungry.*

After eating, they continued into the rainforest as fast as they dared. Toward nightfall, Zalastar was waiting for them in the road. The King of the Aurochs and Aadi went ahead to meet him. Braden and Micah stayed on the horses with G-War and Skirill. They rode slowly to give the others time to talk. When they reached the others, they stopped and waited.

When they finished, it was dark. At least it wasn't raining. They were able to start a fire, so they could see when the Amazonians prepared to take their leave. Zalastar stepped into the firelight for quick greetings with both humans, before hurrying away.

"So, Brandt, what did you guys talk him out of?" Braden was naturally curious. He couldn't read the body language of any of the companions, so he was forced to ask.

There seems to be a rift forming between the various Amazonian clans. The villages are starting to choose sides--those who want to come into the open and those who wish to remain in the depths of the Amazon.' Aadi was narrating a story, probably as he understood it from Zalastar.

'It seems there are more Lizard Men who don't wish to follow Zalastar than we were led to believe.'

"As long as they don't try to kill us, they can hide all they want. It's when they raise their spears against us that I get concerned. And I don't want an accident that hurts one of Zalastar's warriors. I'm still sorry over the one that struck the McCullough woman. I feel like I should have prevented that."

"No. There's nothing you could have done. We were all there. We all let it happen. In the end, it turned out for the best. Maybe that warrior wasn't loyal to Zalastar and was trying to interfere with the trade?" Micah wouldn't allow Braden to wallow in self-pity.

He knew she was right.

"Does Zalastar think we'll have any problems on our way north through the rainforest?"

'No. His people, the loyalists he calls them, are already moving. They will create new villages close to the road. He said that within a moon, they will start clearing the road of undergrowth, filling in holes to allow passage of human carts pulled by the Aurochs,' Brandt replied.

"I think we need to make the best time possible. We need to get out of the rainforest while Zalastar holds his position. Once his people line the road, we'll be safe. Until then, I'm afraid that I'll be suspicious of any Amazonian." At times, Micah was more cautious than Braden while a wild risk-taker at other times. He thought he'd never understand her, but he did. She was just like him--fiercely loyal to her companions, doing anything she thought necessary to keep them safe.

'I agree. I am happiest when I am not in the rainforest,' the 'cat added.

"It's settled then. We do whatever makes the pretty kitty happy." Braden's attempts at chiding the 'cat were usually weak. G-War didn't respond. Skirill bobbed with laughter. He appreciated the sentiment. He didn't like it in the rainforest either. With the vines and intertwined overhead branches, he had difficulty flying. He usually rode, being held upright by one of the humans. It wasn't very dignified for a Hawkoid.

Just like being wet made G-War miserable.

Braden was happy they hadn't fought a battle in the rainforest. The extra weight of being wet would throw off the 'cat's delicate balance. Braden wondered how effective he would be in a fight. The best answer was not to find out. The 'cat was right. They needed to finish this trip quickly.

When the sunrise lessened the darkness on the road, they set out at a slow jog, running more quickly where they could. Braden activated his neural implant, asking the hologram if he knew where they were and how far they had to go. Holly, with infinite patience, described to both he and Micah how they could activate a map and highlight their position. They could then expand the view to show the entire rainforest.

Micah almost fell out of the saddle as she intently stared at the map. She shook her head and closed her window. She wasn't sure she'd ever be comfortable with Old Tech, while Braden seemed right at home. Sometimes that scared her, but she had forced him into getting the implant. Maybe she had made a mistake, but it was done. She would keep him from going too far.

'Yes, I will, because you will,' he responded in his thought voice.

"Ahh! You're getting better at it!" Micah exclaimed. She was a natural at the mindlink, where Braden had to work at it.

"I've only had ten cycles practice, so I think I should be insulted by that." He smiled at her, his tone playful. His goal in life had always been to do a little bit better tomorrow than today. You can't get better without knowing you have shortcomings, his mother used to say.

'I like that,' Micah said. *'Balance is important, too. I wouldn't be me without you. I look forward to the day we can go to my village, to Trent, and show them what we've accomplished, show them what's possible.'*

'When we go, we'll be riding in a wagon filled with goods to trade. I think I'd like to try some of your ocean fish.'

'I'm surprised you didn't ask Holly if you could bring a fabricator along. Besides taking over the world, is there nothing else you think about besides eating?' Micah replied.

'I asked him about the fabricator. He said it wouldn't work. Something about raw materials.' He hesitated for a moment, then continued, *'And there are other things I think about.'* He grinned at her as she blushed, seeing images that

popped into his mind. She had no clothes on in any of them. When she thought of him, he was shooting his bow, talking a villager into a trade, or arguing with G-War. He was leading them. Suddenly, his images of her changed as she fought with her sword, stood with her hand on an Amazonian's chest, punching Braden.

And laughter. The images were replaced by feelings of joy.

'It's giving me a headache. Stop now or I may have to give it a good scratch,' G-War interjected. Braden and Micah looked at each other.

"You're getting much better with our mindlink," Micah said finally.

And then the rain started. They had plodded through turns of rain before, but nothing like this. It rained so hard that they couldn't see more than a few strides ahead of the horse's nose. G-War sunk into a black pit of despair, despite Braden leaning over him with his body. Wet Aurochs smell would have been bad, but it was washed away instantly in another avalanche of water.

It only continued like that for a full turn, before lightening to a more normal downpour. They traveled in the daylight and the dark of night. Aadi led during the night, as he was unaffected by the rain and could see in the dark. It helped that the road was straight. Braden used his implant often to track their progress and read. He wanted to know everything there was about the ancients. He found too much information on the animal research, finally settling on a compendium of modifications, as the ancients called it.

Hundreds of animal species had been modified, their DNA changed to satisfy a particular need that the settlers had. Many of the animals weren't native to Vii, but were introduced by the settlers, as the ancients called themselves.

The Hawkoids and the Hillcats were both developed for the same purpose, to limit a growing rat infestation. The rats of Vii were rather voracious, it seemed. Braden thought the ancients' approach worked because he had never heard of a rat problem during any of his travels.

The Tortoids were developed because one of the laboratory technicians liked turtles. She increased their intelligence exponentially, but dabbling with their brains delivered the unintended side effect of the focused thunderclap, or sonic blast as it was called in the database. It was generated in their mind! She lightened their shells and gave them the ability to float. That's why his shell seemed so much larger than needed for his head and body. He could use his mind to keep himself from blowing away.

The Aurochs were native to Vii. They were bred as a food source, but with the vast grasslands available, they ran wild to feed. The ancients used mechanical craft to harvest the herd when the need arose. The engineers raised their intelligence, which helped their reasoning ability. Previously, they would eat everything in one area, then starve to death. The Aurochs were receptive to the modifications and their intelligence grew quickly until they were sentient. At that point, they were no longer used as a food source, and they were left alone. Braden thought there should have been more, but when he found the entry on the mutie birds, he knew why the numbers were so low.

The Bat-Ravens, as the ancients called them, represented the first attempt to control the rats. They were naturally intelligent, aggressive, and could be bred in sufficient number. They were hearty and could survive any environment, but they couldn't be controlled. They would just as readily attack humans as they would rats. The ancients decided to exterminate them. According to Holly's database, they thought they were successful.

But the Bat-Ravens survived. Maybe that was why there were so few large creatures in the south. The Bat-Ravens killed the rest. Brandt Earthshaker might lead the last herd of Aurochs on Planet Vii.

When Braden shared what he found with the companions, Brandt was even more convinced that they were doing the right thing. The Bat-Ravens could not be allowed to exist.

'*Vulnerabilities?*' Aadi asked.

Braden opened his window and asked the question. Now that he knew the right terms, he could get more information. The ancients tried to poison their food supply. The ones that survived may have been immune. Poisoning probably wouldn't work again.

They linked their minds when they flew in search of food, but in their nests, they were alone. *How do they nest?* he asked the database. In the hills, high trees, low branches. Braden pulled up the map and noted where the mutie birds had attacked their group on the two occasions. He noted where they first saw the cloud of birds. He traced a route north on the map until he came to a small range of hills that bordered the Great Desert, Devaney's Barren. These were far to the west of where he had crossed.

He looked closer, finding the forest on the west side of the hills, lining ravines, spreading into the Plains of Propiscius. "I know where they are. I'm sorry, Brandt, but it looks like we need to make a big fire and burn down a forest."

'If it eliminates these evil creatures, then I approve.'

"We have a ways to go. We know when they last left their nesting ground. We know they leave once or twice a moon to feed. We need to get going if we want to catch them in their nests. And once we get to the plains, we will have to travel at night. They fly both in the daylight and in the dark, although when they hunt, daylight is best for them." Braden shuddered. If the Bat-Ravens had caught the companions at night, they would not have survived.

The long conversation about the Bat-Ravens and the way ahead made the time go by quickly. They traveled with few breaks and were soon back in the sunshine north of the rainforest. They found a stream and rested, drinking their fill, grazing, hunting.

Micah awoke after sunrise, reaching next to her, but Braden was already up. He stood looking north, his thoughts dark. The fire of vengeance burned within him. The Bat-Ravens tried to kill him twice. He knew there would be a third time, but this time, he brought the war to them. The Bat-Ravens had said, 'You will all die.' *No,* he thought, *you will. All of you.*

58 – The Fires Raged

After a turn of rest, they departed in the evening and set a strong pace under the rising full moon. With the humans' implants, they headed unerringly in the direction of the Bat-Raven's nesting ground.

With the mindlink, they planned as they traveled. Brandt and the horses would be the most vulnerable. G-War's role was undetermined, but he was also vulnerable if they chose to attack him in force. Skirill could be a liability as well as a benefit. It all depended on what they found in how well nature protected the birds.

Braden and Micah checked and rechecked their blasters. Besides them, Aadi had the only weapon that could affect the Bat-Ravens as they flew. He could use it twice, then he was spent. Braden and Micah knew they would have to split up. They needed to keep the Bat-Ravens from escaping once the attack started. They could use a hundred more people to do it right, but then they'd never be able to surprise the creatures.

Surprise. Without it, their attack would fail. The muties would spread out and the companions might never get another chance to rid Vii of the threat. How many more would die if they failed? All of the Aurochs? Max and Pack? The deer, wild boar, people…

'Stop it,' Micah said directly into his mind. *'We won't kill them all. Accept that. But we're going to kill so many that it will be a long time before they can threaten us again. Then we'll come back, with more people, more fire.*

'We'll treat them like weeds. Whenever they pop up, we'll rip them out by the roots. And they'll show up again somewhere else. In between, we live peacefully. Trade.' Micah finished her speech on a strong note, appealing to Braden's definition of success--a good trade.

'As usual, you're right. We will kill them with fire, with our blasters as long as they

have power, then we'll kill them with our blades.' Braden finished with determination.

'When Aadi knocks them to the ground, I will crush them.' Brandt wanted to be involved, demanded to be involved.

A plan took shape in Braden's mind where Aadi, Brandt, and G-War would be a target on an escape route. When the Bat-Ravens swooped toward the vulnerable Aurochs, Aadi could knock them out of the sky, then Brandt and G-War could dispatch them while they lay vulnerable.

Once they viewed the terrain, they'd see if this could be part of the plan.

They hurried through the darkness, crossing the grasslands in great leaps the first two nights. By the third morning, sunrise showed them the forested hills, closer than they expected. As normal, they hid themselves, but today was special. With Skirill's help, they would get a bird's eye view of their target.

Skirill flew low, to the northeast, away from the Bat-Raven nesting area. He then flew high, far to the east, exposing himself only briefly as he kept the hill top between him and the nesting ground. He flew up and down, looking at different areas, but never getting too close. Then he dove to the ground, heading east away from the Bat-Ravens. After flying away, he rose and circled to make sure he wasn't being followed. Then he dove to the ground again, returning to the copse where the companions were hidden.

They had seen what he had.

When he returned, he perched on the lowest branch, overlooking a map that Braden and Micah built on the ground.

"Thanks, Skirill. Nice flying, by the way." Braden nodded to the Hawkoid, who bobbed his head in response.

"Okay. I couldn't count the number of Bat-Ravens, but I don't think I'm exaggerating if I say there might be thousands of them. We'll need one person on this ridge, overlooking their nesting area. That will be me. I'll start the attack by lighting these trees on fire. If I saw right, Ess, the wind blew in this direction?" Braden asked for confirmation.

"'esss," he replied.

"Okay. That means the fire should travel in this direction." Braden put a small branch across his map. "I'll need to be up here."

He pointed to a spot high on the ridge. "Micah. You'll need to be here, to the side, not downwind. The fire should race down and out of the valley." He placed another branch.

"Brandt, Aadi, and G-War, you will be here…" They went through their plan, attacking it, looking for weaknesses. At the end, many unknowns remained, but fewer than when they started.

They slept, as much as they could, but they were worried.

Too much could go wrong.

Braden had a long climb, in the dark, without the aid of the horses. The horses! They'd turn them loose when they approached and would hope they ran for their lives. They could worry about collecting them later.

They gathered their things and rode out after dark. Braden relied almost entirely on his implant while Micah watched for any night flyers. They came in from the hill side to shield their approach, but Micah and the companions would be forced into the open getting into position on both sides of the valley. That couldn't be helped. If they had more people, the problem would be worse. Micah, crossing the opening by herself, was less likely to be seen. The others would stay close to the hillside.

As they approached, Aadi and G-War said they couldn't see anything flying. So they split up. Braden rode hard to the northeast while Micah and Brandt slowed, walking the approach to limit their exposure. No sudden movements.

Braden jumped off Max after they climbed a short distance. He pointed his nose to the east and smacked his rump, letting him run into the darkness. His hooves made little sound in the dirt.

Braden started climbing, taking care not to disturb any rocks or dirt. And he climbed, and climbed with grim determination. He tired from lack of sleep, but couldn't let the others down. At the moment of sunrise, he had to be in place and ready.

He knew the others would be. If he did what he planned to do, he'd flush a thousand Bat-Ravens directly toward his partner and his friends. It was the best plan they could come up with. He no longer liked the plan and wished that Micah was climbing the hill instead of him.

After chasing Speckles away, Micah jogged to keep up with Brandt as he walked toward his position. G-War and Skirill rode on him, while Aadi swam close by.

When the time was right, Micah veered west, while the others continued north, remaining on the eastern side of the valley mouth. Micah walked steadily, deliberately, crouched low. Her legs ached from the effort as the sky started lightening. Dawn approached.

She let herself smile. And when it got here, they'd unleash the fire. They'd cleanse the world of this evil.

Braden worried that he wouldn't make it. The hill got steep quickly with more loose stone and soil. The faster he needed to go, the more he was prevented from doing so. He gritted his teeth and pushed forward.

The sun was peeking over the horizon as he approached the top of the hill, which crested with a rock parapet. He clambered the last few strides to the top, only to see the valley still bathed in shadowy darkness. His sunrise was earlier than the rest. The forest was dark and silent. In there, the Bat-Ravens nested.

'I'm in place,' he said using their mindlink.

'As are we,' Brandt's loud voice boomed. Braden ducked involuntarily even though the sound was completely within his head.

'Just made it myself; I'm in position. Sunrise looks to be coming soon.' Micah crouched low behind a bush, the only cover she could find.

'It's already here where I am. Ten heartbeats, then we fire.' Braden concentrated to slow his heart down. He opened the window within his eye. Pulse 94.

Deep breaths. Pulse 86. Slowly. Pulse 80. Aim. Pulse 76. He closed the window.

Fire.

Micah saw a stream of flame erupt from a point on the hill high above the trees. It washed over the trees from her left to her right.

Aim. Fire. Her blaster launched its own line of flame into the trees, right to left, skimming the tops as Braden was doing. Letting off the trigger, she changed her aim and started again, right to left, just above the base of the trees.

The trunks blocked much of the blaster's power from reaching all the way to the hillside.

'FIRE!' A thousand voices screamed into the companions' minds. *'FLY FOR YOUR LIVES!'*

Braden's blaster ran out of power and the line of fire abruptly stopped. He put it in its holster and pulled the second blaster out, waiting.

His mind exploded, and death screams overwhelmed him. He redoubled his efforts to pierce the growing fog of pain clouding his mind.

Micah stopped firing. She couldn't see through the pain behind her eyes.

Bat-Ravens started appearing from among the trees, they were unorganized, every bird for itself, until they were clear. They screeched to rally the survivors to them as they hovered beyond the growing smoke of the forest fire.

More came from below and from within the smoke. Some made it away from the flames, only to succumb to the smoke and fall as they cleared the dark billows.

Very few Bat-Ravens had escaped. As they died, the volume of screams lessened, the pain in the heads of the humans drifted away. The fires on Braden's side of the forest had already burned away from him. He saw a route along the trees to the valley below. He vaulted over the rock face in front of him and started running downhill, the blaster ready to fire when needed.

The Bat-Ravens hovered in a mini-cloud when they saw the King of the Aurochs, standing there snorting loudly, hoof pawing the ground. They saw the Hillcat on his back, but that didn't concern them. They wanted revenge. They never saw the Tortoid floating motionlessly to the side.

They dove, nearly as one, toward their target. A line of flame shot toward them from the side, but missed behind them. They were flying too fast.

A thunderclap slammed into the Bat-Ravens. More than half of them fell, while the others were disoriented, barely able to keep flying.

The King of the Aurochs charged like the oversized bull he was, ripping up the ground where the stunned Bat-Ravens lay. He turned and twisted, jumped and pranced, turning the ground red and black, blood and feathers.

More Bat-Ravens appeared out of the forest and joined the others. Their numbers continued to grow. They spread into a long thin line and flew cautiously toward the beast below.

Aadi loosed his final thunderclap at the line, knocking a pitiful few from the air. The survivors increased speed as they dove toward the Aurochs. Fifty Bat-Ravens raked him at one time, the Hillcat able to only kill two on that pass. They were fast and their numbers overwhelming.

Skirill had been far above the fray, but he could wait no longer. His friends were in pain.

A blaster flame reached out and ripped through a number of Bat-Ravens as they turned for another pass. Then another shot from the blaster and another. The shots were short, but came rapidly.

Then those stopped.

The remaining Bat-Ravens headed toward Brandt from all directions. They surrounded him. No matter which way he faced, the Bat-Ravens were coming. *'Good,'* he thought. *'I swing my horns, evil will die.'*

The Bat-Ravens were unimpressed. They were too quick to be hit by the huge horns. They attacked, again and again, knocking G-War to the ground, and then they swarmed him. Micah was running full speed toward the companions with her sword ready. A couple Bat-Ravens came for her and were sliced in half for their efforts.

Skirill swooped low and raked three of the Bat-Ravens off G-War in one pass. He climbed sharply, banked and dove again. More Bat-Ravens came out of nowhere to attack the Hillcat. G-War's claws flashed as he was able to stand and attack. He whirled and slashed. Front and back claws ripping at his enemies. Then they overwhelmed him and dragged him down.

Skirill was there again, pulling them off. He was knocked down and the Bat-Ravens were on him.

Braden came down the slope toward them, each step four strides long as his Old Tech boots propelled him downward. He dove the last distance, using his body as a battering ram to drive the Bat-Ravens away from the 'cat. He crushed many, but others leapt away at the last instant. Micah swung her sword, cleanly slicing away the birds attacking Skirill. As she got close to the Hawkoid, she pulled off a Bat-Raven with one hand, hacked it with the sword, then reached for the next.

Aadi was there as well, biting with his beak, trying to get his shell between the Bat-Ravens and his friends.

Micah was bitten and clawed. She kept pulling the vile birds away, until Skirill was able to get his wings under him and fly off toward Braden and G-War.

Brandt stamped and swung his head. Bat-Ravens lined his back, biting and clawing, but they needed the speed of a dive to dig deeply into his thick hide. He then dropped, pushing himself sideways with his mighty legs until he rolled onto his back, crushing the mutie birds who wouldn't let go.

A bloodied and battered Hillcat stood and with two final sweeps of his claws dispatched the remaining Bat-Ravens. Braden staggered a few steps, catching the 'cat as he toppled. He hugged the 'cat to his chest, tears filling his eyes. He fumbled at his pouch for the numbweed and started rubbing it into the deepest wounds. The 'cat hung limp in his arms.

Braden's tears fell onto the bloody orange fur. Skirill back winged to a landing next to him and hopped close, rubbing G-War's head with his beak. Micah ran up and fell to her knees at their side, digging in her pouch for numbweed to add to Braden's.

Blood ran down her arms from her own cuts. Braden's hair was matted with blood from the slashes across his head. They wouldn't use any of the numbweed on themselves.

'My name is Prince Axial De'atesh. Today is not my day to die, because you, my human, saved me,' the 'cat said in a very tired but determined voice.

Brandt loomed large over them, red streaks on his side as blood trickled from the numerous wounds lining his back. His huge muzzle shoved past Braden to nose the 'cat. *'I will carry you, my friend,'* he boomed in his large voice.

Braden blinked the tears away and looked into the sky, where a few Bat-Ravens circled, then darted to the north past the billowing clouds from the forest fire.

"Ess?" Braden asked, although he suspected he knew the answer.

'I'm sorry, Master Human. I'm in no shape to catch them.' Skirill unfolded his wings, showing missing feathers and some small skin tears. *'I can fly, but not well. I'm off to catch the horses.'*

It took Skirill an agonizingly long time to return with Max and Pack. Probably half the daylight passed. They recovered the rest of their water and numbweed, putting it all to good use, which meant that most of it went to the 'cat. No one would have it any other way. They used bits of blanket and clothing to bandage their own wounds. Then they climbed into the saddle, carrying G-War and Skirill, and headed home.

59 – Home

"What did you do?" screamed the little girl, crying as she rushed from one companion to another, looking at their vicious wounds. Although Braden had expected it, he wasn't prepared for her near-hysterical rage.

'Ho, little one!' Brandt thundered. *'What he did was save us all. The mutie birds that you fear? You may never see another one in your lifetime. That's what he did.'*

"But look at all of you," she pleaded, her voice getting smaller. She reached out a tentative hand to touch G-War, held tenderly in Braden's arms. She looked at the pink streaks along the King's back and sides, Skirill's missing feathers.

'Keeping you safe takes sacrifice. It was only our blood and flesh, not our lives. You apologize to Braden, little one. Then you go with me to see my people, yes?' She shook her head, tears falling freely down her face. Then she wiped them away and stood up straight.

"I'm sorry, Braden. Thank you for saving me." She darted off toward the Earthshaker Herd without waiting. Brandt snorted and dipped his head, then strolled after her.

The Aurochs' wounds were much better. Once they found a stream and cleaned his back, the skin scabbed over quickly. The scabs peeled away after seeing enough sunlight, leaving bright pink rents through his dark brown hair. It looked like the skin was splitting off his back. He assured them that it was unimportant if the hair grew back or not. They had won a great battle and his legend as King would be forever etched in the minds of the Aurochs. His scars would be a reminder of the epic battle.

G-War was able to walk but Braden carried him into Village Greentree to make sure that the children didn't bother him. He had no strength to play. Braden asked Ditarod, the Village Elder, if there was a place they could put the 'cat where he'd be safe and could rest.

The Elder seemed to glow as he smiled broadly. A crowd of villagers led Braden and Micah to a new stone, wood, and thatch building, behind a new stall in what they now called the Market Square. In the building were a few things that Braden and Micah had left behind, along with a handcrafted bed. The mattress was made from intertwined vines and a spongy material they knew was unique to the rainforest. They looked at it questioningly.

"The Amazonians," he said. "When they learned that you wished to live here, they wanted to contribute. Bronwyn talked with them and made all the arrangements. We built this for you, all of us, Amazonians, humans, Aurochs. All of us."

Micah was the first to speak. "We don't know what to say." She hugged the Elder until he gasped for air. Braden put the 'cat in the middle of the bed, covering him with a thin sheet, before shaking everyone's hand and thanking each of them for the incredible gift.

When the villagers learned of the destruction of the Bat-Raven nesting grounds, they wanted to celebrate, but Braden and Micah asked if they would wait. Braden needed to prepare more numbweed, as much as he could get. Micah would stay with G-War and Skirill.

Braden took two villagers with him as he hunted for numbweed bushes. They were quickly rewarded. To help the villagers build their trade stock, he showed the two volunteers how to process the numbweed, adding the leaves, adding water, close to a boil but not boiling… The villagers had pots made of stone while Braden's was iron. Theirs took longer to heat, but the heat wasn't as intense and for them, easier to keep at a constant temperature.

The supply of numbweed quickly increased. Braden took what he needed for the companions. Although the wounds had started healing, the numbweed would greatly improve the final stage. He applied it liberally to Skirill and G-War, then he headed to the grasslands where the Aurochs had gathered.

Brandt nudged Bronwyn toward Braden where he showed her how to apply the numbweed. She took a great interest and committed herself to being a healer. Braden and Micah approved. There were animals throughout

Vii who could benefit from her attention. She had the potential to be the best animal healer ever, but she needed to learn about the plants and minerals that could help her. They would address that later with her and her parents.

"Well. It looks like we have a home," Micah said as she hugged her partner. "Where does that leave us?"

"It leaves us looking for a wagon!" During their long, slow trip back to Greentree, Braden thought about the trades. With the Bat-Raven threat eliminated, the trade routes were open. All he needed to do was get out there with goods.

"We need to go to Dwyer, see if they've made progress. And we could use some of those people from Westerly. If they are willing to work, there is going to be plenty of work in all these villages. You will see these places boom!" Micah watched as Braden spoke. His excitement about trading was infectious. His dream became his vision which became their new reality.

"As soon as the Prince is healthy enough to travel, we leave?" She said it as a question, but it was really a statement. They heard each other's thoughts, so there were fewer and fewer surprises between them. That didn't mean their relationship was stale. It was stronger than ever, although it wasn't a bond between just two people. The six of them shared a bond that was battle-tested; five different species, one family.

'I'm fine to travel. It is exhausting sitting around here, doing nothing, getting fed whenever I want. Truly. Exhausting.' The 'cat was getting back to his old self, although he was more congenial and had stopped referring to the humans as 'it.'

Near death experiences have a way of changing a person. Or a 'cat.

Brandt came running into the village, alarming a couple villagers who bolted for their huts. *'I heard we're leaving. I'm ready.'*

"I guess this is our life now," Braden said. "Even when we don't have secrets, our plans run wild. Sorry, Brandt, probably with the sunrise, we'll head out for McCullough, then Dwyer. I expect you're curious how your people are doing over there."

'Yes, curious. If there were any problems, they would have come back here, so things must be going reasonably well.'

"I hope they have a wagon ready," Braden mused.

"We all hope they have a wagon ready, so we don't have to put up with your pouting," Micah added.

"I don't pout!" Braden stuck out his lower lip. "Do I?"

Skirill and Aadi shared a laugh at Braden's expense. The King of the Aurochs went away in good humor.

"Whaddya think? Fill the cart? Trade our way there? Take Bronwyn with us?" Micah threw the questions at Braden to make him think about the things he liked, with the little girl added at the end to make her presence more palatable.

Braden wasn't fooled. "If we take her, you have to watch her, make sure she doesn't kill me in my sleep." Braden smiled to himself. Having the gifted little girl along made him more aware of everything he did. Just like Micah, she made him better. Just like all the companions.

"I'll talk with her parents, but I'm sure it will be okay. You fill the cart." Micah walked away in search of Bronwyn's parents.

In the end, the cart was filled with tanned hides, dyed material they acquired from Coldstream, leafy-bags of processed numbweed, and three young men with their tools, looking for something to build.

As well as looking for wives.

Micah made them ride in the cart. Only Bronwyn and the 'cat rode on Brandt. Braden and Micah weren't going to double up on the horses. Braden wouldn't be comfortable with another man riding with her, as she wouldn't be. They'd avoid it altogether.

They committed to make it to McCullough before nightfall. With the horses, the villages were less than one daylight's travel apart. Brandt helped them travel even more quickly. His walk was a trot for the horses. His trot, their gallop.

With sunrise, the caravan set out, the companions plus three and a full cart. Braden could not have been happier. His vision was coming true.

The trip from Greentree to McCullough was pleasantly uneventful. They did not stop to visit the Amazonians. They knew that Zalastar had problems he was working through, so they'd stick with meeting on the arranged schedule. That also would prevent a surprise from the anti-human Lizard Men.

Skirill flew ahead as usual. When a villager saw him, he waved his wings. She rallied everyone to expect the traders' arrival. Braden beamed, smiling ear to ear when the ladies of Village McCullough, led by Elder McCullough, were waiting for them and gave a hearty cheer. The companions waved back. Even Brandt bobbed his huge head, happily surprised by the human greeting.

Micah watched it all. She saw it all, including a few new men in the group. Did they need any more husbands? She hoped the three in the cart wouldn't be disappointed. The last thing they needed was a battle over the women. They'd already had that once and all the men lost. Micah had seen to that personally.

She would do it again if she had to. *We need to talk with all these men,'* she passed to Braden over their mindlink.

'I think so. We can't have them fighting or trying to take over from the Elder.'

Micah looked at the cart behind her. The three men had been expecting eligible women, ready to couple at first sight. What they found was competition. They looked pathetic, almost like slaves in a cage, their faces sad. Micah tried not to laugh. At least there wouldn't be an uprising from these three.

Eventually, the men got out of the cart. Bronwyn climbed down from the King of the Aurochs. She passed his greetings to the Elder and the others present who he recognized. Braden unhooked the cart from Speckles. He shook his head. Speckles.

He rolled the cart back and belted out his oft-stated call to trade. Elder McCullough was first up. The villagers completed one of two blankets that would protect a horse's back and flanks. He took that and doled out various items that he knew they needed. A few of the skins and some numbweed. A couple of the younger women were already wearing tanned deer hide, and it didn't cover well. It seemed they enjoyed the attention they got, maybe too much.

They needed to talk with the men sooner rather than later.

The blanket fit Speckles nicely and replaced the other blanket they'd been using underneath the saddle. They could keep it themselves, but then they'd miss out on the chance to trade. How many horse blankets did they need?

So it went into the pile with everything else that could be had. No one needed it. They'd take it and the rest of the items to Village Dwyer and trade afresh. That's how it worked. Braden couldn't keep from smiling.

Micah took charge and rallied the men for a get-together. She was surprised to see that the men outnumbered the women of Village McCullough. She shook her head and started in on them, pointedly addressing each one in turn. Braden watched from behind. He felt bad and he wasn't the one getting yelled at.

When Elder McCullough got wind of what was going on, she stormed in. She wasn't pleased with Micah's interference. The Elder talked to each man as they arrived, laying down the law for them. They all agreed. She thought Micah's speech was overkill.

Braden hesitated to get in the middle of it, but in the end, he had to.

"Listen!" he shouted to get everyone's attention. "Everyone's heart is in the right place. I remember the first time we entered this village. Five men were already dead, the sixth and seventh died right here. I don't ever want to see something like that again. Neither do you," he said, pointing to the Elder, then Micah, then to the men. "You either. We need more people, not less. There is a lot of work to do. You'll help each other and in the end, everyone's lives will be better. That's what we want. That's what we'll have. Now get back to work."

None of the men hesitated. They hustled away, glancing furtively in the direction of Micah and the Elder.

The two women looked like they wanted to fight, but Braden stepped between them. "Stop it," he said quietly. "We support you and whatever you need, Mel-Ash. Please." He stepped closer, then pulled her in for a hug. Micah joined them quickly.

"I know how to control those boys," the Elder said in her scratchy voice. "I control all the women and that's what those boys are here for. I keep them busy. That's the secret. No matter what they get done, there's always more to do." She smiled, conceding Micah's intentions. The Elder had a way about her, subtle but effective.

"I'm sorry. I just want all this to work," Micah started. It looked like she wanted to say more. Braden stopped her.

"Just like an angry Aurochs in the Market Square! Elder McCullough, if you would be so kind, if you have any issues with any of the men that you can't resolve yourself, you'll let us know?" She nodded, still smiling. "Then we'll stay out of your way."

60 – Dwyer

"I don't care!" a man screamed at Fen, one of Village Dwyer's leaders. Destiny ran to support her fellow on the leadership council. "I'm not doing it!"

"But somebody has to clean the outhouse and it's your turn!" Fen screamed back, her voice a little shrill. Braden and Micah looked at each other, wondering how long this yelling match had gone on.

The group stopped arguing when they realized that Braden and Micah were there, watching. Micah climbed down from Speckles. Her ears took on a red hue as she became angry. Braden made sure she didn't take out her sword, but otherwise let her go.

"Has it been fair? Everybody takes their turn?" Both Destiny and Fen nodded. The man thrust his nose in the air.

"I ain't doing it."

With a quick move, Micah drove her hand under the man's chin, while twisting her leg behind his knee. She pushed forward with her other leg. She drove his chin up, taking his head on a long trip that ended as his body slammed into the ground. With both hands, she pounded his head against the ground two then three more times. As he lay there stunned, she calmly picked herself up, reared back, and punched him in the mouth, splitting his lip and breaking a tooth.

"Feel like doing it now?" she growled into his face.

"You farging crap…" There was more that he intended to say, but once Micah smashed her fist into his nose, his words came out as a gurgle. She rolled him onto his face and started twisting his arm behind him.

"If you break it and he can't work, then you'll be the one cleaning the outhouse," Braden said calmly.

She added more pressure until he squirmed, but he stopped spewing profanity.

Mick arrived, the third member of the leadership council. He looked at the man on the ground, only briefly, before smiling and giving Braden and Micah his warmest greetings.

"Welcome back! It is always so good to see you. I hope you are pleased with the progress that Tom has made with his smithy. Most of all, we'd love to show you your new wagon!"

Braden let out a whoop of joy. Micah let go of the man so she could give each of them a hug. Braden jumped down to do the same thing.

"If you'll do the honors," the older man said, waving at Fen, "I'll take care of this." He helped the man up, before twisting his arm again and dragging him away. Destiny went with them, berating the man with each step.

"Brandt would like to see his people. Are they near?"

"They're at the mine, I think. Not far. Tom had to expand already, so some things have changed, but we're growing rather rapidly. Everyone needs more people to help them do what they need to do.

The three men from Greentree decided to try their fortune someplace other than Village McCullough and were in the cart. Braden stepped aside so Fen could see. "Well, aren't you young men welcome! Come on over and let us take a look at you."

The men had seen Micah in action in two different villages. They were certain they didn't want to get on her bad side, and kept their distance as they approached Fen.

"We have our tools, ma'am. We're ready to work," the group spokesman offered. "We initially thought we'd try our hand in McCullough, but there were too many there already."

"Men, you mean?" She looked at them with a knowing glance. "There were too many men. Yes, they left here thinking things would be easier. If you're here, then maybe they are easy over in McCullough. But there are some available ladies who might appreciate a hard-working man."

"No, ma'am! They were working like slaves over there," one of the others blurted out. Everyone found the good humor in that. Micah threw her hands up in surrender. The others knew that she didn't let people take it easy. Whether there, here, or in Greentree, people earned their keep. Fen reached out to welcome each of the three.

Fen waved down a woman passing by with a basket of greens. "Show these nice young men around. They've come to find work." The young woman pulled futilely at her hair, then tried straightening her clothes before introducing herself and leading the men away.

Micah shook her head. "I suppose she's one of those available." Fen nodded and shrugged.

"If we hadn't been so quick to mete out punishment of the man who used to not clean outhouses, one of those three might have done it for a price. That is what trade is all about, is it not?" Braden offered as a teaching moment.

"No, dear," Fen answered. "He needed to be put in his place. He probably would have cheated the man who took his place."

"Was that one of Gravenin's partners?"

"Bullseye," Fen said while nodding.

Micah had kicked him in the groin and stomped on his head. Maybe his ears were still ringing. She wondered if Gravenin had put him up to refusing work. Braden thought they'd best have a word with Betty Dwyer. She had taken responsibility for the three. Braden had wondered if she could control them.

As soon as Brandt heard that the Aurochs were at the mine, he took off, Bronwyn still astride his neck. Skirill flew ahead of them to help see the way safely. The 'cat went with them because he hated the dogs who were numerous and ran freely through the village. Only Aadi stayed behind.

"Mick said you have a wagon for us?" Braden asked Fen.

Fen led the way. The Market Square had been almost completely taken over by Old Tom's smithy. A huge pile of stones filled the square, while additional roofing had been put over the area around the smelter and the forge. They walked around the iron ore pile and behind the forge. A new wagon stood there, wheels on and ready to roll.

Braden was initially disappointed as he compared it to his old wagon. This one wasn't covered, the wheels looked like they'd give a rough ride, and the buck board wasn't high. Micah, who'd never seen his old wagon, was in awe. Her mouth hung open as she looked it. "Isn't she beautiful!"

"Yes, she is," he said, only partly talking about his new wagon. The fact that Tom and the others had been able to build this without having seen one before was a marvel. Braden needed to appreciate that. They could improve over time, but they had to start somewhere and this was far better than the cart.

"We tested it with the Aurochs and one pulled it without any problem. Look here." Fen pointed to a harness. They had made it adjustable, because there was a big difference between the cow and the bull Aurochs. "With this, it doesn't matter who pulls. A perfect fit every time!"

Braden lightened up, shaking off his initial discontent. The people of Dwyer had done right by him.

61 – Next Leg of the Journey

Brandt was less than pleased with how the other Aurochs had been treated. The cow and the bull tolerated the human's bad behavior, but only because they knew the King would return and they'd be able to express their dismay. Probably the most disconcerting thing for the men working the mine was that they were getting chewed on by a little girl, while the massive Aurochs stomped and snorted at them.

The King loomed, putting the point of his horn a finger-width from one of the miner's eyes until the man peed himself. The King was gratified and more laws were laid down to clarify the Aurochs' role as a partner.

The whole truth was usually different from the story one first hears. The King's initial response may have been more than the situation called for. One man yelled at the cow Aurochs to get out of his way. Once. And when they put them in the harness, the Aurochs thought they were rougher than they needed to be, although once the pulling was done, the men removed the harness quickly.

Brandt had some choice words for his people, and the language caused Bronwyn to wince. Once he knew he upset the little girl, he let it go. Maybe he'd been spending too much time with Micah. Not everyone needed a beating.

G-War and Skirill wanted to hunt, so they committed to making their own way back to the village. Brandt took Bronwyn and headed from the mines, leaving a group of miners and Aurochs to make up and get back to work.

When they returned, they found the Market Square impassable. Braden had set up the cart to the side and was calling all to trade. Brandt squatted until he was lying on the ground so he could watch. He found Braden's love of trade fascinating. Aurochs were intelligent, but lived far simpler lives.

The humans needed their stuff. Since people could not be an expert in everything, trade made it possible to get good things and good food without knowing exactly where it all came from or how it was made. Every individual was good at something. When they found that, then they could produce for trade.

Brandt saw the wisdom in it all. He also saw how close it brought the villages together. He never thought that possible, because everyone kept to themselves. Everyone lived in fear. Used to, anyway.

Braden and Micah opened the southerner's eyes to a whole new world. So the King of the Aurochs watched, fascinated.

The 'cat showed up from nowhere and leaped to the top of the Aurochs' head. He had successfully avoided the dog pack, but was still nauseated by the smell. *'Don't puke on me, little friend,'* Brandt cautioned.

They all settled in to watch Braden ply his wares, trade for goods that he would bring to the other villages. Tom had been productive and there were a few iron items that Braden would be taking with him.

Braden told Tom how he had seen blacksmiths in the north crush charcoal into their metal to make it stronger. He knew that they added other metals to the iron, which further improved the strength. They called that metal steel. At some point in the past, someone in the south knew the process because there were steel items in the south, like the small carving knives. Those could have been scavenged, but Tom would make them available to everyone.

Tom accepted the knowledge as part of his trade with Braden. They shook on it and the deal was sealed.

Once all the trading was complete, Braden transferred some things to the wagon. When they left, they'd have the wagon and the cart with them. With Bronwyn, no one needed to guide any of the animals. She'd tell them what to do and for some reason, they always did it. Even the King would do as she asked.

"Where to next, fellow traders?" Braden asked the companions. Micah, like Braden, had not thought that far ahead. Brandt didn't care, but both

Aurochs were coming with them. He needed to keep swapping them out so every one of his people got their turn in the mines. Skirill, Aadi, and G-War had nothing to say on the matter. They trusted Braden and Micah. They knew that wherever they went, if they were together, they would be better off.

"To Westerly and beyond!" Braden exclaimed. "We take the wagon all the way west, then come back, trading the whole way. I'd like to bring some of those people from Westerly. We could use them here. There's so much to do. We go to the Western Ocean, and then someday, I'd like to see the Eastern Ocean."

Micah stiffened, her mouth drawn tightly closed. "Not yet," she said quietly. Braden put his hand on her arm.

"We'll go when you're ready. Not before." He leaned back and looked at the others. "Westerly it is, my fellow companions. The caravan rolls at first light!"

They always left with sunrise. Braden liked getting that last night's sleep before hitting the road, even though in the south, there weren't any roads. Not yet anyway. They were wearing down a trail between Dwyer, McCullough, the rainforest, and Greentree. As they grew, they could improve the trail until it became a road. And then they'd widen it so wagons could pass each other going in opposite directions.

With the construction of the first wagon, the eventuality of a robust trading network was that much closer.

In the meantime, they needed to talk with Betty Dwyer.

No one was in the hut, but they eventually found her tending one of the fields. When Braden and Micah walked up to her, she hung her head.

"I heard. Are you going to beat me, too?" she said it as if she both expected and deserved punishment. Micah instantly felt bad, although the man seemed to need the beat-down.

"We can't have them acting up," Braden said, physically lifting Betty's face so she'd look at him. "Can you control them or not?"

"We have our moments." She would commit no further.

"Where are they?" Micah asked.

"The river. My boy's arm still hasn't healed right. And the other boy's arm is ruined. Fishing is the only thing they can do with one arm." Betty started to get defiant.

"Better than dead," Micah snapped and stormed off. Braden gave Betty a harsh look before turning away.

The men were at the river, but seemed to be spending more time lamenting their misfortunes than fishing. They stopped completely when they saw Braden and Micah. She added an extra swing to her step as she sauntered toward them.

"He cleaned it so leave him alone!" Gravenin said, his arm held stiffly at his side. But it wasn't bandaged like his companion's, which was wrapped tightly against his body. The third man already had two black eyes from his broken nose. Both his lips were split and puffy. He backed away involuntarily, glaring at Micah.

She put her hand on the hilt of her sword, any pretense of a smile gone.

"Gravenin!" Braden shouted to break the stare-down. Everyone looked at him. "Even your mother won't protect you. What do you have to say about that?

"I didn't do anything!" His good hand flexed and his eyes darted from face to face.

"We can see that you don't do anything," Braden started. "Maybe you should think about contributing more than the next person. Make yourself welcome in this village. Instead of being here with all your friends. Why aren't you trying to make your mother proud?"

"Not much I can do with this arm," he grumbled.

"Instead of crying about it, why don't you figure out how you can contribute?" Micah asked.

"I'm not talking with you," he said pointedly. Micah responded by pulling her sword out.

"I think you understand that we would prefer to kill you all, rather than babysit. Here's the deal. You bring back a basket of fish for everyone's dinner, or don't come back at all." Braden wasn't serious, but he wanted them to provide something for the village.

"You can't do that. We wouldn't survive out here like this."

"Of course we can because we don't care if you survive or not. Since you know you can't survive out here, maybe you ought to look at ways you can survive in the village. Now, fill that basket with fish. We'll be waiting." Braden nodded to Micah, who backed away from the men, her sword in front of her. When they were far enough, she put the sword away.

"I don't know about them. We'll see if they can catch anything. I think having them hobbled keeps them relatively harmless." He looked at Micah. Her face was hard. "I know, I know. You still want to kill them." He pulled her close.

"We can't. That's the easy answer but it won't solve our problem, which is we need more people, not less. Let it go, lover. It seems like Mick, Fen, and Destiny had things under control. They didn't back down. Isn't that what we wanted? Good people to take control and keep control?"

"I guess so," she muttered. Braden knew she had a problem with men. If she hadn't then he would have never met her. She was supposed to be a dutiful wife in a loveless marriage.

"We make great companions," he finally said. He hoped Gravenin and his witless friends came through with the fish. Otherwise, maybe they would have to kill them.

62 – The New Traders

The village's celebration was a feast, headlined by Gravenin's banner catch. This was a huge weight off Braden's shoulders. Braden led the way in congratulating Gravenin and his friends on their catch. Others followed suit and the men looked like they appreciated it. Maybe they could contribute. Braden had a quick word with Mick about keeping a closer eye. If they were capable of catching this much fish, then the village should welcome them, appreciate what they provided.

The companions set out from Village Dwyer at sunrise with a fully loaded wagon. Braden felt odd not riding the buckboard, but that's how it had to be. The young bull Aurochs was first to pull the wagon. He made it look effortless.

Bronwyn sat astride Brandt's huge neck with G-War, as usual. She directed all the companions, so Braden and Micah rode without holding the reins.

Braden rode Max, as usual, while Micah rode Speckles, who pulled the cart with a Dwyer couple who wanted to learn the trade business. Braden could not have been more pleased. They needed traders to ply the routes.

Braden thought they needed a Caravan Guild to enforce the trade standards, but he didn't want to run it. Maybe this couple could trade for a cycle or two and then move into an oversight role. There could even be a training center for any trader.

Micah looked at him. "We aren't ready for that here. Maybe we can just have open trade. Anyone can trade. Village leaders can enforce the trade standards. You establish those. You dictate. They'll follow."

Braden stroked his braid as he thought. Micah had good points. People in the south had lost the ability to read. He was teaching Micah so that she could better use her neural implant, but it was taking time. He conceded that none of the village leaders would be able to read, ever.

So the trade rules had to be simple. They had to be spoken and correctly repeated. People remembered in threes.

"One. Two parties negotiate the terms of the trade.

"Two. Both agree to the terms and finish with a handshake.

"Three. If a deal fails, both parties return their part of the trade. No exceptions."

Micah thought it over. Was it simple enough? "How about this. One: Negotiate. Two: Agree. Three: Trade and be done. I'm not sure I like the failed deal. Don't negotiate if you can't follow through. Delivery is king, which means you have to know that you can deliver to start negotiating."

"Well, now. Isn't my partner the queen of the trade?" He gave her an approving look. "You're right. Negotiate, agree, and deliver. Even Gravenin can remember that!"

"After a couple more head stomps maybe." Braden could feel that in a certain way, Micah wasn't proud of the beatings she delivered. She took pride in her physical abilities and her superiority as a warrior, but knew that she disappointed Braden when she chose to fight.

"A head stomp may be in order, but as a last resort. We'll give the villagers a chance first and see if they can embrace it. Aadi, how do you think the Amazonians will feel about the Three Laws of Trade?" Braden called.

'It would be most convenient as they have three talons. Negotiate, agree, deliver. Yes. I will be able to share that with them. Does this mean we're stopping in the rainforest?'

"Yes, Aadi, we'll stop there. We'll stop at every trading square all the way to Westerly. What do you think about that?" Braden let Max fall back until he was even with the cart where the couple looked wide-eyed at the world as it passed.

'How about you Skirill, what do you think?' Braden asked over their mindlink while the Hawkoid flew far ahead.

'Wherever my friends go, I will follow.' Skirill didn't participate in the trades. He kept his eyes open, like G-War, and protected the companions as they traded. They owed each other their lives. If only there were Hawkoids in the south. He missed his people, even though had he remained in the north, he would be an outcast. Maybe he was better off here.

"What do you two think about the Three Laws of Trade?"

The young couple looked surprised. "We were trying not to listen as you talked with your mate. We know that you are used to traveling alone," the man, Tanner, said softly. "Can you tell us again?" Braden repeated the Three Laws.

"Negotiate, Agree, Deliver. It makes sense. You trade that way," the young lady, Candela, said with more confidence than her partner showed. "We'll trade that way, too. What other secrets can you share, you know, to help get our feet under us?"

Braden was in his element, regaling the young couple with stories of his trades in the north, gold for swords, swords for saffrimander, saffrimander and his wagon for the horses. How to trade each time for just a little bit more, cutting yourself a slice out of the trade as your profit. Trade could never be a completely even exchange. Without improving on the terms, you'd end with nothing.

Plus, here in the south, the Aurochs got an equal share of the profit for their part in pulling the wagon. So far that meant food, but it was a start. Later it could mean more.

As Braden thought about it, the miners owed the Aurochs for their work hauling the ore to the village. No, that wasn't right. The trade was for the labor to build the wagon.

They were all in this together. They all had a wagon and they all had nothing else.

Village McCullough welcomed them back. Braden told them that Tanner and Candela would be leading the trade, which meant he let them set up the trade stall while he and Micah went elsewhere and goofed off.

When they returned, a few trades had been made, with most having gotten more than they cost. Braden would not have made all the trades the same way, but that wasn't important. The young couple was off to a good start.

At the next stop, Tanner and Candela saw their first Amazonians. With Aadi, Brandt, and Bronwyn, they handled the trade well. Braden encouraged them to get as much rope as they could. It helped that Braden had brought down a couple fattened bucks to sweeten the deal.

After their second trade stop, the wagon and cart had more in them than when they started.

It was coming together nicely. But they would never realize their full potential if they couldn't document the trades. They needed to learn how to read.

When they arrived at Greentree, Braden started their lessons in the alphabet and basic math. After seven turns, Micah had improved greatly. Her neural implant showed her the letters and words as she asked for them so she had a constant source of reinforcement. Her head hurt at the end of the day, but her learning speed had increased exponentially.

The young couple had no such advantage. They learned the hard way, through repetition. Braden scratched the numbers on tree bark for them so they could review.

His determination in teaching them to read and write was driven by the fact that they weren't coming to Westerly. They would go as far as Coldstream, then return to Dwyer with the Aurochs and the wagon. That would be their route until Braden and Micah could open trade all the way to the far west.

Bronwyn would have to travel with them so they could communicate with the Aurochs. Brandt insisted on this. He also suggested that two cows accompany the team back to Dwyer where they would help the miners. As long as Bronwyn was with them, no one would get out of line.

Brandt seemed to swell with pride and pranced into the grasslands like a puppy as he joined the Earthshaker Herd. Braden thought it was because he was happy to be with his people, even if only for a short time. Until it became clear that an untold number of cows were in heat. Braden and Micah left him alone at that point, figuring he'd show up when his affairs were concluded.

This delayed their departure, but allowed Braden to spend more time teaching. Micah wasn't surprised that he was an excellent teacher. He inspired the students. If only he had a way to make paper. He wondered if New Sanctuary could print books to teach reading, writing, and basic math. He still carried his rudder and updated it as a way to show Tanner and Candela both how to do it and why it was important.

Whenever they made it back to New Sanctuary, he'd have to remember to check. Then he remembered that he didn't have to remember.

He brought up his neural implant window and asked the question regarding paper and books. The database showed a limitless spectrum of material. He asked Holly if they could print certain ones into books as well as create some blank books. Of course they could. Using wood pulp, they had a fabricator that could create almost anything. These items would be prepared and ready for him when next he returned.

"What?" Micah asked. When she couldn't hear him think, she knew he had the interface active. It blocked their mindlink, and she didn't like it.

"Just asking Holly if he could print some books to help people learn how to read and write. He'll include blank ones too that they can use as rudders."

"Oh," was all she said. Of course Braden would think like that. He wasn't bothered to think two or three turns ahead for himself, but he always took care of other people. This was another example of something she would have never thought of.

And that was why they made good partners. She was feeling amorous, but expected that was from Brandt's emotions overflowing into all of the companions. G-War had started to yowl. Skirill was flying high and fast in circles around the village and far above the rainforest. Only Aadi seemed immune, floating and blinking slowly, keeping his thoughts to himself.

Braden was getting overly adventurous with his hands, so they retired to their house to see if they could forget about the King of the Aurochs.

63 – Fighting to the Western Ocean

The trip to Coldstream was uneventful. The village welcome was unspectacular. The trades were marginal as few items were available, although it was far more than what they'd previously offered. The new traders secured tanned hides and a gourd of colored dye, and Braden worked a side deal for their special sweetened pork. He took as much as he could carry in two leaf bags. Micah suggested he'd make himself sick eating that much. He said he'd share. She knew he wouldn't.

They didn't stay long. Bronwyn was sad to part ways with Brandt. He considered her one of his own. When he talked with her, he would lie on the ground and she'd sit on his horn, her back against his head. Braden and Micah didn't know what they talked about, but sometimes their conversations went on for a long time.

Brandt helped the little girl climb onto the back of an older cow Aurochs who had assumed responsibility for pulling the wagon. He wanted an elder member of the herd to take care of his little girl. Tanner and Candela vowed to take good care of her, too. Micah convinced her parents to join the caravan when it passed back through. Having them along would help both Braden and Micah sleep better at night. If you asked Bronwyn, she was fine without other humans.

The companions knew this to be true, but adults had responsibilities, even for children who were protected by the world's creatures.

Braden's caravan watched Candela's caravan leave on the trade route to the west. Even G-War looked sad.

"When did I stop being fun?" Braden asked the companions. Micah shrugged.

"The innocence of youth. You and I carry all the burdens of Vii on our shoulders. It's not that we stopped being fun. She doesn't carry that weight.

It doesn't darken her thoughts. Her mind is pure, refreshing to touch," Micah answered.

'We have news to share,' Brandt said in his overly loud thought voice. Braden raised an eyebrow.

'Yes, we have news,' Aadi added. *'We wanted to wait until Bronwyn was gone. The news would upset her. Zalastar said that the Amazonian tribes have broken into factions. Zalastar controls the area from Greentree east, or so we were able to gather. The way they reference directions and locations has me befuddled.*

'In any case, the other tribes have taken over the areas to the west. Zalastar thought they'd moved inland to avoid contact with humans or other intelligent creatures. If we run into any Lizard Men, I mean Amazonians, from here west, they may not be friendly.'

Brandt shook his head, swinging his massive horns through the air. They were right, telling by how agitated the Aurochs was, that Bronwyn would have been upset, possibly even inconsolable.

"What changes for us?" Braden asked, concern clouding his face. He wanted to continue west, but didn't want to fight his way there.

'We go to Westerly and beyond, of course,' Brandt said. The King of the Aurochs wasn't to be dissuaded.

"Simple as that?" Braden shrugged as he looked from face to face. This reinforced what he already knew.

He knew that he could not read the body language of his companions.

"Maybe we don't have to travel so close to the rainforest, but yes, off to Westerly!" Micah added with a dramatic smile and hand wave.

So they pressed on.

They traveled more slowly than they had before because they pulled the cart this time and they also marked the trail for future traders. It was just a path of travel at present, but at some point, it would become a real road.

Brandt was exceptional at removing obstacles to the cart's travel. He could plow up any size rock and roll it aside. He even ran back and forth a few times to better mark a trail. When they looked back, it was easy to see where they'd passed. With Skirill flying ahead, they did not have to backtrack. They chose the best way ahead the first time, every time.

With their neural implants, Braden and Micah were able to track progress on maps shown directly in their minds. They updated details on the maps with what they saw, helping Holly to build a real-life view of the trade route.

Micah used the travel time to practice reading. As she learned, she was able to open up more and more areas of the database. After Braden guided her to the school books, she was unleashed. She learned in the course of turns what it took children cycles to do.

Braden kept his window closed to watch over them while Micah studied. By teaching her to read, he opened a vast part of his world to her. She could read his rudders. For him, that was the ultimate expression of trust. That was how he was raised.

She could hear his thoughts and finally, he could hear hers. Maybe reading the rudders was only symbolic, but it was important to him. He looked at the watch he wore. Old Tech. He could finally read the time and know what it meant, thanks to a short lesson from the database. With his neural implant, he could always check the time, which rendered the watch unnecessary.

Like his rudders, the watch, the bracelet they called it, was a physical part of his story. It gave him access and authority with the first hologram. It gave him a title that he liked. Caretaker. Maybe it was time to change from Free Trader to Caretaker Braden. As Micah kept telling him, he took responsibility for the well-being of humanity's current and future generations.

Skirill squawked an alarm, alerting all the companions. Braden and Micah shook off their individual distractions and looked about. "Ess?"

'Fighting. At the edge of the rainforest.' He flew slowly past to show everyone what he saw. Amazonians were engaged with each other. Braden and Micah couldn't tell them apart. It looked like every creature fought for himself.

'They are killing each other, Master Human. We must stop them.' Aadi said, his thought voice pleading.

'I agree. We cannot allow this to go on,' Brandt decided for them as he snorted once and ran toward the trees. Max and Pack followed in his wake at a full gallop. Braden and Micah held on for the ride, hoping the cart wouldn't be damaged as it bounced along.

Ears flat, G-War crouched low as he clung to the King's head. Aadi bounced along behind Speckles as they raced over uneven ground.

Brandt skidded to a stop at the very edge of the rainforest, raised his head and bellowed into the mass of Amazonians.

Braden learned how loud the King's voice could really be.

Braden and Micah rode up to the Aurochs, stopping abruptly to jump off. They each pulled a blaster.

"Stop!" Braden yelled, pointing his blaster haphazardly toward the Amazonians.

A spear appeared out of nowhere. Braden dodged it. Micah fired a short burst at a point above where the spear originated. It scorched the bark of a tree, but didn't start a fire. Braden looked at her in alarm, but she was calm.

A second spear flew from the trees, this time at Brandt. Then a third. Brandt knocked the second spear away with a sweep of his horns, but the third spear hit his side and stuck there. He shook with fury. The spear flipped away from him as did G-War, who landed gracefully in the middle of surprised Amazonians. He bolted in an orange flash up the nearest tree.

The King pawed the ground once and surged forward into a smaller tree, his back legs driving hard. As the tree cracked and went down, Amazonians scattered. Others weren't impressed.

Spears flew from both sides, peppering the Aurochs' sides.

"Get out of there!" Braden yelled as he unleashed the power of the blaster. Micah followed his lead less than a heartbeat later. Braden held the trigger down, sending a line of fire through the Amazonians he could see.

Micah was firing single shots, short bursts, picking her targets carefully.

But they were both on one side of the King of the Aurochs. The Amazonians on the other side were safe.

Brandt's eyes shot wide as the pain finally registered. He stumbled and pulled backwards trying to pull himself from the confines of the rainforest. The Amazonians moved forward tentatively to drive their spears into the Aurochs.

The enraged Amazonians wanted to kill the great beast.

Aadi floated upward quickly and once he saw the attackers, he let loose with his focused thunderclap. The Amazonians staggered, many fell, but others did not. A second group of Amazonians raced forward. Aadi wasn't ready for a second thunderclap. He watched helplessly.

But the second group wasn't trying to attack Brandt. They speared the Amazonians who were helpless from Aadi's attack.

'They are friends! Help them!' Aadi shouted over the mindlink. Braden stopped firing. The power of his blaster was dangerously low. Micah had conserved her power, so she ran, trying to get to the other side of the Aurochs. She swung wide behind him as he kept backing up.

The attack from Brandt's left side had been shattered, although if there were any friends, they counted among the dead as readily as their enemies. Braden ran forward, knowing he would have a shot as soon as Brandt cleared the trees.

Braden was behind the Amazonians when Brandt was finally free. Turning his great head, his hooves ripped the ground as he ran back toward the grasslands.

One Amazonian turned, saw Braden, and immediately thrust his spear at him. The human had been looking past this group toward their enemies. He was surprised and the spear jammed him in the chest, his tunic deflecting some of the blow. The speartip ripped through the special material and creased along his ribs, tearing his flesh as it passed.

He went down, pulling the spear from the Amazonian's hand.

Two others joined the fight against the human, stepping forward to add more power to their spear thrust. G-War landed between the Amazonians and the human, then jumped into the face of the closest enemy. The surprise made the group hesitate. Braden snapped a quick shot with his blaster at the second attacker, blowing a ragged hole into his chest. He fell backward.

G-War shredded the creature's face, but the Amazonian was able to get a grip and throw the 'cat to the side. But he could no longer see, his face covered in blood, one eye missing. G-War turned and leapt high. As he landed on the Amazonian's shoulder, he slashed its throat and jumped away.

"Aadi!" Micah yelled as she barreled into the rainforest to get between the Amazonians and her mate. She fired a few shots toward the Amazonians hovering at the edge of light within the rainforest. They lost their stomach for the fight and disappeared into the murkiness beyond.

That left four Amazonians with clearly mixed loyalties.

Braden stayed down. His chest hurt too much to move. As he looked at the Amazonians, he realized they weren't friends at all. *The enemy of my enemy is still my enemy. I only hate him a little bit less,* Braden thought. After they dispatched their enemy Amazonians, they probably would have resumed the attack on Brandt.

"Aadi?" Micah asked, her blaster pointed at the remaining Amazonians. They remained still, but their spears were leveled, at the ready.

Aadi floated forward until he was in front of the group. He stayed there. As a fellow reptile, the Amazonians had an innate respect for him. As soon as they saw him, they stood their spears on end. Micah didn't relax. She used the time to get into a better position to shoot them.

Aadi spoke with the creatures. Micah stayed where she was, getting more and more anxious as time went by. Braden had not yet gotten up and his blood was spreading into a greater pool around him.

A bleeding Brandt returned, probably summoned by the 'cat, who had moved himself behind the Amazonians. Skirill flew in and perched on a branch directly over their heads. Micah finally put her blaster away and ran to her partner.

"Sorry, lover. I was too slow," Braden said weakly. He let her sit him upright so she could get his ruined tunic and shirt off. She was shocked by the wound. The cut wasn't clean. It was a long gash that needed to be stitched, something she'd never done before. She pulled all the numbweed from her pouch and started packing it into the wound, helping Braden press down on it, which slowed the blood flow.

She turned red with rage. Braden grabbed her arm and shook his head. "Two of those three are dead. These four might follow them into the great beyond, but not yet. Aadi, can you tell us something which might save their lives?"

Micah looked at the group. One stood there without his spear. He was the one. Micah stood and pulled her sword.

"Aadi?" Braden asked again.

'Hold, Micah,' Brandt's thought voice boomed. She stopped moving toward the Amazonian, who stood his ground, head up. 'They are telling Aadi about the war. We need to hear this and then we need to let these four go.'

Micah looked at the Aurochs as if he had grown a third horn from the middle of his forehead.

'We have fewer allies than you realize. If you consider New Sanctuary important and you want to see it again, you'll let these four go.'

"I look forward to hearing more of that story, don't you, Micah?" Braden asked, voice barely above a whisper. She took a deep breath and made a show of putting her sword away. "Help me up and let's get out of here. Brandt needs some attention, too. Hey! Grab that numbweed bush, too." Braden pointed with his right hand, still holding his side tightly with his left.

That's when Micah knew that Braden would be all right. He left a great deal of blood behind, but none of it was the dark blood of a deep wound. She got down on a knee so Braden could get his arm over her shoulder. They stood up together, Braden grimacing in pain, gasping for breath

She kept him from falling down. She dropped the bush at the edge of the rainforest as she needed both hands to steady Braden. He seemed to be getting weaker with each step. *'Skirill, can you bring the horses back?'* she asked in her thought voice. They'd run off during the fight. Skirill immediately took wing and flew toward the grasslands. Speckles was pulling the cart, so he wouldn't be far.

She put Braden against a lone tree away from the rainforest. G-War settled in next to his nearly unconscious human. Micah wanted to get him further away from the rainforest and their potential enemies. She needed the cart.

Brandt stopped menacing the Amazonians and joined the humans by the tree. The Aurochs bled from numerous wounds on his sides, but none of them were deep. Some painful, but not life-threatening.

Her neural implant pinged incessantly. While she waited for the cart, she maintained pressure on Braden's wounds and opened the window. Holly sent a note saying that Braden's life signs were alarming. She responded to him sarcastically, then simplified it to say that she was doing what she could.

Holly used her view to assess the wound. He then recommended giving Braden water, as much as he could hold, then lay him down and keep him that way. Then she could close the wound. Holly recommended firing short bursts from her blaster at her sword, then use the heated metal on the cut. After that, she wouldn't need to sew. She remembered that Braden had run out of thread earlier, sewing up the cow Aurochs. She couldn't sew up the wound, no matter how much she wanted or needed to.

She had to clean the numbweed out of the wound and that meant more water.

Skirill finally arrived with Max and Pack. She muscled Braden into the cart. He was unconscious and starting to get cold and clammy. She washed the wound; the numbweed was already working and it bled little.

Holding her sword upward, she fired short bursts from her blaster. The beams of light brazed the metal and continued into the sky. Soon the blade shimmered from the heat.

"Forgive me," she said as she rolled the blade across the terrible cut that creased his chest. Braden lurched upright and screamed, then dropped, limp.

She threw the sword out of the cart and held him. He was alive. She gave him water, but he couldn't swallow. She pulled on his braid, stroking it, even though it was matted with blood. "Come on back. Come on back to me." She rocked with him in her arms, tears flowed down her cheeks. A big Aurochs muzzle reached into the cart and nudged them both. She patted his nose, while one of his horns got caught on the side board. He had to work to extricate himself without upsetting the cart.

Aadi reappeared. *'Is there anything I can do, Master Micah?'*

"Let's get away from the rainforest. As far as we can go."

Brandt nudged the horses and the cart bounced once as Speckles pulled it toward the north. Braden woke, but only for a few moments. Micah forced water on him. He was in and out, but every time he could, she gave him more water.

The Golden Warrior, Prince Axial De'atesh, wouldn't leave Braden's side. He leaned against his chest, purring constantly. Micah wondered about that, but the 'cat let her know it would be soothing for him, help Braden calm himself. From there, he could start to recover.

She didn't realize that the cart had stopped moving. Skirill was perched at her side, Aadi hovered overhead, and Brandt stood alongside.

"I smell sweet pork," Braden said groggily, mumbling the words.

"What?" Micah asked. Of all things to think about when he came to…

"Sweet pork. I smell it. Not hungry." Each word was an effort for him.

"Shhh." Micah held up the flask. He nodded. This time, he drank deeply before lying back.

She saw that Braden's pillow was his supply of the special meat from Coldstream. If anything could urge him back to health, it was his favorite food. She covered him with a blanket and climbed out of the cart.

"Now let's take a look at you," she told Brandt.

64 – Heal

It was three turns later before Braden was able to move around on his own. Micah set up camp where they stopped and that's where they stayed. The companions kept them safe as Braden recovered his strength.

Micah had also recharged the blasters, making sure all four were out and ready for use.

Micah used all their numbweed supply on Brandt. He'd been hurt more badly than he let on. Two of the spear tips had bitten deeply between his ribs, although they didn't penetrate his lungs. She still needed him to not move around so much. Aadi went back for the numbweed bush so she could process more. She'd seen Braden do it a few times, but that wasn't the same as doing it yourself.

She had to throw out the first batch.

The second batch was marginal, and finally, the third batch was normal.

Brandt was a powerful creature and wouldn't let his injuries hold him back. He grazed with vigor, acting like the mass quantities of grass he ingested would help him heal.

He was probably right.

Following Braden's lead, he also drank a great deal of water.

Skirill flew a long way both east and west, watching for signs of the Amazonians. He saw many of the Lizard Men, but they moved quickly, not lingering near the Plains of Propiscius. He did not believe they intended to attack the companions.

Aadi once again proved to be their secret weapon. He told Micah what the Amazonians had shared, and then repeated it all when Braden was strong enough to listen. As Zalastar had told them, there were multiple factions. The battle they had the misfortune of joining was between three groups vying for supremacy in this area. Braden and Micah killed all the warriors from one group and most of the members from the second. Brandt's charge was into the middle of the second group, which put the remnants between Brandt and the third group. By not killing those last four, Aadi extracted a right to pass from them. This group, although a long way from the ancients' road, had allies who seized part of the south side of the Amazon.

Zalastar and his people were forced out of the depths of the rainforest. They held the road, most of the way through the Amazon, and all the area to the east where there were far fewer Amazonians. Although Zalastar led the largest of the factions, it wasn't a majority of all Amazonians. If the others could unite, then they could overwhelm him.

"But why?" Braden asked. Micah hung her head. She'd already heard the answer.

'Us, I'm afraid.' Aadi floated close to Braden. *'Many Amazonians consider themselves to be still at war with the humans. When we made contact with Zalastar and started trading, too many others could not live with it. They remembered the stories they were told of doing the ancients' work, only to be abandoned when the war started.*

'Those who shared the croc that night with us have tried to convince the others that you aren't like the ancients. You are a new breed of human, willing to partner as equals with any creature who sees a better world, one free of conflict.'

"Judging by the ongoing war, I believe they weren't successful." Braden laughed, ending with a wince. His side hurt. The burn didn't help, but Micah had stopped the bleeding.

He'd eaten all the sweetened pork, which made him feel as good as he was going to feel, under the conditions.

Micah told him she needed to learn how to shoot the recurve bow. She couldn't hunt deer with a sword and a blaster.

Braden realized that she probably hadn't eaten in quite some time. "When's the last time you ate?" She shrugged him away.

G-War and Skirill set out without another word. Over the next hour, as her neural implant told her, Skirill flew back three times, dropping a freshly-killed rabbit each time.

She cleaned them and started a fire. Brandt rooted up wild vegetables that he found, bringing a mouthful to her. She cleaned off the Aurochs spit in the stream and added the vegetables to the pot. She sliced the meat, adding it as well. She also dug into Braden's pack as he watched, pulling out the vial of saffrimander. She raised her eyebrows and he nodded once. She tapped a minute portion into the pot. Rabbit stew was good for the soul and there was going to be a lot of it.

When G-War returned, he looked as if he'd already eaten his fill, as had Skirill. Game was plentiful on the edge of the rainforest. For that, she was thankful, but it also made her wary. Their enemy lurked in the shadows. She wasn't sure she'd ever be able to enter the rainforest again without having both blasters in hand.

Micah was thankful for the companions. As the stew cooked, she went to each of them, touching them on their heads and letting them know how much she appreciated their help. Braden watched her, knowing she was much better at that stuff than he'd ever be.

'Not true, partner mine. You're pretty good, too, although that's probably Free Trader Braden and not you at all,' she said over their mindlink.

'If I could, I'd make you pay for that!'

'By "if I could," you mean that even if you were healthy, you wouldn't be able to. I'll take that as a compliment.'

He looked at her, desire rising within him. She saw it and stepped back from him, dropping her clothing on the ground one piece at a time until she wore nothing.

"Gentle, lover," Braden said softly. He was certain this would help him heal more quickly. Micah was past her initial scare that Braden would die. Now it was time to celebrate, even if only gently, then they'd try the saffrimander-infused rabbit stew. It was shaping up to be a perfect turn.

65 – Westerly

"Horsehair," Braden said out of the blue. "All this time. We don't need thread. We have the finest horsehair in all the south!"

"What are you talking about?" Micah had just woken from a long night of sound sleep. Braden's good arm was wrapped around her.

"To sew up wounds. Hairs from a horse's tail. They are thinner than the finest thread and probably strong enough. I'll have to ask Max if I can liberate a few to add to my kit. The next one of us that needs sewn up is going to get a little help from Max." Braden wondered why he hadn't thought of that before. He'd ridden mindlessly for incredible distances and all of a sudden, it came to him.

He couldn't help what had passed. At least they didn't need thread and for this, he was thankful. He hoped they didn't need the horsehair either. He had enough of sewing up wounds.

Micah stood, stretching in front of Braden before putting her clothes on. *Ahh*, he thought, *the little things that make life worth living*. Micah smiled back at him, having heard what he thought.

He got up, slowly, still sore but able to move. He then tried to repair his shirt and tunic using one of his own hairs, but it was too brittle. Then he used one from Max's tail, and it held.

Max didn't complain. He had a long tail.

Finally, they started traveling again.

Skirill flew ahead. They wanted to be sure everything was normal before entering the village. Ideally, they would get a number of the villagers to emigrate to Greentree and Dwyer.

They could make it to Westerly before mid-daylight on the second turn. That would give them plenty of time to talk with the villagers. If things got hot, they could leave and put a good distance between them.

The village looked active and normal as Skirill flew high overhead. No one seemed to notice the Hawkoid fly by casually, then turn for another pass. Braden wanted to know if the old man was around, the one who gave them grief last time. Skirill didn't see him. He saw the young man who spoke before. He seemed to be going about his business without a concern.

"Looks like we could get a warm welcome," Braden said. "Shall we?"

He still needed Micah's help to get into the saddle, although he was feeling much better. G-War joined him. Micah climbed aboard Speckles, threw the rope for Aadi to grab, and they were off, with Brandt leading the way.

They topped the final rise before the village. Last time, they stopped to make sure they were noticed before entering. This time they strolled directly into the village. They waved, like old friends.

The villagers waved back. Many cheered. The young man who wanted to build homes was the first to come up to them. He held out his hand for Braden to take.

Braden hesitated. If it was a trick, he was in no condition to fight back. Micah knew what he felt and she edged close, ready to engage. G-War crouched, but he didn't appear alarmed.

Braden grasped the young man's hand firmly. He gave Braden a big smile.

"We stopped giving part of our food to the old man and he stopped sharing his leadership with us. Guess what?" The crowd hooted and cheered. "Things got better!"

"So where's the old man now," Braden asked.

"In the fields, fending for himself." Another cheer.

"What's your name?" Braden asked after the crowd calmed down.

"I'm Felip, Felip of Westerly. And you, Free Trader Braden, and your companions are always welcome in our village."

66 – The Western Ocean

"Is anyone still interested in going with us?" Far fewer hands than he expected went up. Sometimes a change in leadership could work wonders. And no one had to die. Braden nodded to Micah. She smiled back.

"You can go with us if you don't mind walking. There's plenty of work, good homes, villagers who will welcome you and work beside you. You won't be sorry. Get your things ready. We'll leave in a couple turns. First, we want to see the Western Ocean. Then we'll be back." Braden finished his speech. They shook hands and slapped people on the back good-naturedly as the crowd broke up. They spoke to Felip alone for a while to make sure the village was okay.

Braden also wanted to show trade items from the east: rope, woodwork, a few metal items, tanned hides, dye, special tunics.

The villagers from Westerly had never seen anything besides what they themselves made. When Braden and Micah showed the wares in the cart, the villagers were wowed. They saw the power of possibility. Braden smiled at the want in their eyes. He'd set the hook. Westerly would anchor the trade route.

They said that they could fill wagons with vegetables from their fields. Braden told them that the artisans needed to eat and food for items like wood and metal made for a good trade. They left Felip with much to think about.

They celebrated heartily that evening. The next morning, with the sun rising behind them, they rode out.

Skirill showed them the way while they dutifully updated the maps in the database. The terrain started to get rougher as the extensive Plains of Propiscius gave way to the ocean approaches. Hills, cliffs, ravines, and other weather-savaged lands lay before them. They stopped early, well before sunset. They unhooked the cart and hid it. They couldn't drag it further without risking damage to it.

They had no intention of delaying things. They could taste the change in the air as the wind pushed toward them from the yet unseen ocean. Micah breathed deeply, closing her eyes. *It smells like home,* she thought. She missed that smell, the comforting sound of the ocean, but not her village.

'Hungry and many choice meals are close by,' G-War said as he sat, watching them. Braden dropped everything except his recurve bow and made to leave with the 'cat.

"Ahem." Micah stood there, arms crossed. She didn't look happy.

"What?" He didn't know he'd done. She sighed and shook her head.

"Give me the bow. I'm going, and I'll do the shooting."

"But you haven't used the bow," Braden started, still confused.

"Exactly. Remember when I told you I needed to learn to use your bow?" She looked at him, hand still out as she waited for him to give her the bow.

"It's still a little foggy. Maybe…" Micah cut him off by snapping her fingers and waving once more for him to hand over the bow.

G-War stood and started walking away. *Humans…*

Braden surrendered, handing her the bow and one arrow, and then put his hands up. She was right, of course. This was a partnership and in reality, his side still hurt. The muscles were stitching themselves back together.

She started to walk past him, following the 'cat, when he grabbed her with his right arm and pulled her toward him. Their noses touched as he locked his eyes on her. "I love you." She pushed him away, blushing and smiling. It was nice when arguments could end like this.

He stopped smiling very shortly thereafter.

Micah's first three shots were woefully off target, resulting in three broken arrows and no prey. Braden did not have many arrows left. He was down to his last few, when she decided that this wasn't the best way to practice. Her arm pull was shorter than Braden's, but she was physically stronger. She had a tendency to jerk the bowstring back, muscling it into position. When she let go of the arrow, she pushed her arm holding the bow forward, almost like she was trying to throw the arrow at the target. It didn't work. He tried talking with her as she aimed, but that scared the game and made her take a snap shot at a running animal.

She gave the bow back so they could have something to supplement their gracious amount of Westerly vegetables. Braden tested the pull. He tried not to flinch as pain stabbed his side. He'd pull once, when they saw their next target.

G-War guided them impatiently to a smallish boar. Braden figured G-War could probably take it down himself if he wanted. If Braden missed, he felt that was exactly what would happen.

He refused to give the 'cat the satisfaction and dropped the boar with a single clean shot, from which he recovered the intact arrow. They smoked the boar in entirety. They had time and wanted a reserve of meat. They spent the evening with the camaraderie of all the companions.

Micah wanted to hear the story of how G-War and Braden bonded. G-War's version was significantly different from Braden's, but entertaining regardless. Braden reveled in the joy of the road, of the trade. This was how he grew up.

There were no expectations. They traded, they moved on. People welcomed them when they arrived. As they talked, it was easy to forget for that short period of time that the Amazonians had started a war. The least he could do was keep the humans out of it.

These thoughts soured his mood. But the humans started it and then got into the middle of it too. They'd have to think and figure out what to do next, even if the answer was to move the trade routes north, away from the rainforest.

Micah punched him gently in the arm, bringing him back to the moment. *Enjoy right now. It's what we have,* she thought. It was hard to argue with that logic. He hoisted his flask of water and took a deep drink as if it were the finest wine from the best fabricator.

With sunrise, the companions stood on the hill, watching, waiting while Skirill flew ahead. He went all the way to the ocean and was surprised by the number of huts. They stood above the water line, up and down the shore as far as he could see. He didn't find anything that looked like a village, just huts and few people. There seemed to be fewer people than places to live. The companions wondered.

Only one way to find out.

They chose their path, easier without the cart, and headed into the hills and down a ravine. By mid-daylight, the companions stood on the beach. The King of the Aurochs learned the hard way that he couldn't drink the ocean. He was less than pleased that no one stopped him before getting a mouthful of saltwater. They looked at each other. Aadi didn't drink like that and Micah had told Braden and G-War at some point that they couldn't drink the water. Skirill could sense the salt, plus the constant movement of the water kept him from landing anywhere near it.

"Sorry about that, Brandt," they mumbled in apology. They had reached the Western Ocean. They could return to Westerly, but the companions knew there were people here. Braden always wanted to talk with new people.

Which wasn't easy as the villagers scattered when they saw the menagerie of creatures that made up the caravan. They finally enlisted Skirill's aid to see which huts people ran to so they could find them.

Leaving the other companions on the beach, Braden and Micah walked up some shaky stairs to one hut, which looked unremarkably like all the rest.

They looked abandoned. But thanks to Skirill's keen Hawkoid eyes, they knew this one was not.

"Hello! I'm Free Trader Braden and we'd like to talk with you. We mean you no harm." He waited. They listened carefully but didn't hear a sound. "We know you're in there. Please don't make us come in. We do not wish to get hurt." What he meant was that he didn't want to hurt them.

"Go away! We don't want your kind around here," a gruff voice shouted from inside.

"What? What problem do you have with humans?" Micah said calmly, a little taken aback by their fear.

"Not you, you farging lunkhead, those other beasts." Micah looked at Braden, then held her hands up, offering that he take over.

"They are our friends. They are kind souls who wish no harm upon their fellow creatures. We are honored that they travel with us. Now that that is settled, we're coming in." Braden pushed on the door, it moved, but something was blocking it from opening all the way. He gave it an angry shove and it slid open. He almost fell. Micah was right behind him, ready to act.

A man and a boy cowered under a table. The man pointed a three-pronged spear at them, but they noted that he wasn't in a position to fight. The only way they'd get hurt is if they fell on the trident. She relaxed.

"Please," she said in a soothing voice. "We don't want anything from you except to talk. What happened here? Why so many empty huts?" She sat down, encouraging Braden to do the same. Micah watched the boy closely. He seemed less afraid than the man, who didn't appear to be much older than Braden. The boy couldn't have been his son, could he?

They hesitated. She continued, "There's no one else coming. It's just us and our friends. We'll soon leave and go back to Westerly, Coldstream, and Greentree. We've established a trade route between the villages from here, I mean Westerly, all the way to Dwyer in the east."

The man started to talk, as if telling a story. Micah was sure he hadn't heard what she'd said.

"They're all gone. The ocean terrors got 'em," the man said quietly. "They came out of the sea, creaking and belching fire. Light shining from their eyes. No one's seen 'em still alive."

"You sound like you've seen them?" Braden asked, skeptical of what was shaping up as a fish story.

"Up close, no. When they broke the surf yonder--" He pointed at an arbitrary spot on the wall of the hut. "I ran. From up there--" Another wild point of a rough finger. "I seen 'em sweeping up our people, before dragging backwards into the surf."

"Daylight or night?"

"They only come at night," he said so quietly they almost didn't hear him.

'G, Brandt, Ess, and Aadi, are you hearing this? Does any of it make sense?' Braden asked over the mindlink.

'Sounds like Old Tech. Have him describe the light shining from the eyes better,' Aadi said. Braden and Micah could feel the curiosity in the others.

"Tell me more about the shining eyes," Micah asked, while Braden accessed his implant.

"The light came out of them and brightened the area in front as if it were daylight. I saw that and ducked. If it shined on me, I'd die!"

Holly suggested it was a research vessel that was used before the war. There were two ocean research facilities, one in the Eastern Ocean and one in the Western. The vessels traveled along the ocean bottom and could drive directly onto the beach. It wasn't capable of driving in the hills.

Holly spent enough time with Braden and Micah that he was starting to understand the technology of their world. He agreed with Braden's mental characterization. A wagon without a horse, but more like the armored vehicle they saw in the armory, just much larger.

"When did these attacks on the people start?" Braden asked.

"A couple cycles ago. Rare at first. Now, it seems like the terrors are cleaning out the rest of us."

"You can come with us. Right now, we have no way of stopping this vehicle, I mean, the ocean terrors. We believe that it can't climb the hills. Come with us and we'll take you away from here."

The man thought about it for a heartbeat or three. Then nodded.

"Your son?" Micah asked.

"No, not my son, not my relation. We're the only two left from our families. Better take care o' each other."

"What are your names?" Braden asked. They needed to hurry if they were going to sweep the surviving humans off the beach and get them to the hills before nightfall. Braden and Micah needed these two to help. They probably knew which humans survived.

"I'm Sand Crab, they call me Crabby, and this is Yellowfin."

"I'm from the Eastern Ocean," Micah said to establish herself. "Aren't those fish and such that you catch?"

"Sure, but over the years, we gave up on the old names. I knew a Bill once and a Devon. But they were really old. They died when I was young."

"If that's your names, then that's what we'll call you. Crabby? Yellowfin? If you're ready, let's go save some lives!" Braden had a way about him that Micah adored. He made this simple task of running to the high ground a noble quest, a great adventure. She wondered why they hadn't run away before, but people do what they know. From the smell and the look of the man's trident, the three-pronged fishing spear, they were fishermen. Always were. They didn't know any other way to survive.

The people of White Beach had lost their way. Sometimes you have to give up what you do to save what you love.

They had devolved into anarchy. Braden would fill their leadership void. They would teach these people how to survive in the grasslands of the Plains of Propiscius. They would join villages and have new lives.

Micah took Yellowfin with her on Pack and Braden took Crabby. They each rode a different direction along the beach. They shouted. Crabby knew everyone's name and called as they passed. They stopped and talked with quite a few people. By the time Braden and Crabby reached the end of the occupied huts, there was a stream of people on the beach walking toward the King of the Aurochs. He stood as a marker for all to see. There was a great deal of trepidation because of the so-called muties, but the hope of salvation won the day.

Micah had the same luck. Although Yellowfin didn't remember the people's names, they knew him. Micah and the boy were persuasive, sending people with their meager belongings down the beach toward the huge beast who was to guide them to the ravine. And their freedom.

It seemed to be taking forever. Many would end up climbing the slope in the dark, but there were more people than they originally thought. They couldn't count the numbers who joined the march from the sea.

Micah led the way behind the King of the Aurochs. G-War rode and Aadi swam by himself. The crowd was moving slowly enough that he could keep up without any trouble. Braden waited at the bottom for the last of the people to enter the ravine. He had to keep them from straying. They had a little bit of everything--young, old, tall, short, strong, weak, mothers with babies, and the frail--but they walked with determination, even though the look on their faces was that of defeat.

As darkness fell, people continued to travel away from the beach and up the ravine. Crabby had long since joined those walking and Braden was left alone. He watched as the last walked off the beach. It had gotten dark and the climb would be tough. He watched the sea for any sign of the ocean terrors, as the villagers called them.

The surf started to churn and Braden's head buzzed. Old Tech trying to communicate with Old Tech. He opened his implant and asked Holly for help. The vehicle continued to climb out of the surf. Holly wasn't having any luck reaching out.

Braden pulled out his blaster and fired a number of short bursts into the sand in front of the vehicle. It stopped, then settled into a gentle rocking motion as the surf pushed and pulled.

'Anything yet, Holly?' Braden thought within the open window.

'Yes, I have it now. These are automated. Inside are a number of Development Units. They have expanded their undersea laboratory and the people of White Beach are being used to repopulate it.' Holly scrolled the information through his open window.

'These Bots are programmed to not harm humans. According to the laboratory, it estimated that the people on White Beach will die out within two generations if not tended to.'

'Can you tell them to leave these people alone? We're going to take them inland to Coldstream, Greentree, McCullough, Dwyer, and anywhere in between where they want to build homes. Will that keep them from dying off?' Braden asked, hoping he could get a look inside the ancients' vehicle that could travel on the ocean floor.

He forgot that Micah couldn't hear him while he was talking with Holly. He closed the window.

'That thing showed up,' he said in his thought voice. *'Holly was able to talk with it. Old Tech taking the villagers to repopulate an ancients' outpost on the bottom of the ocean! I'm going to try to get a look inside.'*

'You better not go inside that thing!' If one could shout over a thought voice, it was clear she just had. Getting trapped under the ocean was not something she wanted to risk. He needed to tell the villagers of White Beach that if their loved ones were taken, they were still alive. He'd have to have that conversation before they went too far inland. For that, he needed to navigate the ravines and climb the hills.

Micah was right. He couldn't risk getting a look inside. He'd leave it alone.

With a last glance at the ancients' sea vehicle, he spurred Max into the ravine.

67 – Splitting

They did the best they could getting people settled, but there were too many. They slept on the ground. With the sunrise, they could take all the food they had, vegetables and smoked boar, and share it with villagers of White Beach. What seemed like a great deal of food the turn before was pathetically small as their numbers grew.

After they ate what would be meager portions, he'd tell them what he learned. If they wanted to go back, that would make things more manageable for him, but they needed the people inland, where there was more work than people.

The power of trade.

When the sun rose, it showed a large and ragged group of refugees wondering if there was anything to eat.

Braden and Micah had gotten themselves in deep.

They called everyone together. Braden stood on a rock and waited until they were quiet. "People of White Beach! I don't know how to tell you this, so I'll just say it. The ocean terror is Old Tech. It's not a living creature.

"The ancients, with their technology and their intelligence, built a village on the floor of the ocean. The ocean terror is a vehicle that has taken your people to that village. I believe they are all alive, just living beyond your reach. To go to them, you have to wait for the Old Tech to appear and go with it." That's when the grumbling started.

"You and your mutie bunch are with them!" screamed an ugly voice. "Let's get 'em!" The people crowded together and started surging forward. The fire from a blaster erupted, drawing a line on the ground in front of the crowd. Many flinched, toes slightly singed. Micah held a blaster in each hand and glared at the crowd.

"We're not with them. Settle down!" Braden roared. "The one thing we guarantee you is your freedom to choose. It's light, go back if you want. Come with us. Go your own way. That's your business. We brought you all here so you could figure out what you want to do. Cowering in fear is no way to live. We offer you the opportunity to do more with your lives. If you want to go back to the beach and wait for the ocean terror, do that. If you come with us, you'll see new and different things. There will be some hardship. We have a long way to travel, but once we get there, you can start your lives fresh, with new people. You'll learn new skills, become more than you are."

"I'm a fisherman. It's all I know. Too old to turn my hand different." It was the initial instigator, speaking in a loud voice but not screaming, not inciting the crowd. "I'm going home. If it takes me, it takes me, but one thing I know for sure... I'll have fish for dinner tonight!" He started to elbow others aside as he pushed his way toward the downhill path.

More cries and others followed.

"I'm hungry. I'm going."

"Me, too."

"My partner's alive! I have to see him."

After the initial wave of people flooded down the hill, others trickled after them. Micah put her blasters away.

G-War never moved from the King of the Auroch's great head. Brandt had been ready to storm through the crowd if the people got too close to Braden.

Micah moved next to her partner. "At least they aren't afraid anymore," she said blandly. Braden snorted and shook his head.

Crabby and Yellowfin were among those who remained. "We have nothing back there. Even if our families are alive, not sure we want to live under the ocean. We'll try our hand in the dirt instead."

"And we'll make sure you get that opportunity," Braden said and stuck out his hand. They shook warmly.

When the dust settled, only about twenty people remained. Braden and Micah both thought the same thing: that was a manageable number. These were the younger ones, those who were willing to change, maybe even those who sought adventure. Everyone who had nothing to live for went back to the beach. Micah was right, though. At least they weren't afraid.

They'd embrace that as the victory and then celebrate when the good people of White Beach joined the eastern villages.

68 – Hope and Fear

There was no reason to wait. Braden hooked the cart behind Pack and told the people the next stop was the Village of Westerly.

'You'll have to slow your pace, my friend. The good people with us won't be able to keep up,' Braden said to Brandt over their mindlink.

'You lead, I will follow,' the King of the Aurochs answered.

Without fanfare, the group set off at a slow walk. Braden opened the map in his neural interface and did the calculations. *We'll make it before dark,* he thought. Holly confirmed it. Braden quickly closed the window by telling it to Sleep.

Did I need to use Old Tech to figure that out? He was instantly angry with himself. The easy way lured him in and trapped him. Micah listened as he struggled with his thoughts. She peeked at him, to make sure that he wasn't getting too depressed. He needed to wean himself off the Old Tech.

'What do you think of going back to New Sanctuary? Maybe we can take a couple turns to ourselves in the luxury of the Presidential Suite? And then we can have them take these things out of our heads?' Micah wrestled with the Old Tech, too. It was too easy to pull up something, read something else, get completely lost.

Sometimes the real world didn't exist. She had to drag herself back, remind herself that she was riding a horse. She needed to wean herself off it, too.

'I think we need to do something. When we get back, let's turn all four blasters in to the armory. Maybe you can get a recurve bow for yourself. I'd like that better. No Bat-Ravens, no need for the blasters,' Braden responded. To Micah, it sounded like he was talking himself through a problem, not discussing it with her.

'The Amazonians. Could we have stopped them from hurting Brandt without our

blasters? Look at the Old Tech vehicle that came from the sea. Would it have stopped if you didn't have your blaster?'

'That's the easy answer, Micah. I could have simply ridden into the ravine. It could not have followed. The Amazonians? We'll need the companions to better control themselves. If Brandt and Aadi hadn't rushed in, we wouldn't have been in that situation. Brandt and I wouldn't have been speared. Life would have been better. Unless the Amazonians are wearing McCullough tunics or leggings, we stay away from them. Brandt? Can I get you to agree?' Braden thought through the battle again and again while he recovered. He always came to the same conclusion. The only way to win was not to fight.

'Yes, my friends. I made a mistake that I shall not make again. We cannot save the Amazonians from themselves. Only if they ask, will I try to help.' Brandt was determined. His mistake almost cost Braden his life. The King of the Aurochs was harder on himself than anyone else could ever be. His run into the rainforest caused him many sleepless nights.

'And me, too, Master Humans. I shall be far more judicious when assisting the Lizard Men,' Aadi added.

"I have an idea!" Braden blurted out loud. White Beach villagers walking nearby were startled. They looked oddly at him.

'I have an idea,' Braden said, switching back to his thought voice. *'In order to help us help ourselves, why don't we train those who travel with us as an army? I've seen a couple demonstrations in the north. I've often thought how an army should fight. We can train as we walk, you know, attack formations, defensive formations. We've seen how the Amazonians fight. We have enough people. They all have spears or tridents. We can fight back in a better way, where we won't have to rely on the Old Tech.'*

Micah was having a hard time keeping up as Braden's thoughts flowed. She watched him stroke his braid as he continued.

'Two ranks…low and high… a line of spear points that no one can get through…' Braden imagined how the fishermen could hold back the larger Amazonians. *'If the enemy didn't have too many warriors, then the fishermen could win.'*

'They can also win if they don't go anywhere near the rainforest,' Micah

interjected. *'Do you really want to play with their lives?'*

'You're right, lover. We can't play, but we need to be ready. The alternative is that we count on Old Tech to keep us safe.' Braden reached under his tunic to feel the scar across his ribs. Max was ambling, but the villagers were keeping up. Those who left White Beach behind were hearty.

He looked at the individual faces, forcing himself to take in each person's details. Tall and thin, a scar on his forehead. Crabby, bow legged and sturdy, face tanned like leather. The young boy, Yellowfin, ready with a smile. Hope brought him a new happiness.

No, Braden thought, *he couldn't play with these people's lives.* Maybe they could practice a spear wall as they got closer to the Village of Bliss. Bliss, Coldstream, and Greentree were close to the rainforest. Braden didn't know if the Amazonians would attack. The least they could do is help the people to help themselves.

He couldn't let anything happen to these villagers. They put their trust in him and the companions. They left their homes because of him.

'We won't let anything happen to them!' Brandt's thought voice boomed in his head. The ground trembled as Brandt snorted and ran a wide circle around the group. *'See? Is there anything that can get past me? I'm the King of the Aurochs!'* Brandt launched himself into the air, shaking his mighty head.

'If you don't want a Hillcat clawing your ear to shreds, you'll settle down.' G-War's voice came through the mindlink clearly, cutting Brandt's playfulness short. Braden and Micah looked closer. The 'cat was sprawled across Brandt's head. His orange ears were back, his tail puffed out as he readied himself to be thrown to the ground.

Brandt snorted in laughter and stopped. He held his head high, then bowed gracefully to the group of humans.

"Brandt, King of the Aurochs, is showing you that he is here to protect you all," Micah said in a loud voice. The villagers recovered from their initial alarm at the great beast's antics. They returned his courtesy by bowing as they passed.

"Thank you, my friend! We can ask for no one of greater stature to take responsibility for us," Micah said as she bowed in her saddle.

Skirill stopped circling high above the group and dove toward the Aurochs. As he accelerated toward the ground, he banked sharply, cutting a tight corner around the group. He completed his circle, then back winged to a soft landing on one of Brandt's horns.

'What fun!' Aadi exclaimed as he swam serenely alongside Max. Age and wisdom kept him from any masterful displays of physical prowess.

Plus, he was a Tortoid, and they didn't do those things.

Braden spurred Max forward for a quick gallop to the top of the next rolling hill, where he turned back, the sun shining brightly behind him. The villagers squinted as they looked at the man on his horse, the one who was leading them to new lives, lives filled with the promise of a bright future.

69 – A Long Road Ahead

The people of Westerly welcomed the villagers of White Beach with food and friendship. There was no better reception as the villagers had eaten little since they left their homes. The two groups shared laughs as well as harrowing stories of adventure.

Braden and Micah were the consistent theme throughout all conversations. Strangers with strange creatures came out of nowhere to show them how life could be. As evening approached, the people from two villages gave a hearty cheer for the Traders from Warren Deep. Braden was humbled. Micah felt his discomfort. The crowd grew silent as they waited.

They wanted him to talk.

'Go ahead, lover. Tell them what their future looks like,' Micah encouraged him.

He nodded to her, then found a stump to stand on.

"Great people of Westerly and White Beach. I thank you both for your kind words and for your willingness to share with each other. Micah and I only opened the door. You walked through it and only you can make your futures.

"As a trader, I've seen that people who work together get further in life. Everyone is good at something. When you trade, you take what you're good at and share with someone who's good at something else. Trade is the way we get the most from everyone. Maybe someone makes more or better. That doesn't matter. What you do and how you do it does.

"Trust is at the heart of every trade. In the north, we have the Caravan Guild that guarantees trade. We don't need that in the south, because here, when we put our hand to something, we stand behind it. When we shake on the deal, it's done.

"There are three Trade Laws: Negotiate, Agree, Deliver. It's as simple as that. But how do we find others to trade with?

"The King of the Aurochs has partnered with us. His people are pulling a wagon right now from Dwyer to Coldstream. Soon, the wagons will come all the way here. Westerly will anchor this end of the trade route. You'll see woodwork like you've never seen before. You'll trade for rope, light and strong, for metal shovels and axes. You don't even know you need something until you see it. Bring your best. Get the best.

"We've come a long way already. The villages--Dwyer in the east, then McCullough, the Amazonians, Greentree, Coldstream, Bliss, and now Westerly--are all committed to the trade route. We've been marking a road for future traders to follow.

"What does that mean for you? Soon, there will be more wagons and regular trade. I see a wagon coming through every ten turns. I see people learning more about each other. I see you, working, making the most of yourselves, making things better for your families. I see some of you riding in the wagons, being the links that hold this world together.

"And I see friends, friends at every stop, smiles and greetings when we enter a village. That's what was missing. Visitors aren't to be feared, but embraced. We've lived with too much fear. I say no more." Braden ended quietly. No one made a sound. The speech was long for Braden, but everyone listened. The silence continued for a few heartbeats, then the crowd broke into applause. They stood and cheered, moving closer to him.

'Nice speech. I think you have admirers,' Micah thought, giving Braden a big smile. He nodded to her. They'd be traveling with a large number of people. They'd have to have regular food, water, and bathroom stops. They'd have to find food each day.

'We'll share the duties, with the villagers, too. Everyone will contribute. You can hunt for us all because no one does it better than you and G-War. Ten turns is all we'll need. Don't worry, we have a lot of smart people with us. I think we're going to learn a lot on this trip,' Micah added with a final nod.

"We leave at sunrise. Bring what you have to. Try to carry enough food for the day." Braden ended awkwardly, waving as he finished. He got down from the stump, but wasn't able to escape. He was intercepted by the throng, everyone asking questions at the same time. He calmed them down, then went through one by one.

It was well into the night when he freed himself from the last of the villagers. Many changed their minds back to going with Braden and Micah. According to Braden's tired mind, he counted forty people, give or take, that would travel east with them. He'd count them at sunrise and then they'd see who was ready to walk across the Plains of Propiscius.

'Hungry...' was the last voice Braden heard before he drifted off to sleep.

70 – The Walk to Bliss

Only thirty-seven stalwart souls stood in the dawn. A few others turned out to wave good-bye. Not good-bye, but good luck. They'd be back. Braden and Micah didn't wait. They mounted Max and Speckles and turned their noses toward the sun.

Skirill flew ahead, Aadi swam alongside, and G-War, having hunted during the night, was plump and resting on the King's head.

"Why do you let him do that?" Braden asked.

'My friend stood on my back to fight off the Bat-Ravens. He also makes it possible for me to talk with all the companions,' Brandt replied. *'Most of the time, I forget he's up there. He weighs as much as the morning fog.'*

Braden and Micah both looked at the great horns towering over them. Compared to those, everything else was insignificant.

They looked back at the cart where two new mothers and their three small children rode. There was a limited amount of food and some personal items that would have been too heavy to carry on people's backs. The villagers from White Beach carried all of their own gear. They had already traveled two days by foot. They had nothing left to put in the cart.

Braden and Micah determined that routine would serve the group best. They hiked at a steady pace for half the morning, then they'd take a break, shift things about. They'd hike until mid-daylight when they would break again. Then they powered through until early evening. Braden and the companions would race ahead to hunt and build a fire. When the villagers arrived, their meal was cooking.

Skirill flew back and forth to keep everyone going in the right direction. The King of the Aurochs ensured that the road was passable for their cart.

Braden and Micah let the children ride with them, in turns. Maybe that was a necessary import from the north to the south. They needed horses for personal travel and for small caravans. They didn't want to break up the Earthshaker Herd. Braden saw a time in the near future where all of them could be plying the routes at the same time.

Yes, horses. They had to return north. Braden wasn't ready, like Micah wasn't ready to return to Trent. Braden knew for sure that he didn't want to bring Old Tech, unless he could have New Sanctuary manufacture something that didn't look like Old Tech but would fetch a good price. He'd need it to trade for a herd of horses and a tent big enough to cover them all as they traveled through the Great Desert.

'Whatcha thinking about?' Micah asked. Braden looked at her in surprise. She knew what he was thinking about, unless his thoughts were too jumbled to make sense. They rambled, even for him. He laughed to himself. So much to do.

'What do the next couple cycles hold for us, Micah?'

'More than you know, lover. They hold change. Many changes, while much will also remain the same.'

'I'm not following you. I want to go to the Traveler, once Holly says we can. We need to go north, get horses and bring them back. I would like to see your village, and maybe others in the east to join the trade routes. The people with us will help build up Greentree and maybe even Dwyer. We'll have a smithy and then as young men and women learn, they'll set up more metalworks, woodworks, and the towns will grow. Maybe the Amazonians can resolve their differences, end their war. That bothers me the most. I'm not worried about the Bat-Ravens. It'll be generations before they're a threat again.' Braden's thoughts started coming together. He was learning to think far into the future.

'Sounds like a good plan,' Brandt added. Braden thought he was just talking with Micah, but he never knew for sure. She was good at the thought voice. He used it, but didn't think about it.

'Clearly,' the 'cat said. *'Maybe you need to listen better.'*

'Hey! Can't a man think to himself?' Braden smiled, knowing the answer to

his question was no, he couldn't think to himself. Those days were long past. What did G-War mean with that last quip?

'Braden. I'm pregnant.'

Braden stopped Max and sat there. Sparks appeared in front of his eyes. A loud roaring filled his ears. He felt hot.

If Micah was a normal woman, she may have worried, but she had the benefit of the companions. She had the benefit of the mindlink. She could see and feel her partner. He had to think through it and then he'd be fine. She knew that a part of him was ecstatic. The part that was confused was his planning side. To him, this changed everything. To her, this changed very little. Hadn't he been raised on the trade routes?

'When,' was all he managed to say. She threw back her head and laughed. Villagers nearby looked at her, but their spirits were high and they joined her, not knowing what she found funny.

'I think our first time,' she answered.

'So you were procreating.' Aadi had finally joined the conversation.

'I guess so, Master Aadi, I mean Aadi. I guess so.'

Brandt thundered up to Max and stood with his horns dangerously close to Braden. The Villagers stopped, not knowing why.

The King of the Aurochs locked eyes with Braden. *We shall raise our bulls to be strong, lead this world into the future!'* he bellowed in his thought voice.

'You, too, huh?' Braden mumbled. Micah was starting to get angry with him. She wasn't going to allow the men to sit around the campfire lamenting the misfortune of their families.

Micah spurred Speckles forward. The cart bounced along and the people inside clung tightly. She pulled up next to him. He still hadn't moved.

She made a fist and reared back.

'This will be fun to watch,' G-War announced over the mindlink.

'What? Oh, hey! What are you doing?' Braden leaned away from her. He heard the companions laughing. Micah pursed her lips. If she hadn't been pulling the cart, she would have been able to get closer to him and he probably would have already been punched.

'If I may extend my hearty congratulations to you both and you, great King, on your incredible news, on the new additions to our family!' Aadi said. He was the wise one.

Braden finally internalized the message. He was going to be a father and they were going to be parents. The child would be raised by all the companions. What child wouldn't want that? He smiled, thinking back on the joys of his childhood. He jumped off Max and pulled Micah off Pack into his arms. Her eyes sparkled as they embraced each other and their future.

He let her go and looked at the gathered villagers. "We're pregnant!" he shouted. The villagers cheered and pressed in to hug and shake hands. Then they quieted down and stood there, looking at each other.

"Well, shall we continue? We have a great deal of daylight left. I think we'll reach Village Bliss in another two turns?" He avoided the Old Tech. One turn or three turns, it didn't matter. He urged everyone forward and the group started walking again, slowly at first, but then with a purpose.

'Will he have his mother's ability to mindlink?' Braden asked G-War, who seemed to know most about these things.

'Thank the heavens they both will. More like Bronwyn and less like you.'

"Both?" Braden and Micah exclaimed out loud.

"Why didn't you say anything?" Micah asked G-War sharply.

'It was unimportant. Before you ask, a boy and a girl, both are already quite loud with their thought voices. It's getting to be a great deal of noise, so if you would, please get your children under control. Hungry. Tired. Hungry. Warm. It's incessant.'

"Ass!" Micah said aloud. *'Those are my children!'*

'OUR children,' came five voices in unison. The warmth of their commitment washed over her.

'We approach the area of the Amazonian attack. Be sharp!' Skirill cautioned.

Instantly, they were alert. Brandt ran forward under Skirill's direction to leave a trail further north than the last time they passed. Braden urged the villagers to quicken their pace. They needed to prepare defenses, just in case.

He gave Micah a proud smile, and then bolted ahead. He had to hunt and find a place they could defend. Brandt joined him, jogging easily to keep pace with a galloping Max.

71 – Traders' Rest

Skirill suggested the edge of a stream, not far away, but due north. They changed direction under the Hawkoid's guidance and soon arrived. It wasn't a stream at all, but a wide river. It came from the north and turned east where Braden and Brandt stood, before splitting into multiple branches that headed south into the rainforest. They had crossed those on previous trips without issue. If they had to cross at this point, it may not be possible. The river's flow was strong. Max and Brandt waded side by side into an eddy pool where they both drank deeply.

Sparkles from the sun reflected from fish scales. Braden shaded his eyes. There were fish and plenty of them. There were twenty fishermen who would soon arrive, and they would get their chance to provide for the group and to teach a little about fishing to the rest.

The riverbanks were heavy with trees and bushes. G-War, perched on Brandt's head, confirmed that there was game to be had. With that thought, the 'cat ran down the Aurochs' back and jumped onto dry land. He quickly disappeared into the undergrowth.

"This looks like the place, my friend. Can you dig a hole for the outhouse? There will be no house, of course…" Braden laughed at his own joke. Life on the road was rough. Women and men traveled together. They enforced personal space, and no one was allowed to look while others relieved themselves. It was important in keeping the peace. When they arrived at the end of this journey, everyone needed their dignity intact.

Braden hobbled Max on the riverbank where he could graze on the thick, green grass. With his bow in hand, he joined G-War where he enjoyed flushing a pair of wild boar. He took one with a close shot, but the second he took down while it was running and some distance away. He was proud of that shot. The wound on his chest had finally healed to where he felt no pain, felt no limit to his draw on his recurve bow.

Braden was still cleaning the first hog when the villagers arrived. Two from Westerly immediately relieved him of the cleaning duties. Others went to work finding deadfall for the fire. But the villagers from White Beach, they watched the river flow, mesmerized by the sight of fish. Once they decided, they lined up along the beach and turned to using their tridents to spear the fish.

Micah had to stop them once they landed more than the group needed.

"We'll smoke the hogs to give us a supply of meat to take with us." Braden told those preparing the spit. The fishermen said that their catch could also be smoked. They'd show the land-locked folk how.

The competition for best meal commenced. A number of the farmers headed into the woods to look for edible tubers and plants. They returned shortly after finding success.

Pots materialized and they started two smaller fires for stew.

The only thing they lacked was bread, but they didn't miss it. They celebrated Braden and Micah's announcement and they celebrated the opportunity to fish.

Braden didn't want to spoil things, so he waited until after they ate. He gathered everyone together.

"Just south of here, we were attacked by the Amazonians." Braden lifted his tunic and shirt, turning so everyone could see the ugly scar. "I don't think they'll come this far north, but they could move through the woods. I think we need to post a watch. Everyone have your spears ready. Micah and I will have our weapons ready, too. I don't think we'll need them, but better to have them and not need them than to need them and be caught unaware."

The villagers nodded, almost indifferently. Those from White Beach had lived through the night terrors. Watching for a flesh and blood enemy was not too much to ask. They accepted it and started mapping out the watches.

Braden was happy that he didn't have to say anything else. After they worked out the details between all the villagers, a few people came to

Braden and Micah.

Crabby led the group, mostly White Beach villagers, but a couple from Westerly. "Good place here. We want to stay," Crabby said.

"How long? We need to keep moving to get to safer areas, Bliss, Coldstream, and Greentree." Braden was okay with a longer break. The villagers from White Beach had traveled four long turns on foot, although they didn't seem worn out.

They weren't.

"No. I mean we stay, build a village. We have fisherfolk and farmers, everything we need. This'll be a good trading stop. By foot, it's barely more than three turns from Westerly and another couple to Bliss?" Braden nodded. Crabby continued, "Imagine fields over there, with grain for bread. Right here, we catch and process fish. The woods on both sides of the river for game. There are fifteen of us ready to settle right now."

Braden and Micah looked at each other. There was no reason not to start a new village. They hoped the people would help out the already established villages, but freedom of opportunity was what they had promised.

"I can't think of a better place to build a new village," Micah said, not waiting for Braden to answer.

"Congratulations," Braden said with a smile, offering his hand to Crabby. They shook, firmly. "Sleep on it and after sunrise, maybe you can give it a name. We'll proudly add it to the trade route maps."

Braden and Micah finally had time to themselves. "How could I not have noticed?" he asked simply. "How long have you known? Never mind. The 'cat knew, didn't he?"

"Yes. You've been busy. You always notice me, but the change has been gradual. What, did you think I was eating too much?" she said without accusing Braden.

"I didn't notice. I don't care about that!" He was defensive. She punched him softly in the arm.

Sleep, then they'd come up with a new plan over the next few turns. Everything was changing, yet nothing changed. Ever since he met Micah, he simply hung on as the raft of life rushed down the whitewater rapids. Things used to be so calm.

'*G?*' Braden asked as an afterthought.

'*Aadi moved into the forest to watch over us all. The Amazonians won't harm him,*' the 'cat answered.

'*Sleep well, friends. I've got this,*' Aadi assured them.

72 – River Crook

With the departure of so many from the caravan, they didn't leave with the sunrise. They waited to make sure things were sorted out. Braden gave them his trusty shovel that had helped them cross the Great Desert. He also gave them all of the remaining Amazonian rope.

Their excitement grew as the two groups intermingled and said their goodbyes. Braden assured them that with the trade routes, someone would always be coming through. They'd left a good trail from Westerly for anyone to follow. They were going to continue building the road to Village Bliss, then to the rest of the villages on their new trade route.

Soon, someone would be back, and maybe with a wagon load of implements--plows, axes, maybe even a saw blade. Braden was most proud that these people saw the possibilities and seized them. Crabby was going to be a great leader. He watched as the settlers looked over their new home and made plans.

Braden cautioned them to set up a watch each night, and keep their spears close.

Aadi told the companions that there had been no movement in the woods along the river. He even looked for signs that the Lizard Men had been there, but couldn't find anything. Braden didn't share this with Crabby. He wanted them to stay alert. Maybe someday soon, the Amazonian war would end and people could sleep soundly. Until then, he wanted them ready to keep themselves safe.

The settlers stood back as the remaining villagers shouldered their burdens and prepared for the morning's hike. Braden and Micah sat on their horses, while G-War curled up in his usual spot on Brandt's head. Skirill watched from a distant tree limb. Aadi stayed close to the cart.

Traders did not like saying goodbye. Successful trades needed to be repeated. They vowed to return. The best traders always found a way to make it back, bringing more or better of what the people wanted. As Braden waved, Crabby came up to him for one last handshake.

"River Crook is the name. It's where there's a crook in the river before it divides into the five streams. White Beach? The beach is white. I'm afraid we're not very imaginative."

"River Crook is what it shall be. What matters is that you named it and you will make it what it will be. We will see you again and soon."

They waved and set off at their regular pace. Twenty-two villagers remained with the caravan, which included the two women and three children in the cart. It wasn't as many as they planned for, but more than the villages had.

'It'll be what it is. These are good people. They'll be welcomed wherever they decide to settle,' Micah said simply over their mindlink.

"Of course you are right, partner mine." Braden nodded and gave Max a nudge forward. They trotted ahead of the people as he looked for the best way across the streams ahead.

Skirill helped, but he couldn't judge the depth. Brandt jogged ahead and tried a number of crossing sites before Braden arrived. They picked the best ones and marked them with boulders and freshly scored earth. They continued until the route across the streams was easily followed.

Skirill flew ahead to check on Village Bliss. Braden thought they were less than a full turn away. He didn't verify that with the Old Tech, because he refused to open his neural implant. The Old Tech didn't scare him, but his reliance on it did.

The companions made sure that he knew what he needed to know.

'I see no people at Bliss. It looks like the village is abandoned,' Skirill told him. He hadn't been flying long, so maybe they were less than a turn away. But if the people were gone, Braden didn't need to rush in. He was afraid to ask, but he had to.

'Do you see any bodies, Ess?'

'No. I see no one. Let me get closer.'

'Be careful, Ess! Don't get too close to the rainforest,' Braden cautioned.

'Master Human, if I may. Zalastar or Akhmiyar would have warned the humans away if it looked like the fighting would get close. They may have contacted Bronwyn so she could tell the humans to run.' The Tortoid's logic was sound. Zalastar was a good friend to the humans and wouldn't let them get in the middle of a battle.

'Nothing. It looks like they simply left and not even in a hurry. I think Aadi is right,' the Hawkoid agreed. He didn't see anything that suggested the Amazonians had attacked Village Bliss.

'Let's head straight for Coldstream. We can be there in three turns if we don't dally,' Micah agreed and encouraged the seventeen people walking to move more quickly. They obliged her when she explained that Bliss had been abandoned, and they were on their way to Coldstream. She shared the good news that Bliss wasn't a victim of the Amazonian war.

For the next three turns, they limited their stops, slept briefly at night, and always stayed alert.

Their arrival at Coldstream wasn't what they expected.

Amazonians were standing guard, just inside the rainforest. They lined the heavier trees, but they faced inward. The villagers welcomed the group, not with cheers but questions.

"Did you see them? Are you the people from Bliss?"

Once Braden got the people to make sense, he discovered a grim truth. Their guess at what happened to the villagers from Bliss was wrong. They'd been taken by hostile Amazonians. Akhmiyar and his people were standing guard to guarantee the safety of Coldstream. Bronwyn had come through with Tanner and Candela. That's when Akhmiyar showed up. The little girl was shocked at the turn of events. If she only had the chance to talk with all the Amazonians, she was sure she could have changed their minds.

Akhmiyar tried to convince her that she would not have made a difference.

Only the Amazonians could resolve their differences.

Bronwyn had left only two turns prior with the older cow Aurochs and the trader couple. They hurried away to inform the Greentree villagers of current events. Akhmiyar assured her that Greentree and the other villages were well within the area that Zalastar controlled.

The good people of Westerly and the few that remained from White Beach committed to staying in Coldstream, to help them should a hostile force of Amazonians arrive. The extra people were welcomed by Coldstream.

Braden and Micah looked to Aadi, who led them to Akhmiyar. After talking with the Amazonian leader, they were convinced what needed to be done. They had to go after the villagers. Braden didn't want Micah to come along.

That earned him a hard punch in the chest. It was lucky he was healed.

She negotiated some sweetened pork and with that, they committed to leaving at first light. Skirill and Brandt would travel to Greentree, catch up with Bronwyn, and rally the Aurochs. Max and Speckles would remain in Coldstream and await the companions' return. Aadi and G-War would accompany Braden and Micah, with Akhmiyar and a band of his warriors leading the way into the Amazon.

They prepared to travel light, carrying the absolute minimum. Akhmiyar assured them that they didn't have to travel far, although the Amazonian way of measuring distance was lost on the humans. They simply agreed. They'd get there when they got there.

73 – The Rescue

It was still dark when Akhmiyar roused them from their sleep. Braden wasn't sure if it was past the middle of the night. The Amazonian told them that he'd received a report that the enemy was moving, so they needed to hurry before they got too far into the depths of the rainforest.

They put their weapons on, Braden with his recurve bow across his back, his remaining hardwood arrows in the quiver, two blasters, and a long knife on his belt. He filled his pouch with numbweed and mushrooms. He was ready.

The scabbard for Micah's sword wasn't made for running, so she slung it across her back instead. This freed her hands in case she needed her blasters. They were fully charged. She did not bring the recharger. If they couldn't rescue them with what they had, then they couldn't be rescued.

Braden heard her grim thoughts, but didn't comment. He agreed with them. There was only one chance to get this right.

They were ready quickly. Akhmiyar and his warriors set off at a brisk pace. The humans struggled to keep up as their feet weren't made for slopping through the tree roots, underbrush, and muck. Aadi grasped a roped that one of the Amazonians carried. He floated as he was pulled along. He often bounced off trees, but his shell protected him.

G-War raced through the tree branches. Judging by what little they could see, Braden revised his opinion of how well the 'cat could see in the dark. He had no problems keeping up and on occasion raced ahead.

Akhmiyar stopped so the humans could catch their breath. Each time, Akhmiyar told Aadi that the humans needed to be quiet. Braden and Micah felt bad, but they couldn't see and the footing was treacherous. Aadi suggested the Amazonians carry them, which they reluctantly agreed to. Braden told Micah to protect the babies, but she was already ahead of him on that.

When their human eyes didn't have to look at the ground, they saw the rainforest in amazing detail. When they were running, they missed much of what the rainforest was.

As sunrise approached, Akhmiyar told them that they were close. Braden wanted as much detail as they could give him so he could best devise a plan of attack. Micah knew that his plan would be good. He was gifted at tactics, even though he detested fighting.

The villagers were holding the Amazonian enemy back. The Bliss villagers couldn't and wouldn't move quickly through the trees and swamps.

Akhmiyar didn't have a way to see the enemy. He knew the villagers were there because of his keen hearing and sensing the rainforest around him. That didn't prevent G-War from going ahead. With the sunrise, he ran, flitting from branch to branch as quick as a bird.

Braden and Micah got down from the Amazonians who'd been carrying them.

Not many heartbeats later, G-War shared his view of the villagers, huddled together in a mass with the larger Amazonians circling them. The Lizard Men used their spears as prods on the people, but they refused to move. They were too tired, too sore, maybe even too fed up. As Akhmiyar and his warriors stealthily moved forward, Braden and Micah had time to think.

'They are too close to the villagers for us to use our blasters. I can use my bow, but can't shoot fast enough. There are too many. We can't let Akhmiyar and his warriors engage. They are outnumbered. As long as they're fighting, we can't use our blasters. Aadi, can you ask Akhmiyar to wait? We don't have a plan.'

'I'm afraid it's too late,' Aadi replied.

They had cleared a final row of trees when they were spotted. Those closest turned and readied to throw their spears.

Aadi swam forward to get in between the two groups of Amazonians. A hurled spear bounced off his shell and ricocheted harmlessly into the trees. Akhmiyar and his warriors crouched, preparing to thrust their spears. Behind the enemy, the villagers cowered.

Braden jumped to the side until he had a clear line of sight in front of the villagers. He could fire across the front of the group. He pulled the trigger and instantly let go. A tight beam of light hit an enemy warrior in the chest.

He went down.

The others turned and threw their spears as one, at Braden.

He stepped behind the tree he'd used to brace the blaster for his first shot.

Akhmiyar and his warriors rushed forward into the unarmed enemy. Each spear found a target and five Amazonian enemy wriggled on the points as they died. Others stepped from around the villagers.

"Get down!" Braden yelled. The villagers went to their knees and huddled over top each other.

A spear thrust forward and Akhmiyar went down. The point had driven through his back leg. He lost his spear, but held the shaft of his enemy's weapon to keep him from pulling it out.

Braden picked another target and dropped him with a short beam from his blaster. Micah had moved to the other side, to the left of Akhmiyar, which gave her a good angle to shoot without endangering the villagers. She aimed at the Amazonian who wrestled with Akhmiyar and pulled the trigger. The enemy toppled over.

Akhmiyar pulled the spear from his leg and crouched, ready for another attacker. His warriors were bunched up, parrying and thrusting with the enemy, neither gaining an advantage.

Braden moved to find a clean shot. He took it and another Amazonian died. One of Akhmiyar's warriors was stabbed in the throat and he went down. Then another. Then one of the enemy.

Micah took two more shots, wounding two of the enemy. Braden kept moving, trying to clear his targets.

Akhmiyar and another were wounded. Two of his warriors were dead. The enemy still had double their number in the fight. When they rushed Akhmiyar, Braden and Micah each shot one.

The enemy Amazonians decided that if they were to die, they'd take the humans with them. Not the ones with the deadly Old Tech, but the unarmed villagers.

G-War flew from a tree, landing on the Amazonian furthest from Braden and Micah. He attacked with a Hillcat scream, shredding before leaping away. Braden and Micah ran forward, shooting at a range of only an arm-span, killing one, then another. The last Amazonian turned and dashed into the shadows, but was tripped up by a flying orange fur ball. Braden continued around the villagers until he was over the Amazonian, who lay stunned from his fall.

Aadi rushed forward and hovered finger widths from the creature's face.

He tried to push the Tortoid away, but Aadi swam back, time and time again. Then he delivered a focused thunderclap, from that close, directly into the Amazonian's head, which cracked from the force of the blow.

"Aadi!" Micah exclaimed.

'Sorry, sorry. He wasn't very cooperative, I'm afraid.'

"It's over. It's over." Braden put his hand on their arms and shoulders as he urged the villagers to stand. Two didn't. Blood ran from spear wounds that the desperate enemy had delivered at the last moment.

"How many others?" Micah asked.

"Two more, right after they herded us into the rainforest. We lost four total," an elder lamented. "But we would have all been lost if you hadn't come for us."

"You can thank Akhmiyar and his warriors. If it wasn't for them, we wouldn't be here." Braden nodded to Akhmiyar, who was on one knee.

Braden had forgotten about his horrific wound.

He rushed over and pulled numbweed from his pouch. He applied it to ease the pain. Then he pulled the numbweed out and sewed up the wound using hairs from Max's tail. And he reapplied numbweed. Akhmiyar never flinched through the entire process.

'These Amazonians are tough! I'm glad they're on our side,' Braden told Micah in his thought voice. *'How about you? Are you okay?'*

'We're just fine.' She smiled at him as he stitched a shallow wound on the other warrior's front arm. G-War sat and watched them both, while Aadi talked with Akhmiyar.

'Master Humans, with the war, Akhmiyar is very interested in your medical skills. Could you teach him how you repaired their wounds?'

"Yes, no problem. I can teach him, but I'm afraid they won't be able to make the numbweed. You need fire for that. But we can make it for them, especially if they can bring us the bushes. You can show them which ones I'm talking about."

Braden and Micah looked over the villagers. Some scratches and plenty of bruises, but nothing that would keep them from making the journey to freedom.

Akhmiyar limped slightly, but led them on a shorter route out of the rainforest. They were far to the west of Coldstream, but not quite to Bliss. They decided to continue walking to Coldstream. Village Bliss remained in contested territory. Until it was safe, they couldn't go back.

Akhmiyar said that he and his two warriors would travel inside the rainforest and meet them in Coldstream. They said their good-byes and watched as the Amazonians faded into the dark of the rainforest day.

Braden felt bad making Micah walk all that way. Skirill and Brandt were too far away to be any help, so he held her hand as they strolled. She said it was refreshing and she should do more of it. She felt like she sat too much. Braden looked closely at her and he could see that she was showing. How had he missed that?

Maybe he didn't look at her with such a critical eye. He didn't care that she had scars down both arms and on her neck. He didn't care if she had a thin waist. She was his partner, an equal who challenged him.

He liked to think that he was a far better man than the one who rode from the north, seeking fame and fortune. He looked at the villagers walking along quietly. Before, they wouldn't have been rescued because no one would have known they were taken. They had a place to go because the trade route had been established and people were introduced by way of their trade goods.

Although the Amazonians blamed him for the war, he suspected that it was there all along. If it weren't for him, then something else would have been the catalyst. The war was inevitable, he realized. And he hoped that he was helping to bring it to a swift and sound conclusion. He hated taking lives, but they gave him no choice. Kill or be killed. He wasn't about to be killed. There was too much to do.

He had children on the way and he wanted more than anything that they grow up in a world free from conflict, where people made their lives better by working with others.

He'd gone a long way toward creating that world. He and Micah, that was. He couldn't have done any of it without her.

She gripped his hand tightly, knowing that the future was going to be okay. She felt a furry body run into her from behind. G-War rubbed against her leg, almost tripping her.

'I have so much to teach my kittens, so you take care of them. It won't be too much longer now before we get a look. What's with the humans and their hairless kittens? Maybe we don't want a look until they are more presentable.' G-War contemplated life with little ones around. He decided that it would be okay. If they pulled his tail, he'd give Braden a good scratch. There's wasn't much of the human's body left unscratched. In that, he and Braden were alike. They both looked rough.

'One too many battles, my friend,' Braden said over their mindlink.

As Braden didn't care how Micah looked, she didn't care how he looked. She knew where nearly every one of his scars came from. She was there, cleaning them for him as he cleaned her wounds.

"Crap, Braden! If you would have told me what dangerous business trading was, I would have never let you take me away from that lake!"

Craig Martelle

74 – Settling In

After the rescue of the Bliss villagers, Coldstream was overwhelmed with people. The new additions from White Beach and Westerly readily packed up for the trip to Greentree and McCullough. Even some people from Bliss joined them. Leaving Coldstream and the sweetened pork behind, Braden and Micah rode on Max and Speckles as they continued leading the caravan of refugees east.

Brandt and Skirill found Bronwyn and the new traders. They had taken good care of the wagon. All was well. Everyone made progress, although the smithy was still working on a formula for the strongest metal. They had not produced much, but expected over the next few moons to leap forward. Tom thought they were close to success. Maybe Braden and Micah would take some of the metal to New Sanctuary and have it analyzed to see exactly what Tom needed to do.

With his growing family, he was more inclined to find an Old Tech solution. He only wanted the best world for his children. He also learned that they could not have recovered the villagers without the blasters, or freed Brandt, or destroyed the Bat-Ravens.

The good guys needed Old Tech weapons. If they didn't use them for the right purpose, the King of the Aurochs would run them over. Braden shuddered at the thought. The King was a magnificently large creature.

With Micah at his side, for the first time in a long time, he opened his neural implant. Holly immediately greeted him.

Braden requested that a number of saw blades be manufactured that they could pick up the next time they were in New Sanctuary. Holly said the wheel hubs for the wagons were ready, and the printed books had been manufactured and were ready for pick up as well.

Braden asked about Cygnus VI. Holly said that the data had been

264

transmitting nonstop since they last talked with the outpost, although it wouldn't be analyzed until after the download was complete. The humans seemed to be in good spirits knowing that the last four hundred cycles of work was not wasted, and they looked forward to transporting to Cygnus VII when the matter transfer equipment was functional.

He wasn't comfortable with ancients and the Old Tech at New Sanctuary. Not until they had the failsafe in place. Since they didn't know what the war prevention failsafe looked like, it could be quite some time before the last remaining humans from the before time could return home.

"Stop worrying, lover. It will be okay." She couldn't hear his thoughts when he used his neural implant, but she guessed. The troubled look on his face told her all she needed. He agreed, wished Holly a good night, and closed the window. "Let's take some time, let other people lead for a while."

He looked at her and sighed. If he could only do that.

75 – The Traders Return

During Braden and Micah's trip to the west coast, Candela and Tanner made two complete passes through the villages from Dwyer to Coldstream. Each time, they improved their trades. They traveled with a full wagon, trading all the food while it was still fresh. The Aurochs made the trips go quickly.

Bronwyn made sure they had no problems with any creature they came across. She kept the Aurochs happy and they made her happy. She spent most of her time riding on the older cow, stroking her ears and rubbing her neck.

They even successfully traded with the Amazonians. Bronwyn shared that many warriors were fighting and it disturbed her. Zalastar personally assured them that the road was safe and would always remain so. Trade with the humans was critical as they needed all the tunics and limb protection they could get. These identified Zalastar and his loyalists to the average human. The friendly Amazonians were committed to keeping the humans out of the war.

The raid on Village Bliss had not yet happened, but it wouldn't change his commitment, only the reality of the situation. Akhmiyar took action to protect Coldstream, to ensure the conservative Amazonians came no farther east.

Having completed their trades, Candela and Tanner wished everyone well, packed up, and in the spirit of tradition, they left at sunrise for Village McCullough. The trip was less than a single daylight thanks to the Aurochs. The younger cow pulled the wagon, while the older cow led the way, with Bronwyn safely astride her wide neck.

The wagon was filled with vegetables and meats, but most significantly, two new shovels made from Tom's latest metal. These were sturdy and his best products yet. He said he could produce many of these in a single day. He celebrated with his crew as they had worked relentlessly for moons to produce one functional shovel. Everything else paled in comparison.

The traders knew that Tom's smithy would be the single most influential trading stop in the south. They made sure he received the choicest crops and extra tidbits whenever they passed through.

As the Canavan, as Candela and Tanner called their caravan, approached McCullough, a familiar figure flew overhead.

"Skirill!" yelled the little girl, waving her arms furiously. Skirill swooped low to pass over them then circled and with the cow's permission, landed on one of her horns.

"Good to see you, 'ronwyn!" the Hawkoid said in his best human speech. Bronwyn crawled forward until she perched on top of the Aurochs' head where she could scratch Skirill's chest and neck.

'Your feathers have grown in very well! You are the most magnificent bird in all the land,' she exclaimed in her thought voice.

'You are also too kind, precious one. The others are in McCullough and await your arrival. They have much to share.'

'I know of the war. I know it's terrible.' She hesitated. Skirill knew that she was deep in his mind, looking at the images of their travels. *'Oh no! My Brandt...more scars. Even Braden.'* She sat up straight, surprise on her face.

'Micah?' she asked. The Hawkoid bobbed his head happily as the Aurochs broke into a run. Skirill jumped from the bouncing horn before he was thrown off. The young cow pulling the wagon also started running. The trader couple was alarmed. They thought something was wrong and kept yelling for Bronwyn to explain.

She didn't hear them. She crouched low over the Aurochs' head as the great creature raced forward. Bronwyn was going to be a big sister to others just like her and she couldn't wait to talk with them.

76 – Trade Routes and More

"They are so precious! I love them!" Bronwyn exclaimed to Micah's belly.

"Am I the only one who can't talk to my children?" Micah asked.

'Appears so,' G-War interjected.

"Ass!" Micah blurted out. Bronwyn gave her a sharp look so she mumbled a quick apology.

'Although you don't think you can talk with them, you are closer to them than any of us will ever be.' Aadi always knew the right thing to say. Tears welled up in her eyes.

Braden watched everything. Silence was his key to survival. He'd never traveled with a pregnant woman before, but he'd heard stories. He maintained a certain level of fear-based respect as his partner went through her changes.

"You are more beautiful than ever," was what he settled for. Safe, but true. He was proud of her, of them.

"Enough with the baby stuff. How'd the trades go?" Braden asked Candela and Tanner. Micah was interested, too. They had shed blood and invested a great deal of themselves in getting the trade route set up. She most wanted to hear that it was successful without Braden. She didn't want to live on the road.

She wasn't disappointed. The young couple's excitement was infectious. As Braden listened, he was both excited and saddened.

'Give them the wagon, lover. Trade them something for it. Then they can own it and go about their business, the business you made possible for them,' Micah told Braden

over their mindlink. Braden nodded. Then he made the offer.

The young couple could not have been happier. They agreed to a percentage of the goods over the next cycle. All that meant was that Braden and Micah would get vegetables and mushrooms, which was no different than their current situation, but he had done the right thing. If he wanted trade to flourish, then he had to help new traders get established. It didn't hurt that Tom was building another wagon.

He'd be surprised when they brought the Old Tech wheel hubs. Which begged the question, when were they going back to New Sanctuary?

"We can go in the next turn or so?" Micah offered, once they were alone.

"Are you okay to travel?" Braden asked, unsure of what was different.

"Of course. Let's take the cart and I'll ride in that, sitting using the leather strap. That may be a little easier on my backside. As long as the Prince is with us, I'll know that the babies are okay." Braden nodded.

"And sooner is better. We know that Zalastar controls the road. Let's go while that remains true. I wonder if the Medical Lab can check you out, make sure everything is okay?"

"And maybe we can get the neural implants removed?" Micah suggested noncommittally. Braden was ready for that, but not ready. He liked having the maps in his head. Until they could get them down on paper, he didn't want to lose his hard-gained knowledge.

They also needed the implants to control the Old Tech in New Sanctuary. As long as they had it, no one else could get it. By carrying it inside them, they protected the world.

"I don't know," Braden finally said. Micah knew that meant they wouldn't. They'd keep the Old Tech and she'd watch closely, making sure that it didn't take over their lives. For now, they had resisted its call. She was convinced they used the Old Tech for good. Braden's trade of his coveted wagon demonstrated once again that his personal power wasn't a goal. He was a rarity in the south and from what she understood, in all of

Planet Vii.

77 – New Sanctuary

"I think that's the best decision, Brandt," Braden told the King of the Aurochs. They had discussed who would go to New Sanctuary. In the end, only Braden, Micah, G-War, and Aadi would travel together. If Brandt went, then Bronwyn would insist on going. Skirill couldn't fly in the rainforest and if they spent any time at New Sanctuary, he would have nothing to do. By staying, he could watch over Bronwyn and all the villages.

Bronwyn knew about New Sanctuary because she had seen it in their minds, but she didn't talk about it. First-hand knowledge was different. They didn't think she was ready for that.

She was the first of a new generation who didn't need the Old Tech to be superior. They wanted her to thrive on her own. Braden also saw the darkness that the Old Tech could bring. He and Micah carried it with them, but they had each other for support, to fight its seductive draw.

They left at first light, Max in the lead and Pack behind with Micah holding the reins from her position across the leather strap at the front of the cart. G-War was in the cart on a soft blanket, while Aadi held a small length of Amazonian rope tied to Braden's saddle. For this trip, Braden insisted on a cover for the cart, to keep the interior dry. If they were to carry a load of books, those wouldn't fit in a case like the one he used to carry his rudder. If rain got to them, they'd be ruined. G-War agreed. He was looking forward to a trip through the rainforest that didn't end with a wet 'cat.

Braden brought an oiled deerskin with him, hoping that he could stay dry, too. Max and Pack unfortunately were left to the weather. But if they were attacked, the special material from Village McCullough covered them from their ears to their tails and down below their bellies. Micah expected Bronwyn had something to do with the extensive coverings for Max and Speckles, as she called him.

Having traveled this route before, they were well prepared. What they didn't expect was the work the Amazonians had done on the road. Zalastar had told them moons ago that his people would repair the road, but that was before the war. They were surprised that he could fight a war and fix the road. Maybe the war wasn't as extensive as they believed. Or Zalastar had more Amazonians at his command than they knew of.

It made the travel easy and quick. The horses trotted much of the time. The cart was light as they carried no load, and it rolled along the surface smoothly. The Amazonians even improved the crowning of the road so the nonstop rain ran off, leaving the middle of the road firm.

They still traveled for three turns in the rain. G-War never left the cart. Aadi remained indifferent. Max and Pack were only slightly miserable. The protective material kept off most of the rain.

Everyone appreciated seeing the sunlight peeking through the Amazon's southern border. Without Skirill flying ahead, leaving the rainforest was less exuberant than usual. They missed him and the King. During their trip, they discovered that they could talk over their mindlink until they were most of a turn distant from their friends. Then they couldn't hear them anymore.

There was nothing to worry about. The trade route had been established and Brandt suggested that before the moon was out, he'd lead the caravan back to Westerly. They were all curious to see how Crabby and the village of River Crook was progressing. They also wanted to know if the rest of the people from White Beach had gone to the village under the water.

So many questions.

They'd see what Holly knew, but in person, not through their neural implants.

As they approached New Sanctuary, the Security Bot hovered out to greet them. When they asked why he did that, he said that was in his programming. Their close proximity to the Bot helped confirm their identities through something it called DNA sampling. The President was welcomed back, as were her companions.

They left the cart in the open area by the buildings, and they turned the horses loose to graze. Work expanding the fields was well underway, so Max and Pack could eat to their hearts' content. G-War helped himself to a fresh meal of rabbit upon their arrival, then settled on the beach to sleep in the warm shade. Aadi floated around, doing as he did. The humans expected he waited for them to engage the Old Tech, so he could continue to learn and study. If anyone could design the failsafe against war, they expected it was the Tortoid. They hoped he would find an answer.

The first thing Braden wanted to do was visit the Medical Laboratory. They climbed aboard the elevator and told it where to take them.

Micah dutifully climbed on the table in the lab, while various Bots and other equipment moved around her. Holly stood nearby explaining what diagnostic procedures were underway, but Braden still watched carefully, not sure what many of the words meant.

Holly pointed to the screen which showed a black and white image of the two babies, curled against each other. The final verdict was that they were healthy and they would be born in four to five moons, months as Holly called them.

But then Holly suggested something they hadn't thought of: have the babies at New Sanctuary where the medical equipment could guarantee that both mother and children would survive the process with the least amount of pain. In fact, Holly insisted that the President not risk her life by giving birth in the wild.

"We're going to have to think about that, Holly. As long as the decision is ours, we will consider it. If we feel pressured, we'll have this whole facility dismantled. Do you understand?" Braden asked.

"I shall only offer options," Holly conceded.

"It's not you, Holly. We don't want any Old Tech to make us like the ancients, where they decided a war was the best course of action. Whatever they did to get there, we don't want to repeat. Can you understand that?" Braden tried to reason with Holly, thinking of him as a human who lived somewhere else.

"Can you talk with our Tortoid friend, Aadi?" Micah asked Holly. "If not, what would it take so you could? I want you two to talk about the failsafe, the procedures we have to follow where war cannot happen. That is my number one priority."

"I will explore options and will return to you with them." Holly seemed firm in his commitment. Micah reclined on the laboratory examination bed. The relief of hearing that the babies were healthy combined with the warmth of the room was making her drowsy.

"Let's go to our room so you can get some rest."

78 – Change Is Constant

They decided to stay, with conditions of course. The south could do without books and Old Tech wheel hubs for another six or seven moons. He wondered if Skirill could fly over the rainforest if he needed to talk with them.

Braden used the Command Center to look in on the villages. With Holly's help, he watched each village go about their business. The view was from far above, as if Skirill flew high. He even found River Crook and dedicated a monitor to them. With the Old Tech, he could watch everything and know that the world moved on without him and Micah.

He never saw a human on the monitors showing White Beach. The people were all gone. Holly tried to contact the underwater vehicle, but once it had gathered the last of the humans, it disappeared. Thanks to Braden and Micah, the villagers were willing to go, and it expedited the process.

Braden hadn't intended that to happen. He wasn't sure if he liked being obsolete as a trader either. He sat in the New Command Center by himself, his unhappy thoughts poor company.

He also watched the villages and towns in the north. It was hard to tell if things were normal or not. He didn't see anything that looked like war, but the market squares were less crowded than he thought they should be.

The elevator arrived and Micah stepped out. She walked with a purpose, a scowl on her face. The babies were growing well. They were at a size where she could no longer walk like a warrior. He stood, scolding himself for looking at another world, when everything he needed was walking toward him.

She brightened as she heard his thoughts.

"There's no need for me to be down here. Let's go outside and enjoy the sun." Braden took her hand, but she led him to the wall of monitors instead.

"Tell me what's going on in all the trade villages, then we'll go outside." He hesitated. She was showing him that if it was important to him, it was important to her, so he talked through each monitor. Holly blew up the pictures for each village, where nine monitors showed one view. They panned the view until they could see the Aurochs herd. They saw the wagon in Coldstream's market square. River Crook had its first two buildings. New buildings had appeared in Westerly. The smoke from Tom's forge obscured much of Dwyer.

"We might have to move the village or move Tom." They both saw the humor in trying to root Tom out of his smithy. It would probably be easiest to move the village. They were sure there were plenty of engaging conversation between Tom and his nearest neighbors.

Braden even dedicated monitors to Trent and Cornwall. Both villages looked normal, people doing what they do. They looked peaceful from the view Holly provided.

The rainforest was impenetrable. They wouldn't know how the Amazonian war went until they returned through the rainforest.

"What did the lab say?" Braden asked.

"It said any day now. I have to keep my neural implant open for it, so I made it small and stuffed it in the corner."

They went outside and walked. They stripped naked and swam. Micah's back hurt. Swimming helped, so she was in the lake or in their suite's pool whenever she got the chance. Her fingers seemed to be permanently shriveled. They floated by the shore, teasing fish that came too close.

"A little more than a cycle ago, G-War and I planned to cross the Great Desert. Look at us now." The 'cat sat upright in the shade on the beach, watching his humans carefully. "What are they saying, G?"

They are ready to greet their parents. The time has come. Aadi and I will be with you, down below. We expect you need a great deal of help.'

Braden helped Micah out of the water and into the robe she'd been wearing, while he threw on his clothes without drying off. "I don't know what you're worried about. Micah will be fine," he told the 'cat as they waddled toward the building with the elevator.

'You are correct. Micah will be fine. It's you who will need help.' G-War padded after them and Aadi met them at the door. In order to fit, the humans crouched while Aadi floated over their heads. Micah started to get uncomfortable. She hadn't had her freedom of movement for a couple moons, but this was different. The children were taking over her body and the contractions were painful.

They made it to the Medical Laboratory, where the Bots took charge of making Micah comfortable. Braden was surprised at how quickly it was happening. After moons of waiting, all of a sudden, it was time.

He wasn't ready.

Micah started screaming at him. "You better be ready!" She followed that with a long howl of pain. Braden stood still, his mouth open, eyes wide, heart pounding. The color left his face. Darkness crowded the edges of his vision until he only saw two pinpoints of light. There was no sound.

Micah watched as the Tortoid, perfectly positioned thanks to G-War, let Braden fall on him. Aadi slowly dropped until the human rolled gently to the floor.

"You didn't!" she yelled at Braden's unconscious form. Then she laughed as G-War appeared at her side, finishing the laugh with a contortion and a gasp as another contraction came.

'I told you,' was all the 'cat said. He purred and nuzzled her cheek as the Bots took over. She drifted as they injected her with something. She felt the pain, but it didn't hurt. She watched dispassionately as first one baby, then the other appeared. Bots with arms held them securely as the babies were cleaned and swaddled.

The table moved itself to where Micah was sitting upright. The Bots handed her the babies and for the first time, she heard their voices in her head.

Aadi banged against Braden once again and he finally shook himself awake. "What happened?"

'Go see your family, Master Braden. They require your presence. And yes, before you ask, you missed it.'

He hurried to his feet, clearing the cobwebs from his mind. He staggered to the table where Micah looked tired, but refreshed. She held a small bundle in each arm while the 'cat lay curled on her chest. Aadi followed him.

"I'm so sorry," he mumbled as he tried to look at his children. They were both sleeping peacefully. She smiled at him.

"Moons ago, G-War told me you'd do that. He even suggested you wouldn't last thirty heartbeats. Holly checked. From the time I got on the table until you hit the floor was thirty-seven heartbeats." Braden snorted and shook his head. There was nothing he could do about it now. The 'cat knew him better than he knew himself.

"We never decided on names." They had talked, but hadn't been able to agree.

"I think they've made that decision for us. The Golden Warrior and Bronwyn have been talking with them for ages. They've picked their own names."

Braden brightened. "You can hear them now?"

"The second they were born." She beamed up at him. They both felt as new parents should feel.

Then it hit him, his smile faded from his face. "No. Please," he pleaded.

She threw her head back and laughed. "Meet your son Axial."

"No," he said weakly.

"And your daughter, De'atesh." G-War purred louder, until Braden swore it shook the whole room.

Postscript

If you liked The Free Trader of Planet Vii, please drop me a line at craig@craigmartelle.com. I am always happy to hear from people who've read my work. I do my very best to answer every email.

If you liked the story, please write a short review for me on Amazon. I greatly appreciate any kind words, even one or two sentences go a long ways. The number of reviews an ebook gets greatly improves how well an ebook does on Amazon.

Amazon – amazon.com/author/craigmartelle
Facebook – facebook.com/authorcraigmartelle
My web page – www.craigmartelle.com
LinkedIn – linkedin.com/in/craigmartelle

Thank you for reading The Free Trader of Planet Vii. This book adds some detail to Braden's southern adventures. The Free Trader and his companions are now prepared for their next great adventure on board the RV Traveler.

The next book fulfills a dream that I've had nearly forty years and that was to take my love of Brian Aldiss' Starship and Robert Heinlein's Orphans of the Sky and create an adventure on an interstellar ship that has been abandoned, yet teems with life. The Free Trader's world expands to the skies! Adventures on RV Traveler will be available in April 2016.

There are other things we need to learn about Planet Vii. We need to find out what's happening in the north. Has someone destroyed the trade-based civilization that Braden was raised to respect? What about the villagers from White Beach who were taken to the Western Ocean Research Facility? How is the Amazonian war going to play out? Will the survivors from Cygnus VI make Vii a safer place?

Before I answer those questions, I need to write the lead book of the Rick Dayman Thrillers. Can petty politics keep Rick from stopping the next terror attack? Taken from today's headlines and my twenty years of experience in the intelligence community, the world is never from tipping out of balance. The smallest events can have the greatest impact. Finding these and stopping them is an ongoing challenge to a free society. And your average citizen doesn't even know what's been done to protect them.

FREE TRADER SERIES
BOOK 3
CRAIG MARTELLE

ADVENTURES
ON
RV TRAVELER

The Adventure on RV Traveler

The following excerpt takes place after Braden and his companions are aboard the RV Traveler…

10 – Transfer to the Traveler

It was time. They crowded into a new room tucked into the manufacturing level. The companions were noticeably upset. The machinery and depth underground weighed heavily on them. Like Braden and Micah, they preferred the outdoors. They hoped Holly was correct, that the spaces would be open and they'd feel free. Otherwise it was going to be a very long trip. G-War told Braden that he'd kill him in his sleep if he was trapped inside for more than a single turn.

Micah told G-War that she wouldn't allow that, so they settled on a simple maiming.

Braden looked to Aadi and Skirill for support, but they avoided his gaze.

"Fine." He wanted everyone to relax. He'd seen pictures and even moving pictures of the ship. With basic maps in his head, he didn't expect any surprises.

They'd arrive in a small room at the aft end of the ship. The matter transfer system consumed great amounts of power, so it was best situated close to the engines. From there, they needed to travel to the bow, where they would change the orientation of the ship to align it for transfer to Cygnus VI. Once the survivors on Cygnus VI were safely aboard, they'd realign the ship for transfer to the New Command Center.

The details of why were lost on Braden. Appear in the back of the ship. Go to the front. Move levers, mash buttons, turn wheels exactly as Holly tells them. Go to the back, prepare a safe place for the people of Cygnus VI. Then back to the front to do as Holly commands. Then one last trip to the back. For perspective, Holly said that it was more than a single turn's walk one way. They had to cover the distance four times.

Through possibly hostile areas.

Four times…

They entered the circular room and the wall slid into place behind them. Braden helped Skirill off Aadi's shell, then carefully put him in one of twelve reclining metal chairs. Aadi floated down until he stood on his chair. G-War jumped into another of the recliners and crouched on it. The two humans got into their chairs. The feet of the chairs pointed inward to the center of the circular room where a single cylinder stood from floor to ceiling. No matter which way they looked, their reflections looked back at them.

They stood in the room while Holly's disembodied voice talked to them. "The panels will shimmer. Stay in your seats and do not move. Do not touch each other under any circumstances. Space between you is important as the device catalogues and deconstructs you. You will be reconstructed on the Traveler. For you, it will seem as if only a moment has passed, while the entire process will take one to two days. Relax. Close your eyes and breathe deeply."

The mirror-like panels on the wall shimmered, as a Mirror Beast might. Then a deep tone pressed in on them. The 'cat struggled to remain still. *'Relax G. We're here together. We'll be there soon and then we can find the open air, maybe bag a rabbit together. Rabbit sounds good…'* Braden's thoughts calmed them all as they thought of their next meal.

11 – Controlled Chaos

'...*Rabbit.*' Braden opened his eyes. He had a massive headache. The room was the same but different. The ceiling colors had changed. The panels shimmered until they didn't. "Holly?"

Braden opened his neural implant. Holly appeared in the window. The transfer was complete.

They were on the RV Traveler.

They needed to exit this room. Next door, there should be people controlling computer systems and maybe engineers keeping the engines running. A door up one level and to the right would put them in a corridor that would take them to a rear core access door. From there. Once they crossed, there would be a pod system, a vehicle to take them to the forward core world access. Across that, into the central non-gravity area, they'd find the Command Decks.

Or so Holly assured them.

"Is everyone okay? Micah?"

She opened her eyes. They remained unfocused as if she had just woken from a long sleep. She flexed her fingers then hands and started stretching each of her muscles. "Yeah. I feel like Brandt ran me over, but besides that, feeling great." She leaned over the side of her chair and heaved her breakfast onto the floor.

Aadi remained motionless, unblinking. "Aadi?" Braden asked as he threw his feet from the chair to the floor. The room started to spin and he dutifully puked up his breakfast. Holly hadn't suggested they'd be sick.

Skirill blinked rapidly and started to flex his wings. *I'm afraid there's no room to fly yet. I shall continue to be a burden to poor Master Aadi.'* The Hawkoid didn't get sick as he flexed his muscles and was soon moving freely.

Braden stood on shaky feet. He staggered to Aadi and held his head in both hands, looking closely at his eyes. A slow blink and a deliberate shake of his head. Braden rubbed the Tortoid's neck. *'Sorry. Fell asleep. What a strange sensation. I dreamed of cactus weevils and water.'* He floated upward and swam around the room without a problem.

Braden shook his head and tapped Aadi's shell. "Holly, can you open this door for us?" They placed a large device Holly had given them so he could directly access systems. He called it a broadband transceiver, whatever that meant. The device needed to be close to the computer and Holly could then talk to it. Without it, he could only access the systems that let him in.

G-War jumped from his chair, hairs on end. Only the humans had gotten sick. *'We were all sick, but we're tougher than you humans, that's all.'*

"We're here ten heartbeats and you're already an ass. Remember, we're guests. Be kind." Braden smiled at his friend. He was happy to see the 'cat more calm than when they left.

"Holly? We're ready to go."

'Almost there,' Holly sent to the window before Braden's eye.

"Holly says he almost has the door open. This is the only one we need him to open. After this, our bands should give us access everywhere we need to go. Be ready." Skirill hopped onto Aadi's back and grasped the harness strap. Braden and Micah pulled their blasters which they'd previously dialed to the weakest setting.

Three panels moved inward and slid along the wall.

Darkness greeted them, darkness speckled with small colored lights. Again, Holly hadn't suggested they'd operate in the darkness although one of many Old Tech toys in their backpacks would help. They stepped to the side of the door, slung their backpacks to the floor and started digging.

'G? Aadi?'

'It's like the New Command Center. I see workstations and screens. No people. There's vegetation in the back, looks like vines. The air is wet, like the rainforest.' G-War told them after looking through the opening. Braden and Micah thought they were hot from the excitement of the transfer. *'I don't see danger. Not right now.'*

The humans pulled out the portable lights from their backpacks and turned them on. It was odd that they didn't flash, but that's what Holly called them – flashlights. The beams penetrated the darkness. With a shrug, the humans walked into the next room, shining the beams left, right, up, down. An empty Command Center. Micah opened the window of her neural implant. *'Are you seeing this Holly?'*

'Yes. I am pleased with the functioning systems, but alarmed at the heat and humidity. These are not good for the systems. I will close the door to the matter transfer room. The instruments in that room are delicate. They must be protected if you are to return.'

'Do you want your box in or out?' Micah asked.

'In is better. I'll close the door. Don't be alarmed,' Holly responded.

"Holly's closing the door. He wants to keep that room dry to make sure we can leave when we're done."

The door to the matter transfer room silently slid shut. The only light remaining shone from the beams of their flashlights. Aadi and G-War moved wide to see anything to their sides while Braden and Micah moved forward, past the work stations. Metal equipment and large devices covered the wall to their front. To the left, their lights faded into the distance as the floor arced toward the ceiling. There was a great deal of space above them.

"Elevator – there." Braden pointed with the light beam. "Up one and then down the platform to the right. He shined the beam along the walkway, but couldn't see the doorway they needed to go through. It was disconcerting seeing the floor slope upwards. Holly explained that the shape was necessary so the ship could spin, creating the appearance of gravity. When they asked what that meant, Holly said without the spin, they would float through the air. They'd get a taste of that when they reached the forward Command Deck.

Skirill launched himself from Aadi's back and flew upward. Braden followed him with his light so the Hawkoid could see. He flew oddly, at an angle and sometimes sideways. He turned tightly and flew back, swooping past them. He made another tight turn, then climbed to the catwalk, as Holly called it, they needed to take. He flew a hundred strides down and landed on the handrail. Braden and G-War waited while Aadi and Micah called the elevator and entered it.

"One floor up please," she said as Holly had told her.

The doors closed and the elevator moved quickly upward. They floated off the floor as it slowed, landing when it stopped. The doors opened and they stepped onto the catwalk. Braden was far below with his light shining past Skirill. Micah waved her flashlight and then pointed it at Skirill. She headed toward him.

Braden and G-War rode the elevator and stepped onto the walkway.

Braden's neural implant buzzed. Holly insisted that they not close the window while they were aboard the RV Traveler. He needed to stay in touch at all times. Braden thought Holly was more worried than he was.

'What, Holly?'

'Braden, thank you for answering.' Was that sarcasm? *'I suggest you go the other way and check on the vines growing down the wall. There shouldn't be any growth in here. You may need to burn that down to preserve the systems in this area. That may be the reason for the high humidity.'*

"Micah!" Braden shouted. She jumped and shushed him.

"Holly wants us to look at the vines and maybe burn them out," he said in a quieter voice. "We have to go back this way." G-War turned, shaking his head, and padded in the new direction.

Skirill flew past them, angling away from the vines, slowing and hovering with great wing beats. The other companions looked through his eyes at the vines. They looked like something straight out of the rainforest. The vines were heavy, with small leaves. Water ran downward puddling on the floor before disappearing through a grating below. Braden leaned around the railing of the catwalk, hanging precariously over the edge. Even with Skirill's help, he couldn't see the base of the vines.

He held his hands up in surrender, then Micah looked. The vines covered the catwalk like a waterfall. If they wanted to pass this way, they couldn't, unless they went back to the main engineering space, down one level. She looked closely, focusing her light on a single thick vine and the small leaves on it. She reached up to touch it.

'STOP!' G-War shouted over their mindlink.

She pulled back as the leaves whipped back and forth where her hand had been a moment before. She pulled her sword and held it close. The leaves whipped against it, ringing as metal struck metal.

She swung at the vine and chopped deeply into it. The leaves slapped the blade in a frenzy. She pulled it back. The Old Tech blade was unscratched. She hacked into the vine until it started spewing red juice that looked too much like blood for her comfort. She backed up as it sprayed toward her.

"That's enough of that." Braden pulled his blaster, changed the setting to wide and depressed the trigger. When the flame hit the vines, they jumped and flew about the space like a tree in a storm. The vines pummeled the catwalk, shaking the companions off their feet. They crawled backwards trying to get away.

They got to their feet and ran. Skirill flew like one possessed. Aadi struggled to move quickly. A vine slapped against him, leaving an ugly scratch down the armor over his shell. Skirill's harness was cut from the Tortoid and fell over the catwalk to the floor below. Braden and Micah dropped to a knee and dialed narrow beams. They fired into the vines in short bursts, cutting through the thick of the vine trunks. When the beams hit a leaf, it was reflected away.

One, then another and another of the vines were cut. The top sections hung, the blood-like juice running freely from them. The bottom parts of the vine fell away from the catwalk, crashing into and through a number of the terminals in the engineering section. Sparks flew. The smell of ozone filled the air. Silence returned. They shined their flashlights on the carnage.

Both their neural implants buzzed.

"What?" Braden asked angrily.

'What just happened? A number of systems have gone critical.'

"That vine acted like it was alive! When I hit it with blaster fire it went nuts, tried to kill us. It needed to die."

'I understand,' Holly said calmly. *'Next time, please take care not to destroy the systems you need to keep you alive.'*

"I'm not sure how I feel about that," Braden said to Micah. "We haven't been here any time at all and we've already tried to destroy the ship."

"More like the ship tried to destroy us. Then again, it didn't bother us until we went after it. I can't blame it," Micah answered.

"So, we take more care then?" Braden offered. She nodded. It was a prudent course of action. She was already certain that she didn't want to spend one more heartbeat on the Traveler than she absolutely had to.

Skirill flew past them to the lower deck. He stayed away from the vines as he looked for Aadi's harness. It was underneath a dying vine, swamped in a growing puddle of the vine's juices.

It was going to be a long trip, he thought.

12 – The Corridor

They stood on the catwalk with the door before them. Micah readied her blaster as Braden waved his bracelet near the pad on the left side. G-War crouched low as the door slid open.

An emergency light flashed somewhere ahead. The wide corridor was filled with debris, but no vines. Nothing moved. G-War nodded and stalked through the door, jumping to the side once in. He stayed in the shadows and watched.

Aadi floated in the middle of the doorway, Skirill holding a rope tied hastily around the Tortoid's shell. The new scratch in his armor provided a notch that kept the rope from slipping.

The lights flashed and they saw the corridor in snippets, like watching during a thunderstorm.

Braden walked forward, staying close to the side of the corridor. Micah followed him in, moving to the other side. Once Aadi and Skirill were in, the door closed. They had to watch out for Aadi, keep him close. He no longer had his access band. The killer vines had seen to that.

Micah leaned down as Braden carefully walked ahead, holding his blaster at the ready, G-War at his side, walking as a 'cat does on a sunny day in the middle of nowhere. This helped Micah relax.

She looked at a box, burst open on the floor. It looked like someone had dropped it. Repair parts for a Bot or an Old Tech system. Holly had tried for the past moon to teach them what they needed for the ship, but she didn't care what any of it was called. She only wanted to know what was dangerous and what wasn't.

She opened her neural implant window. *'Holly? We're in the corridor and the floor is littered with stuff. I'd say a bunch of people dropped what they were carrying and ran off.'*

'These look like repair parts for small motorized systems, like actuators. Over there I see electrical components. But these look like storage boxes. If a technician were going to

291

repair something, they'd bring just the parts they needed, not the whole box. Maybe a group of people raided a storage room and then were stopped by the Security Unit at the end of the corridor.'

"What Security Unit?" She asked out loud. Braden instantly crouched, darting glances into the shadows.

'Behind you, beside the door. See that red dot? That's the unit embedded in the bulkhead, the wall holding the door. You have bracelets. You're safe.' Braden continued to huddle behind a pile of metal plates. G-War sat in the middle of the corridor and looked at him.

"We're safe because of our bracelets and Aadi's safe because he's with us," Micah said, pointing at the wall behind her. Braden squinted, then turned on his flashlight. The beam showed the Security Unit. It had a label that said "Engineering Security."

'We need another access bracelet for Aadi. The vines destroyed his last one.'

'With your bracelet, Master President, you will be able to fabricate one. At the end of this corridor, before you enter one of the main decks you will find crew spaces. In there will be a fabricator you can use.'

"Detour at the end of the corridor. Holly says we can use a fabricator to make another bracelet for Aadi." Micah minimized her window and shoved it into the lower left corner of her vision.

Braden expanded his neural implant window and accessed the ship's map. He saw the way ahead clearly. Another 150 meters along this corridor. Last door on the right. He minimized the window and moved forward.

He'd never get used to the way Holly measured distance. He figured one stride was roughly one meter. He gauged everything else from there. It was close enough for him, but Holly had an annoying tendency for precision.

The corridor cleared further on. It reinforced Holly's impression of why the materials were strewn about.

The red emergency lights flashed, but provided enough continuous light that they could see. Maybe those red lights should have been called flashlights?

Once they passed the debris, they moved quickly to the door at the other end. There were two doors. The one straight ahead gave them access to one of the great open levels of the ship. Braden turned his back to that door. They'd go through it soon enough. For now, they had to find the fabricator.

About the Author

Visit Craig's web page, craigmartelle.com for the latest posts and updates or find him on Facebook, Author Craig Martelle. Send an email to craig@craigmartelle.com to join his mailing list for the latest on new releases, information on old releases, and anything related to his books.

Craig is a successful author, publishing regularly. He's on track to publish ten books in 2016. He's taken his more than twenty years of experience in the Marine Corps, his law degree, and his business consulting career to write believable characters living in a real world.

Although Craig has written in multiple genres, he believes that most important is that compelling characters are critical. Just like Star Trek, the original series used a back drop of space, but the themes related to modern day America. Life lessons of a great story can be applied now or fifty years in the future. Some things are universal.

Craig believes that evil exists. Some people are driven differently and cannot be allowed access to our world. Good people will rise to the occasion, whether it's before or after a crisis. Good will always challenge evil, but will it win in time?

Some writers who've influenced Craig? Robert E. Howard (the original Conan), JRR Tolkien, Andre Norton, Robert Heinlein, Lin Carter, Brian Aldiss, Margaret Weis, Tracy Hickman, Anne McCaffrey, and of late, James Axler, Raymond Weil, Jonathan Brazee, Mark E. Cooper, and David Weber. Craig learned something from each of these authors, story line, compelling issue, characters that you can relate to, beauty of prose, action, and unique tendrils weaving through the book's theme. Craig's prose has been compared to that of Andre Norton and his Free Trader characters to those of McCaffrey's Dragonriders, the Rick Banik Thrillers to the works of Robert Ludlum.

It is humbling, but never the intent. Craig only wants to tell a good story about real people, keep readers engaged, leave them with something to think about – "What would I do in that situation?"

Through a bizarre series of events, Craig ended up in Fairbanks, Alaska. He never expected to retire to a place where golf courses are only open for four months out of the year. But he love it there. It is off the beaten path. He and his wife watch the northern lights from their driveway. Their dog has lots of room to run. And temperatures reach forty below zero. They have from three and a half hours of daylight in the winter to twenty four hours in the summer.

It's all part of the give and take of life. If they didn't have those extremes, then everyone would live there.

Made in the USA
Middletown, DE
03 July 2023

34448820R00182